STRANDS IN THE WEB . . .

The frighteningly erratic behaviour of the climate over the past few years . . . Unidentified Flying Object activity at an all-time peak . . . the continuing pollution and despoliation of planet Earth by overpopulation and industry . . . the mounting incidence of unexplained disappearances of people in mysterious circumstances . . . horrendous new killing techniques — including spontaneous combustion — used by government assassins against those who pose a threat to the security of an ultra-secret organization . . . terrifying advances in mind-control by agencies like the CIA and their use in creating a class of mindless human-robot slaves . . . astounding revelations of clandestine collaboration in space between the USA and the USSR over a period of decades . . . bizarre features observed on the Moon and Mars — *but for some reason barely mentioned in the media* . . .

These and many other sinister features unearthed and examined by those investigating the horrific enigma of ALTERNATIVE 3 are the strands in a web of conspiracy which could only exist in our age of terminal technology. Top journalist Leslie Watkins, making use of the research for the original TV exposé — much of which was not incorporated into the programme itself for various reasons — and of material that has come to light subsequently, has written a book with the grip, pace and compulsion of a thriller. And with the grim bite of terrible truth — a truth which is sure to be denied by those who are themselves terrified that the most explosive secret in human history is about to blow up in their faces . . .

Alternative 3

LESLIE WATKINS

From the Anglia Television Film
ALTERNATIVE 3
Devised by David Ambrose and
Christopher Miles
Written by David Ambrose
Directed by Christopher Miles

WARNER BOOKS

*This book is dedicated to Ann Clark, Robert Patterson
and Brian Pendlebury – wherever they may be*

A *Warner* Book

First published in Great Britain in 1978 by Sphere Books
Reprinted 1979, 1980 (twice), 1987, 1989
This edition published in 1994 by Warner Books

Original television script copyright © David Ambrose & Christopher Miles 1977
Book version copyright © Leslie Watkins 1978

The moral right of the author has been asserted.

A CIP catalogue record for this book is
available from the British Library.

ISBN 0 7515 1009 2

Printed in England by Clays Ltd, St Ives plc

Warner Books
A Division of
Little, Brown and Company (UK) Limited
Brettenham House
Lancaster Place
London WC2E 7EN

SECTION ONE

No newspaper has yet secured the truth behind the operation known as ALTERNATIVE 3. Investigations by journalists have been blocked – by governments on both sides of the Iron Curtain. America and Russia are ruthlessly obsessed with guarding their shared secret and this obsession, as we can now prove, has made them partners in murder.

However, despite this intensive security, fragments of information have been made public. Often they are released inadvertently – by experts who do not appreciate their sinister significance – and these fragments, in isolation, mean little. But when jigsawed together they form a definite pattern – a pattern which appears to emphasise the enormity of this conspiracy of silence.

On May 3, 1977, the *Daily Mirror* published this story:

> President Jimmy Carter has joined the ranks of UFO spotters. He sent in two written reports stating he had seen a flying saucer when he was the Governor of Georgia.
>
> The President has shrugged off the incident since then, perhaps fearing that electors might be wary of a flying saucer freak.
>
> But he was reported as saying after the 'sighting': 'I don't laugh at people any more when they say they've seen UFOs because I've seen one myself.'
>
> Carter described his UFO like this: 'Luminous, not solid, at first bluish, then reddish ... it seemed to move towards us from a distance, stopped, then moved partially away.'

Carter filed two reports on the sighting in 1973, one to the International UFO Bureau and the other to the National Investigations Committee on Aerial Phenomena.

Heydon Hewes, who directs the International UFO Bureau from his home in Oklahoma City, is making speeches praising the President's 'open-mindedness.'

But during his presidential campaign last year Carter was cautious. He admitted he had seen a light in the sky but declined to call it a UFO.

He joked: 'I think it was a light beckoning me to run in the California primary election.'

Why this change in Carter's attitude? Because, by then, he had been briefed on Alternative 3?

A 1966 Gallup Poll showed that five million Americans — including several highly experienced airline pilots — claimed to have seen Flying Saucers. Fighter pilot Thomas Mantell had already died while chasing one over Kentucky — his F.51 aircraft having disintegrated in the violent wash of his quarry's engines. The U.S. Air Force, reluctantly bowing to mounting pressure, asked Dr. Edward Uhler Condon, a professor of astrophysics, to head an investigation team at Colorado University.

Condon's budget was $500,000. Shortly before his report appeared in 1968, this story appeared in the London *Evening Standard:*

The Condon study is making headlines — but for all the wrong reasons. It is losing some of its outstanding members, under circumstances which are mysterious to say the least. Sinister rumours are circulating ... at least four key people have vanished from the Condon team without offering a satisfactory reason for their departure.

The complete story behind the strange events in Colorado is hard to decipher. But a clue, at least, may be found in the recent statements of Dr. James McDonald, the senior physicist at the Institute of Atmospheric Physics at the University of Arizona and widely respected in his field.

In a wary, but ominous, telephone conversation this week, Dr. McDonald told me that he is 'most distressed.'

Condon's 1,485-page report denied the existence of Flying Saucers and a panel of the American National Academy of Sciences endorsed the conclusion that 'further extensive study probably cannot be justified.'

But, curiously, Condon's joint principal investigator, Dr. David Saunders, had not contributed a word to that report. And on January 11, 1969, the *Daily Telegraph* quoted Dr. Saunders as saying of the report: 'It is inconceivable that it can be anything but a cold stew. No matter how long it is, what it includes, how it is said, or what it recommends, it will lack the essential element of credibility.'

Already there were wide-spread suspicions that the Condon investigation had been part of an official cover-up, that the government knew the truth but was determined to keep it from the public. We now know that those suspicions were accurate. And that the secrecy was all because of Alternative 3.

Only a few months after Dr. Saunders made his 'cold stew' statement a journalist with the Columbus (Ohio) *Dispatch* embarrassed the National Aeronautics and Space Agency by photographing a strange craft – looking exactly like a Flying Saucer – at the White Sands missile range in New Mexico.

At first no one at NASA would talk about this mysterious circular craft, 15 feet in diameter, which had been left in the 'missile graveyard' – a section of the range where most experimental vehicles were eventually dumped.

But the Martin Marietta company of Denver, where it was built, acknowledged designing several models, some with ten and twelve engines. And a NASA official, faced with this information, said: 'Actually the engineers used to call it "The Flying Saucer".' That confirmed a statement made by Dr. Garry Henderson, a leading space research scientist: 'All our astronauts have seen these objects but have been ordered not to discuss their findings with anyone.'

Otto Binder was a member of the NASA space team. He has stated that NASA 'killed' significant segments of conversation between Mission Control and Apollo 11 – the space-craft which took Buzz Aldrin and Neil Armstrong to the Moon – and that those segments were deleted from the official record: 'Certain sources with their own VHF receiving facilities that by-passed NASA broadcast outlets claim there was a portion of Earth-Moon dialogue that was quickly cut off by the NASA monitoring staff.'

Binder added: 'It was presumably when the two moon-walkers, Aldrin and Armstrong, were making the rounds some distance from the LEM that Armstrong clutched Aldrin's arm excitedly and exclaimed – "What was it? What the hell was it? That's all I want to know." '

Then, according to Binder, there was this exchange –

MISSION CONTROL: What's there ? . . . malfunction (garble) . . . Mission Control calling Apollo 11 . . .

APOLLO 11: These babies were huge, sir . . . enormous . . . Oh, God you wouldn't believe it! . . . I'm telling you there are other space-craft out there . . . lined up on the far side of the crater edge . . . they're on the Moon watching us . . .

NASA, understandably, has never confirmed Binder's story but Buzz Aldrin was soon complaining bitterly about the Agency having used him as a 'travelling salesman'. And two years after his Moon mission, following reported bouts of heavy drinking, he was admitted to hospital with 'emotional depression'.

'Travelling salesman' ... that's an odd choice of words, isn't it? What, in Aldrin's view, were the NASA authorities trying to sell? And to whom? Could it be that they were using him, and others like him, to sell their *official* version of the truth to ordinary people right across the world?

Was Aldrin's Moon walk one of those great spectaculars, presented with maximum publicity, to justify the billions being poured into space research? Was it part of the American-Russian cover for Alternative 3?

All men who have travelled to the Moon have given indications of knowing about Alternative 3 – and of the reasons which precipitated it.

In May, 1972, James Irwin – *officially* the sixth man to walk on the Moon – resigned to become a Baptist missionary. And he said then: 'The flight made me a deeper religious person and more keenly aware of the fragile nature of our planet.'

Edgar Mitchell, who landed on the Moon with the Apollo 14 mission in February, 1971, also resigned in May, 1972 – to devote himself to parapsychology. Later, at the headquarters of his Institute for Noetic Sciences near San Francisco, he described looking at this world from the Moon: 'I went into a very deep pathos, a kind of anguish. That incredibly beautiful planet that was Earth ... a place no bigger than my thumb was my home ... a blue and white jewel against a velvet black sky ... was being killed off.' And on March 23, 1974, he was quoted in the *Daily Express* as saying that society had only three ways in which to go and that the third was 'the most viable but most difficult alternative'.

Another of the Apollo Moon-walkers, Bob Grodin, was equally specific when interviewed by a Sceptre Television reporter on June 20, 1977: 'You think they need all that crap down in Florida just to put two guys up there on a ... on a bicycle? The hell they do! You know why they need us? So they've got a P.R. story for

9

all that hardware they've been firing into space. We're nothing, man! Nothing!'

On July 11, 1977, the *Los Angeles Times* came near to the heart of the matter – nearer than any other newspaper – when it published a remarkable interview with Dr. Gerard O'Neill. Dr. O'Neill is a Princeton professor who served, during a 1976 sabbatical, as Professor of Aerospace at the Massachusetts Institute of Technology and who gets nearly $500,000 each year in research grants from NASA. Here is a section from that article:

> The United Nations, *he says*, has conservatively estimated that the world's population, now more than 4 billion people, will grow to about 6.5 billion by the year 2000. Today, *he adds*, about 30% of the world's population is in developed nations. But, because most of the projected population growth will occur in underdeveloped countries, that will drop to 22% by the end of the century. The world of 2000 will be poorer and hungrier than the world today, *he says*.

Dr. O'Neill also explained the problems caused by the earth's 4,000-mile atmospheric layer but – presumably because the article was a comparatively short one – he was not quoted on the additional threat posed by the notorious 'greenhouse' syndrome.

His solution? He called it Island 3. And he added: 'There's really no debate about the technology involved in doing it. That's been confirmed by NASA's top people.'

But Dr. O'Neill, a family man with three children who likes to fly sailplanes in his spare time, did not realise that he was slightly off-target. He was right, of course, about the technology. But he knew nothing of the political ramifications and he would have been astounded to learn that NASA was feeding his research to the Russians.

Even eminent political specialists, as respected in their sphere as Dr. O'Neill is in his own, have been

10

puzzled by an undercurrent they have detected in East-West relationships. Professor G. Gordon Broadbent, director of the independently-financed Institute of Political Studies in London and author of a major study of U.S.-Soviet diplomacy since the 1950s, emphasised that fact on June 20, 1977, when he was interviewed on Sceptre Television: 'On the broader issue of Soviet-U.S. relations, I must admit there is an element of mystery which troubles many people in my field.' He added: 'What we're suggesting is that, at the very highest levels of East-West diplomacy, there has been operating a factor of which we know nothing. Now it could just be – and I stress the word "could" – that this unknown factor is some kind of massive but covert operation in space. But as for the reasons behind it . . . we are not in the business of speculation.'

Washington's acute discomfort over O'Neill's revelations through the *Los Angeles Times* can be assessed by the urgency with which a 'suppression' Bill was rushed to the Statute Book. On July 27, 1977 – only sixteen days after publication of the O'Neill interview – columnist Jeremy Campbell reported in the London *Evening Standard* that the Bill would become law that September. He wrote:

> It prohibits the publishing of an official report without permission, arguing that this obstructs the Government's control of its own information. That was precisely the charge brought against Daniel Ellsberg for giving the Pentagon papers to the *New York Times*.
> Most ominous of all, the Bill would make it a crime for any present or former civil servant to tell the Press of Government wrong-doing or pass on any news based on information 'submitted to the Government in private'.

Campbell pointed out that this final clause 'has given serious pain to guardians of American Press freedom

11

because it creates a brand new crime'. Particularly as there was provision in the Bill for offending journalists to be sent to prison for up to six years.

We subsequently discovered that a man called Harman – Leonard Harman – read that item in the newspaper and that later, in a certain television executives' dining-room, he expressed regret that a similar Law had not been passed years earlier by the British government. He was eating treacle tart with custard at the time and he reflected wistfully that he could then have insisted on such a Law being obeyed. That, when it came to Alternative 3, would have saved him from a great deal of trouble . . .

He had chosen treacle tart, not because he particularly liked it, but because it was 2p cheaper than the chocolate sponge. That was typical of Harman.

He was one of the people, as you may have learned already through the Press, who tried to interfere with the publication of this book. We will later be presenting some of the letters received by us from him and his lawyers – together with the replies from our legal advisers. We decided to print these letters in order to give you a thorough insight into our investigation for it is important to stress that we, like Professor Broadbent, are not in the 'business of speculation'.

We are interested only in the *facts*. And it is intriguing to note the pattern of facts relating to astronauts who have been on Moon missions – and who have therefore been exposed to some of the surprises presented by Alternative 3. A number, undermined by the strain of being party to such a horrendous secret, suffered nervous or mental collapses. A high percentage sought sanctuary in excessive drinking or in extra-marital affairs which destroyed what had been secure and successful marriages. Yet these were men originally picked from many thousands precisely because of their stability. Their training and experience, intelligence and physical fitness – all these, of course, were prime

12

considerations in their selection. But the supremely important quality was their balanced temperament.

It would need something stupendous, something almost unimaginable to most people, to flip such men into dramatic personality changes. That something, we have now established, was Alternative 3 and, perhaps more particularly, the nightmarish obscenities involved in the development and perfection of Alternative 3.

We are not suggesting that the President of the United States has had personal knowledge of the terror and clinical cruelties which have been an integral part of the Operation, for that would make him directly responsible for murders and barbarous mutilations.

We are convinced, in fact, that this is not the case. The President and the Russian leader, together with their immediate subordinates, have been concerned only with the broad sweep of policy. They have acted in unison to ensure what they consider to be the best possible future for mankind. And the day-to-day details have been delegated to high-level professionals.

These professionals, we have now established, have been classifying people selected for the Alternative 3 operation into two categories: those who are picked as individuals and those who merely form part of a 'batch consignment'. There have been several 'batch consignments' and it is the treatment meted out to most of these men and women which provides the greatest cause for outrage.

No matter how desperate the circumstances may be – and we reluctantly recognise that they are extremely desperate – no humane society could tolerate what has been done to the innocent and the gullible. That view, fortunately, was taken by one man who was recruited into the Alternative 3 team three years ago. He was, at first, highly enthusiastic and completely dedicated to the Operation. However, he became revolted by some of the atrocities involved. He did not consider that, even in the prevailing circumstances, they could be justified.

Three days after the transmission of that sensational television documentary, his conscience finally goaded him into action. He knew the appalling risk he was taking, for he was aware of what had happened to others who had betrayed the secrets of Alternative 3, but he made telephone contact with television reporter Colin Benson — and offered to provide Benson with evidence of the most astounding nature.

He was calling, he said, from abroad but he was prepared to travel to London. They met two days later. And he then explained to Benson that copies of most orders and memoranda, together with transcripts prepared from tapes of Policy Committee meetings, were filed in triplicate — in Washington, Moscow and Geneva where Alternative 3 had its operational headquarters. The system had been instituted to ensure there was no misunderstanding between the principal partners. He occasionally had access to some of that material — although it was often weeks or even months old before he saw it — and he was willing to supply what he could to Benson. He wanted no money. He merely wanted to alert the public, to help stop the mass atrocities.

Benson's immediate reaction, after he had assessed the value of this offer, was that Sceptre should mount a follow-up programme — one which would expose the horrors of Alternative 3 in far greater depth. He argued bitterly with his superiors at Sceptre but they were adamant. The company was already in serious trouble with the government and there was some doubt about whether its licence would be renewed. They refused to consider the possibility of doing another programme. They had officially disclaimed the Alternative 3 documentary as a hoax and that was where the matter had to rest. Anyway, they pointed out, this character who'd come forward was probably a nut . . .

If you saw the documentary, you will probably realise that Benson is a stubborn man. His friends say

14

he is pig-obstinate. They also say he is a first-class investigative journalist.

He was angry about this attempt to suppress the truth and that is why he agreed to co-operate in the preparation of this book. That co-operation has been invaluable.

Through Benson we met the telephone caller who we now refer to as Trojan. And that meeting resulted in our acquiring documents, which we will be presenting, including transcripts of tapes made at the most secret rendezvous in the world — thirty-five fathoms beneath the ice-cap of the Arctic.

For obvious reasons, we cannot reveal the identity of Trojan. Nor can we give any hint about his function or status in the Operation. We are completely satisfied, however, that his credentials are authentic and that, in breaking his oath of silence, he is prompted by the most honourable of motives. He stands in relation to the Alternative 3 conspiracy in much the same position as the anonymous informant 'Deep Throat' occupied in the Watergate affair.

Most of the 'batch consignments' have been taken from the area known as the Bermuda Triangle but numerous other locations have also been used. On October 6, 1975, the *Daily Telegraph* gave prominence to this story:

> The disappearance in bizarre circumstances in the past two weeks of 20 people from small coastal communities in Oregon was being intensively investigated at the weekend amid reports of an imaginative fraud scheme involving a 'flying saucer' and hints of mass murder.
>
> Sheriff's officers at Newport, Oregon, said that the 20 individuals had vanished without trace after being told to give away all their possessions, including their children, so that they could be transported in a flying saucer 'by UFO to a better life'.

Deputies under Mr. Ron Sutton, chief criminal investigator in surrounding Lincoln County, have traced the story back to a meeting on September 14 in a resort hotel, the Bayshore Inn at Waldport, Oregon ...

Local police have received conflicting reports as to what occurred (at the meeting). But while it is clear that the speaker did not pretend to be from outer space, he told the audience how their souls could be 'saved through a UFO'.

The hall had been reserved for a fee of $50 by a man and a woman who gave false names. Mr. Sutton said witnesses had described them as 'fortyish, well-groomed, straight types'.

The *Telegraph* said that 'selected people would be prepared at a special camp in Colorado for life on another planet' and quoted Investigator Sutton as adding:

'They were told they would have to give away everything, even their children. I'm checking a report of one family who supposedly gave away a 150-acre farm and three children.

'We don't know if it's fraud or whether these people might be killed. There are all sorts of rumours, including some about human sacrifice and that this is sponsored by the (Charles) Manson family.'

Most of the missing 20 were described as being 'hippie types' although there were some older people among them. People of this calibre, we have now discovered, have been what is known as 'scientifically adjusted' to fit them for a new role as a slave species.

There have been equally strange reports of animals — particularly farm animals — disappearing in large numbers. And occasionally it appears that aspects of the Alternative 3 operation have been bungled, that attempts to lift 'batch consignments' of humans or of animals have failed.

On July 15, 1977, the *Daily Mail* – under a 'Flying Saucer' headline – carried this story:

Men in face masks, using metal detectors and a geiger counter, yesterday scoured a remote Dartmoor valley in a bid to solve a macabre mystery.

Their search centred on marshy grassland where 15 wild ponies were found dead, their bodies mangled and torn.

All appeared to have died at about the same time, and many of the bones have been inexplicably shattered. To add to the riddle, their bodies decomposed to virtual skeletons within only 48 hours.

Animal experts confess they are baffled by the deaths at Cherry Brook Valley near Postbridge.

Yesterday's search was carried out by members of the Devon Unidentified Flying Objects centre at Torquay who are trying to prove a link with outer space.

They believe that flying saucers may have flown low over the area and created a vortex which hurled the ponies to their death.

Mr. John Wyse, head of the four-man team, said: 'If a spacecraft has been in the vicinity, there may still be detectable evidence. We wanted to see if there was any sign that the ponies had been shot but we have found nothing. This incident bears an uncanny resemblance to similar events reported in America.'

The *Mail* report concluded with a statement from an official representing The Dartmoor Livestock Protection Society and the Animal Defence Society: 'Whatever happened was violent. We are keeping an open mind. I am fascinated by the UFO theory. There is no reason to reject that possibility since there is no other rational explanation.'

These, then, were typical of the threads which inspired the original television investigation. It needed

17

one person, however, to show how they could be embroidered into a clear picture.

Without the specialist guidance of that person the Sceptre television documentary could never have been produced – and Trojan would never have contacted Colin Benson. And it would have been years, possibly seven years or even longer, before ordinary people started to suspect the devastating truth about this planet on which we live.

That person, of course, is the old man . . .

SECTION TWO

They realise now that they should have killed the old man. That would have been the logical course – to protect the secrecy of Alternative 3.

It is curious, really, that they did not agree his death on that Thursday in February for, as we have stated, they do use murder. Of course, it is not *called* murder – not when it is done jointly by the governments of America and Russia. It is an Act of Expediency.

Many Acts of Expediency are believed to have been ordered by the sixteen men, official representatives of the Pentagon and the Kremlin, who comprise the Policy Committee. Grotesque and apparently inexplicable slayings in various parts of the world – in Germany and Japan, Britain and Australia – are alleged to have been sanctioned by them.

We have not been able to substantiate these suspicions and allegations so we merely record that an *unknown* number of people – including distinguished radio astronomer Sir William Ballantine – have been executed because of this astonishing agreement between the super-powers.

Prominent politicians, including two in Britain, were among those who tried to prevent the publication of this book. They insisted that it is not *necessary* for you, and others like you, to be told the unpalatable facts. They argue that the events of the future are now inevitable, that there is nothing to be gained by prematurely unleashing fear. We concede that they are sincere in their views but we maintain that you ought to know. You have a right to know.

Attempts were also made to neuter the television programme which first focused public attention on

19

Alternative 3. Those attempts were partially successful. And, of course, after the programme was transmitted — when there was that spontaneous explosion of anxiety — Sceptre Television was forced to issue a formal denial. It had all been a hoax. That's what they were told to say. That's what they did say.

Most people were then only too glad to be reassured. They *wanted* to be convinced that the programme had been devised as a joke, that it was merely an elaborate piece of escapist entertainment. It was more comfortable that way.

In fact, the television researchers did uncover far more disturbing material than they were allowed to transmit. The censored information is now in our possession. And, as we have indicated, there was a great deal that Benson and the rest of the television team did not discover — not until after their programme had been screened.

They did not know, for example, that Sir William Ballantine's freakish death — not far from his base at Jodrell Bank — was mirrored by that of an aerospace professor called Peterson near Stanford University at Palo Alto, California. Nor did they know of the monthly conferences beneath the ice of the Arctic.

Alternative 3 appears a preposterous conception — until one analyses the history of the so-called space-race. Right from the start the public have been allowed to know only what is considered *appropriate* for them to know. Many futuristic research developments — and the extent of information pooled between East and West — have been kept strictly classified.

There was a small but typical example in 1951 when living creatures were hurtled into the stratosphere for the very first time. Or, at least, the public were eventually *told* it was for the first time. Four monkeys — code-named Albert 1, 2, 3 and 4 — were launched in a V2 rocket from White Sands, New Mexico.

Remember White Sands? That's where the Columbus *Dispatch* man photographed that strange craft — the one which a NASA official grudgingly admitted was known as 'The Flying Saucer'.

The monkeys were successfully brought back to earth. Three survived. One died, shortly afterwards, of heat prostration.

Much later, when news did leak out, it was explained that Operation Albert had been kept secret for only one reason – to avert any possibility of animal-lovers staging a protest demonstration.

Most people accepted the official story – that the four Alberts really had been this world's first travellers in space. But was that the truth?

By 1951 the V2 rocket, a relic of World War II, had been superseded by far more sophisticated missiles. So would it be logical, or indeed practical, to use an obsolete vehicle for the first launch of living creatures?

Is it not more feasible to argue that Operation Albert was no more than a subsidiary experiment which happened to slip through the security net? That the authorities were not too perturbed about having to confirm it – because it helped conceal the real and gigantic truth?

There is abundant evidence that by 1951 the superpowers were far more advanced in space technology than they have ever admitted. Much of that evidence has been supplied by experienced pilots. By men like Captain Laurence W. Vinther . . .

At 8.30 p.m. on January 20, 1951, Captain Vinther – then with Mid-Continent Airlines – was ordered by the controller at Sioux City Airport to investigate a 'very bright light' above the field.

He and his co-pilot, James F. Bachmeier, took off in a DC3 and headed for the source of the light.

Suddenly the light dived towards them at great speed and passed about 200 feet above them. Then they discovered that it had reversed direction, apparently in a split second, and was flying parallel to the airliner. It was a clear moonlit night and both men could clearly see that the light was emanating from a cigar-shaped object bigger than a B-29. Eventually the strange craft lost altitude, passed under the DC3 and disappeared.

Two months later, on March 15, thousands of people in New Delhi were startled by a strange object, high in the sky, which appeared to be circling the city. One witness was George Franklin Floate, chief engineer with the Delhi Flying Club, who described 'a bullet-nosed, cigar-shaped object about 100 feet long with a ring of flames at the end'. Two Indian Air Force jets were sent up to intercept. But the object suddenly surged upwards at a 'phenomenal speed' and vanished into the heights.

So, despite all official denials, sufficient advances had been made by 1951 to provide the basis for planning Alternative 3.

By the mid-Seventies there were so many rumours about covert information-swapping between East and West — with men like Professor Broadbent becoming progressively more curious — that the American-Russian 'rivals' staged a masterpiece of camouflage. They would show the world, quite openly, how they were prepared to co-operate in space! The result was seen in July, 1975: the first *admitted* International Space Transfer. Television cameras showed the docking of a Soyuz spacecraft with an Apollo — and the crews jubilantly exchanging food and symbolic halves of medals.

Leonid Brezhnev sent this message to the united spacemen: 'Your successful docking confirms the correctness of technical solutions that were worked out and realised in co-operation by Soviet and American scientists, designers and cosmonauts. One can say that Soyuz-Apollo is a prototype of future international orbital stations.'

Gerald Ford expressed the hope that this 'tremendous demonstration of co-operation' would set the pattern for 'what we have to do in the future to make it a better world'. And at his home near Boston, Massachusetts, former Apollo man Bob Grodin switched off his television set in disgust.

Grodin's comment was more succinct than that of either leader. He said: 'How they've got the bloody neck!' Then he poured himself another tumbler of bourbon.

Grodin had cause to be bitter that day. Bitter and also cynically amused. There'd been no television coverage, no glory of any sort, when he'd done the identical manoeuvre – 140 miles above the clouds – on April 20, 1969. He'd shaken hands up there with the Russians and laughed at their bad jokes – exactly like Tom Stafford had just been doing – but there'd been none of this celebrity crap about that operation. It was crazy . . . the way they were kidding people by making it all seem such a big deal! Christ! It hadn't been a big deal even when he'd done it. There'd been all the others before him . . .

We now know, in fact, that this American-Russian docking technique was successfully pioneered in the late Fifties – with specially-designed submarines in the black depths of the North Atlantic. It was pioneered specifically because of Alternative 3. Because of the need for the ultimate in security. The system made it possible for men who were officially enemies, who played the charade of distrusting each other in public, to travel separately and discreetly to meetings far below the waves.

Thursday, February 3, 1977. A landmark. A Policy Committee meeting infiltrated, via the transcript, for the first time by Trojan. Information about earlier meetings, held in variety of locations, still not available. Complete transcript obviously filed in separately-secured sections. Sensible precaution. And frustrating. Trojan obtained only small section. Enough to confirm murder conspiracy. Major break-through.

The venue: the wardroom of a modified Permit nuclear submarine. Thirty-five fathoms beneath ice of Arctic. Permit subs 'seek out and destroy enemy'. So American tax-payers are told. Cold War concepts are readily accepted. They distract from real truth . . .

No names on transcript. No names, apparently, ever used. Only nationalities and numbers. Eight Russians – listed as R ONE through to R EIGHT – and eight Americans.

Procedure shown by subsequent transcripts – A EIGHT and R EIGHT alternate monthly as chairmen.

February 3. Chairman: A EIGHT. Transcript section starts:

A FIVE: You're kill-crazy ... you know that? ... absolutely kill-crazy ...

A TWO: No ... the guy's right ... that old man is dangerous ...

R SIX: I am reminding you that it was agreed ... right from the start it was agreed ... that expediencies would be kept to the minimum ...

A TWO: And the old man, friend, is right there inside that minimum ... the way he talks ... he'll blow the whole goddam thing ...

R ONE: Who do you suppose ever listens to him? Eh? ... nobody ... that's who listens. Come ... he knows nothing ... not after all these years. Theories ... that's all he's got ... theories and memories ...

A FIVE: That just says it, doesn't it? Here we are wasting time and wetting ourselves because of theories that are twenty years old ... Jeez! ... if we start spreading expediencies so low because ...

R FOUR: The theories have not changed so much in twenty years and in my considered opinion ...

A FIVE: ... so low because of a semi-senile and garrulous old man ...

A EIGHT: He's not semi-senile ... he's not even *that* old ... I heard him lecture last year at Cambridge and, you take my word, he's certainly not semi-senile ... What, precisely, has he been saying?

A TWO: About getting air out of the soil ... about how the ice is melting ... people at that university ... they're beginning to listen to him ...

A FIVE: That's no more, for Chrissakes, than he was

24

saying in Alabama back in 1957... hell, I was right there at Huntsville when he said it...

R FOUR: The Huntsville Conference was like this meeting ... the discussions there were not for outsiders and...

A FIVE: Yes ... but not many people took him seriously even then ... and now that he's over the hill...

R FOUR: It is still a serious breach of security ... it is dangerous and it could start a panic among the masses...

A FIVE: So all right! ... Kill him! He's a harmless and doddering old has-been but if it makes you feel better ... go ahead and kill him ...

A EIGHT: Expediencies aren't to make us feel better... and our friend here was right ... we have agreed to restrict them to the minimum ... anything else against this man?

A TWO: Yeah ... the real bad news... I hear he's been dropping hints ... nothing specific but oblique hints about the big bang ... about the earth-air thing being cracked...

R SIX: But it is not possible for him to be knowing that ...

A TWO: Maybe he doesn't know ... not know for sure ... but he's sure done some figuring...

A ONE: You're saying he's guessed ... right? That's what you're saying?

A TWO: Too damned right that's what I'm saying.

R ONE: So it is as I said ... theories and memories and now guesses! We sentence an old man to death because of his guesses? That is how you Americans wish us to work?

A EIGHT: Let's cut the East-West stuff ... we're a team here, remember, and we don't have nationalities ... now, we've got a hell of an agenda to get through and we've spent quite long enough on this Englishman. So let's vote ... Those for an expediency? ...

25

Uh, huh ... And against? ... Well, that's it ... he goes on living. For a while, at least. But I suggest we keep tabs ... agreed? ... Right then ... Now Ballantine and this character Harry Carmell ... looks to me like there's no room for question about either of them ...

R SEVEN: This Harry Carmell ... we are certain that he has stolen that circuit from NASA?

A EIGHT: Positive certain. And heads, I can promise you, have rolled at Houston. We also know that he's somewhere in England ... probably London ... so if he should link up again with Ballantine ...

R SEVEN: I think we are all aware of what could happen if he did link with Ballantine.

A TWO: Especially with Ballantine's contacts in Fleet Street ...

R SEVEN: How was it possible for a man like Carmell to get out of America ... ?

A EIGHT: Don't tell me ... I can say it for you ... he'd never have got out of Russia that easily ... but there it is ... our people goofed and now it's down to us ...

R SEVEN: As you say then, there is no room for question ... both of them have got to be expediencies.

A EIGHT: All agreed? ... Good ... I suggest a couple of hot jobs ... coroners always play them quiet ...

R SEVEN: But first, presumably, we'll have to find Carmell ...

A EIGHT: We'll find him ... London's not that big a town and he'll soon be needing his shots.

A THREE: How hooked is he?

A EIGHT: Hooked enough ... Now what about Peterson? Same deal?

R FOUR: We've all seen the earlier report on Peterson ... what is the latest assessment?

A EIGHT: He's getting more and more paranoiac about the batch consignments ...

R FOUR: You mean the scientific adjustments?

A EIGHT: Yeah ... the scientific adjustments ... he's running off at the mouth about ethics ... that sort of crap ...

A TWO: Ethics! What the hell do some of these guys think we're all at? Jesus! We're smack in the middle of the most vital exercise ever mounted ... with the survival of the whole human race swinging on it ... and they bleat about ethics ...

A EIGHT: That surgery bit ... it really got to him ...

A FIVE: They should never have told him ... he didn't need to know that ... look, we *owe* Peterson ... he's done good work ... couldn't we just get him committed?

A TWO: No way ... much too risky ... he'd squeal his bloody head off.

A EIGHT: I endorse that. I'm sorry because I like the guy ... but there's no choice. Anyone against an expediency for Peterson? ... okay ... that's carried ... now for God's sake let's get down to the big problem ... this stepping-up of the supplies-shuttle. Any word from Geneva?

That was where the transcript section ended. Three murders, quite clearly, had been agreed. No matter what they chose to call them, they were still talking about murder. But scientific adjustments? A great deal had already been published in the Western Press about strange experiments being conducted on inmates – chiefly dissidents and political prisoners – at the Dnepropetrovsk Mental Hospital in the Ukraine. They were barbaric, these experiments, but they had been known about and talked about for years. To push this Peterson to such agony of mind – to push him into risking and forfeiting his life – that surely had to be something new.

Trojan, by that time, had supplied us with information about that 'something new' – for it was precisely that something which had decided him to make his dangerous

27

break and talk to Benson. But he had nothing in writing. Nothing to document or substantiate his claims. We decided they were worth investigating but that it would be irresponsible merely to assume their accuracy.

We sought help from contacts in Washington. Contacts with influence in Senate and Congressional committees. And we were surprised by the speed with which those contacts achieved results. They didn't manage to bring the full story into the open, not at that stage, but they did make it possible for the public to see a glimmering of the truth.

On August 3, 1977, the London *Evening News* carried this story:

> Human 'guinea pigs' have been used by the CIA in experiments to control behaviour and sexual activity.
>
> The American intelligence agency also considered hiring a magician for another secret programme on mind control.
>
> The experiments over the past 20 years are revealed in documents which were thought to have been destroyed, but which have now been released after pressure from United States senate and congressional committees. The attempts to change sex patterns and other behaviour involved using drugs on schizophrenic as well as normal people. Hallucinatory drugs like LSD were used on students.
>
> Another heavily censored document shows that a top magician was considered for work on mind control.
>
> The give-away word was 'prestidigitation' — sleight of hand — which appeared in a 1953 memo written by Sidney Gottlier, then chief of the CIA's chemical division.

That story, we are convinced, would never have appeared if it had not been for the information supplied by Trojan. The 'guinea-pig' facts would have remained as secret as the rest of the Alternative 3 operation.

The following day – August 4 – other newspapers developed the story. Ann Morrow, filing from Washington, wrote in the *Daily Telegraph*:

Some of the more chilling details of the way the Central Intelligence Agency (CIA) tried to control individual behaviour by using drugs on willing and unwilling human 'guinea pigs' were disclosed yesterday by its director, Mr. Stansfield Turner.

In a large wood-panelled room, Mr. Turner, who likes to be known by his rank of Admiral, told the Senate's Intelligence Committee and Human Resources Sub-committee on Health that such tests were abhorrent to him.

He admitted that the tests were carried out in 'safe houses' in San Francisco and New York where unwitting sexual psychopaths were subjected to experiments and attempts were made to change sexual conduct and other forms of human behaviour.

At least 185 private scientists and 80 research institutions, including universities, were involved.

Mr. Turner went on to say that one man had killed himself – by leaping from an hotel window in New York City – after he had 'unknowingly' been used in a 'CIA-sponsored experiment'. The report continued:

Senator Edward Kennedy asked some incisive questions, but like other members of the Senate Committee found it difficult to keep a straight face when asking about the CIA's operations 'Midnight' and 'Climax'.

Questioning two former CIA employees about the experiments which began in the 1950s and ended in 1973, Senator Kennedy read out a bizarre list of accessories for the 'safe houses' in San Francisco and New York where prostitutes organised.

In his flat Bostonian accent he reeled off, straight-faced: 'Rather elaborate dressing table, black

29

velveteen skirt, one French Can-Can dancer's picture, three Toulouse Lautrec etchings, two-way mirrors and recording equipment.' Then he admitted that this was the lighter side of the operation.

Mr. John Gittinger, who was with the CIA for 26 years, trembled and put a handkerchief to his eyes. He just nodded in agreement.

The Times, as you can check for yourself in any good reference library, carried a similar story from Washington that day. It described documents taken from CIA files and added:

> Batches of the documents have been made available to reporters in Washington under the Freedom of Information Act, which guarantees the public access to Government papers. They are nearly all heavily censored.

That's the give-away – there in that last line. *Nearly all heavily censored.* Alternative 3, right from its conception in the Fifties, has always been considered exempt from the Freedom of Information Act. And it is no coincidence that these controversial experiments also started – as is now openly admitted – in the Fifties.

The editors of these newspapers had no way of knowing that their stories, disturbing as they were, had a direct connection with Alternative 3. Nor that they had secured only a fraction of the truth about those CIA experiments.

Information obtained from the *complete* experiments was pooled with that gained at the Dnepropetrovsk Mental Hospital. It was pooled so that factory-production methods could be developed to manufacture a slave species.

Remember that curious statement made by criminal investigator Ron Sutton in October, 1975 – after the disappearance of the 'batch consignment' from Oregon?

'They were told they would have to give away

30

everything, even their children. I'm checking a report of one family who supposedly gave away a 150-acre farm and three children.' That's what he said. And now those words fit into perspective.

In the days before the American Civil War slaves had no right to a family, no right to keep their own children, and they had no property. They *were* property. That horrifying philosophy, we can now prove, has been adopted by the space slave-masters of the Seventies.

Alternative 3 needs regular consignments of slaves. It needs them to labour for the key people. For people like Dr. Ann Clark.

SECTION THREE

Three people unwittingly inspired that television documentary and, although they would be dismayed to realise it, they helped alert the world to the horrors of Alternative 3.

Dr. Ann Clark is a research scientist specialising in solar energy. Brian Pendlebury, a former RAF man, is an electronics expert. Robert Patterson is a senior lecturer in mathematics – or, rather, he *was* until the time of his disappearance. Today, almost certainly, Patterson no longer teaches mathematics but is working full-time for Alternative 3.

So these people, then, were the catalyst for the entire investigation. That is why, although we have never met them, we have dedicated this book to them.

Ann Clark, a raven-haired and attractive woman who was just nudging thirty, made her big decision towards the end of 1975. She would never have made it – although her pride stopped her admitting as much on television – if her fiancé had not unexpectedly broken their engagement.

Her future had seemed all set. She'd intended to soldier on, despite all the frustrations, at the research laboratory in Norwich until they got married. And then, probably, until their first child was born. Conditions at the laboratory were, as she'd often said, 'pretty grotty' but she was prepared to tolerate them. After all, it wasn't going to be for too long . . .

Then Malcolm had shattered her with his news. He'd been astonishingly casual about it. Quite unlike the Malcolm she'd thought she'd known. He'd just told her, brutally, that their engagement was a mistake, that he didn't 'want to get tied down'. And then, only four weeks later, she'd heard he was talking about marrying some girl called Maureen . . .

Suddenly the laboratory, and everything about it, had seemed intolerably depressing. Squalid and almost sordid. All the authorities admitted that their research was important. Particularly with the energy shortage and the climbing cost of oil. But apparently it wasn't important enough to have money poured into it.

Experimental projects often took three times as long as they should because of equipment which was make-shift and, in some cases, almost obsolete. Certain projects could not even be started. 'Maybe in the next financial year but, at the moment, there's no budget available.' That was a stock answer from the administrators. And Ann Clark became progressively more frustrated.

She wanted, now, to throw herself harder than ever into her research, to immerse herself in it completely, but she was increasingly aware that – like the others – she was not being allowed to make full use of her training. She'd never have felt so strongly if it hadn't been for Malcolm. But Malcolm and his plan for marrying this Maureen . . . that's what really decided her to start a new life.

Plenty of others were doing the same that year. They were getting out of Britain, heading for the big-money jobs in Europe and in the Middle East. And in America. They were doubling their salaries and picking up bonus perks like company cars and lavish homes. They were also being offered far better conditions in which to work.

The Brain Drain. That's what it's called. And it is an accurate label. In the twelve years up to December, 1975 – the month Ann Clark reached her decision – nearly 4 million people had evacuated from the United Kingdom. More than a third of them were from the professional and managerial levels of British society.

One of the department heads at Norwich had left for

33

a top post in America at the beginning of that year and, as his occasional letters had shown, he had not regretted the move. His only regret, in fact, was that he'd not made it years earlier. Ann Clark decided to write to him.

To her amazement, he telephoned her from California as soon as he got the letter. There'd be no problem at all, he told her. Not with her ability and experience. She was exactly the type they needed and, if she wanted, he could certainly get her fixed with the right job.

If she wanted! She'd never imagined it could possibly be that easy. Excitement surged through her as she listened. Apparently there was a man in London who was recruiting scientists for the company in California and if she cared to contact this man . . .

She jotted down the name and address of the man in London, together with his telephone number. 'I'll get in touch with him today,' she said. 'I can't tell you how grateful . . .'

'Let me call him first,' he interrupted. 'I'll put him in the picture about you.'

'Thank you,' she said. 'Thank you very much indeed.'

She met the man in London the following day and it was all settled within an hour. She drafted her resignation on the train back to Norwich.

That was the week, as we will explain later, that she was first contacted by Sceptre Television. And, at first, she was more than happy to talk to them about her plans. She didn't mention Malcolm, of course, because the viewers didn't need to know about him. However, it was important, she felt, for people to be told exactly why scientists were flocking away from Britain. She was flattered, in fact, to be given the opportunity and she told herself that, by speaking out, she might help get conditions improved for those she was leaving . . .

Now we reach a mystery which we still have not completely resolved. The information we have fitted

34

together has come from Ann Clark's friends and colleagues in Norwich. It almost provides an answer ... but it also leaves questions.

Shortly after the Sceptre Television film unit arrived at the laboratory in January, 1976 – for the first of a series of interviews – Ann Clark was visited there by a strange American. He'd made no appointment but just turned up and they assumed he was connected, in some way, with her new job. The American talked to her, privately, for a long time and afterwards she seemed upset. She refused to say what he'd wanted or what they'd discussed but she was obviously extremely upset.

That American, we have now established, went to her flat that evening and stayed for three hours. And after that evening her attitude to those around her, and to the Sceptre Television people, changed in the most extraordinary manner. She did her work as conscientiously as ever but she was oddly withdrawn. She refused to be drawn into any conversations. It was as if she had brought a shutter down all around herself.

There was also something else. One of her colleagues, an elderly man, told us: 'I started noticing that she was sometimes looking at me – and at others – with a funny sort of expression in her eyes. It was almost as if, for some reason or other, she felt sorry for us. All a bit odd ...'

All *very* odd. Dr. Ann Clark left Norwich in a self-drive hired car on February 22, 1976. She left without working out her notice because, as she explained, the Americans were in a hurry to have her. So she became part of the Brain Drain. But she has still not joined that company in California.

Brian Pendlebury was thirty-three when he became part of the Brain Drain in July, 1974. His principal reason for leaving was that he disliked the climate, particularly the climate in Manchester. He was very much a sun person.

35

Since leaving university, with a degree in electronics, he'd acquired a taste for travel as a special-projects officer with the RAF.

The Air Force had shown him the world. It had also shown him that he wasn't the type to settle down in any hum-drum routine. Certainly not in Manchester.

Five months after leaving the service he applied for a job with a major electronics firm in Sydney, Australia. And, to the acute disappointment of his parents, he got it.

They were, they now admit, disappointed for a selfish but very understandable reason. He was their only child and they absolutely adored him — having scrimped to get him through university and been so proud over his success — and for years they'd seen so very little of him. They had hoped that now he would live at home, for a year or so, at least. His mother also had this cosy vision of Brian marrying some nice sensible Lancashire girl and of herself becoming a doting grandmother.

'Maybe we can work out some compromise,' he'd told her teasingly. 'I'll try to find myself some nice sensible Australian girl and then you can have a grandson with a touch of aborigine in him . . .'

There was no way of arguing with him, not once he'd made up his mind. He did promise, however, that he'd keep closely in touch. He'd write regularly and he'd send lots of photographs. Yes, he knew that he'd said all that before . . . but this time he really would.

He kept that promise. He kept it for five months after leaving Manchester. Every week they got a letter with news of his life in Australia. The job, it seemed, was going fine and he was really enjoying himself there. They also got photographs: Brian surfing . . . Brian with friends at a nightclub . . . Brian in front of Sydney Harbour bridge. That bridge picture was a particularly good one. They had it framed and they put it on the mantelpiece.

So everything was fine, absolutely fine, except for some disconcerting facts.

Brian Pendlebury did not live at the address shown on his letters. The company for which he claimed to be working insist they have never heard of him. The truth, as far as we can establish it, is that Pendlebury never got to Australia.

Britain's system of taxation was a favourite hate subject with forty-two-year-old Robert Patterson. And, as a mathematician, he always had the latest facts to justify his anger.

His friends at the University of St. Andrews, where he was a senior lecturer, had become accustomed to a regular bombardment of figures:

'Do you realise that in Germany the most a man has to pay on the top slice of his taxable earnings is only 56 per cent! And in America ... now *that's* a country where they really appreciate the value of incentive ... in America it's only 50 per cent!'

Every one of his sentences, when he was talking tax, seemed to finish with a fiery exclamation mark.

'But what's it here in Britain? You ask me that and I'll tell you! Eighty-three per cent ... that's what it is here ... 83 per cent! And you wonder why people here aren't interested in working harder!'

This sort of conversation – with Patterson supplying all the questions and answers – could go on indefinitely without anyone else saying a word. It was a hangover from his lecture-room technique and it made him quite intolerably boring.

Many people at the university were rather relieved when he eventually announced that he was going to follow his own advice. He and his wife Eileen were getting out of Britain. They were taking their two children off to a fresh start in America.

He was unusually reticent about what he was going to do in America, saying no more than that he'd been 'invited on an interesting project'. It seemed obvious, despite his evasiveness, that he'd accepted some really

37

plum post in America. And at the university, they weren't surprised, for he was recognised as one of the most brilliant mathematicians in Britain. It was a pity that he was also such a bore.

Patterson broke his news at the beginning of February, 1976, and a paragraph appeared in the *Guardian*.

One of the researchers at Sceptre Television — the one who'd organised the initial interview with Ann Clark — saw the paragraph and immediately contacted Patterson. He was offering Patterson the best platform he'd ever had to air his views on taxation for the programme *Science Report* was networked right across the country.

'Thank you for the invitation,' said Patterson. 'Normally I'd love to take it up but I've got a time problem. We're flying at the end of next week and there's so much I've got to do . . .'

'We wouldn't need all that much of your time,' persisted the researcher. He'd had trouble enough finding the right people and he wasn't going to let a prize like Robert Patterson slip away too easily. 'We could send a reporter and film unit up to Scotland and do it, perhaps, at the university or at your home.' Harman, he knew, would probably squeal about the cost of sending a unit all that way from London — just for one interview — but let him bloody squeal.

They couldn't expect to hold a network slot without spending a few bob. Anyway, he thought, Chris Clements could fight that out with Harman. That's what producers were for. His job was to get the right people and he was damned well doing it. 'It wouldn't take long, Mr. Patterson,' he said. 'And we could do it almost any time to suit you.'

Patterson hesitated. 'How about next Tuesday morning?' he said.

'Fine. What time?'

'Eleven o'clock?'

'Right. And where?'

'It would be more convenient here at my house.'

'Then your house it is, Mr. Patterson. We'll be there at eleven. And thank you.'

Colin Benson, now co-operating with us, was the TV reporter who went to Patterson's home on that Tuesday morning. He found the house locked and obviously empty. The Pattersons, according to neighbours, had driven off in a hurry at lunchtime on the Saturday.

If you watched that particular edition of *Science Report*, you will probably recall that the family's car was later found abandoned in London. But the Pattersons — Robert, Eileen, sixteen-year-old Julian and fourteen-year-old Kate — have not been seen since.

February 6, 1977. Sir William Ballantine kept looking nervously at his watch. He couldn't understand why Carmell hadn't telephoned. That, quite specifically, had been the arrangement. He should have telephoned — and fixed the meeting — as soon as he arrived in England.

From his study window, stark against the unseasonably bright blue of the afternoon sky, Ballantine could see the gigantic listening saucer of the Jodrell Bank radio telescope.

He stared at it now, trying to stifle the conviction that something had gone dreadfully wrong. For days he'd had this premonition that somehow *they* had discovered what he was planning, that time was draining fast away.

It had been a mistake, a terrible mistake, to have kept the tape a secret for so long. He should have told the public, months earlier, what was *really* happening in space. He should have done it that day when — at NASA headquarters in America — he saw the undeniable proof ... that men had achieved the impossible.

But, there again, who would have believed him? The facts were so fantastic that, despite his international standing as a radio astronomer, there would have been scepticism. Particularly if NASA denied the story – and Harry Carmell had warned him that NASA would deny it most emphatically.

Carmell had helped him. He'd been nervous about doing so but – without seeking permission from his superiors – he had helped. He'd played Ballantine's Jodrell Bank tape through one of the NASA electronic decoding circuits. And then they'd seen, just the two of them, the astounding pictures which were suddenly flowing from the unscrambled tape.

Carmell, immediately, had been terrified. 'Don't yap about this – not to anybody,' he'd said. 'These bastards would kill us if they knew what we've just seen. Take a word of advice, friend, and destroy that damned tape ...'

We have those words, exactly as they were spoken, for they made a big impression on Ballantine. Enough of an impression for him to record them in his 1976 diary.

Carmell had refused to get involved any further. And Ballantine, disturbed by the vehemence of his warnings, had taken the tape back to Jodrell Bank. It had stayed there, locked in a drawer of his desk, since his return from America.

Ballantine did not speak of what he'd seen at NASA. He tried to forget. But, of course, he could not forget.

On Wednesday, January 26, 1977, Ballantine got an unexpected telephone call from Carmell in America. Most of Ballantine's telephone conversations contained such a mass of technical information that he taped them for future reference. He taped this particular one and now, by permission of Lady Ballantine, we are able to present it:

CARMELL: Did you do like I said? ... Did you destroy that tape?

BALLANTINE: I haven't told anybody about it ... but I've still got it safe ...

CARMELL: Thank Christ! Then we can burst the whole bloody thing ...

BALLANTINE: I'm sorry ... what *are* you talking about?

CARMELL: Batch consignments ... that's what I'm talking about ... I tell you, friend, it's incredible what these goons are doing ...

BALLANTINE: Batch consignments? ... I don't know what that means ...

CARMELL: Stinking atrocities ... that's what it means ... But I don't want to say no more, not on the wire ... I'll tell you when I get to you ...

BALLANTINE: You're coming to England?

CARMELL: By the first damned flight I can ... I've quit NASA and I've borrowed a baby juke-box ...

BALLANTINE: I don't think I caught that ...

CARMELL: A juke-box ... you know ... a de-coder like we used last year ... I've got one and I'm bringing it to England ...

BALLANTINE: But what's happened? ... And what are batch consignments?

CARMELL: Wait till we meet, friend, and it'll blow your mind ... Jesus, I knew these bastards were evil but I never imagined ... look, I'll ring you when I get to London, okay?

BALLANTINE: You expect to get here tomorrow?

CARMELL: Can't rightly say ... they know I've got this baby and they're looking for me ... so I gotta play it smart. I might get up through Canada and out that way ... give me till ... well, let's say a week Sunday ... I should have made it before then ...

BALLANTINE: You know, I find this very hard to credit ... you really are in some danger?

CARMELL: Not *some* danger, friend ... the worst danger possible ... but I couldn't stand by and just let them do what they're doing ... now, look, I gotta go ... so a week Sunday at the outside, okay?

41

BALLANTINE: That'll be February 6 . . .

CARMELL: Yeah . . . but with luck it'll be earlier . . . if you haven't heard from me again by February 6 — let's say by four in the afternoon — you'll know it's all screwed up . . .

BALLANTINE: And what does that mean?

CARMELL: That I'll be dead, friend, that's what it means.

BALLANTINE: Good Lord! . . . but if that were to happen . . . what should I do?

CARMELL: If you give a damn about decency or human dignity . . . you'll go right ahead and expose the whole stinking shebang . . . there's a guy in Geneva who'll help you . . . his name is . . .

That was the core of the conversation. We are not printing the name mentioned at that stage by Harry Carmell for it is that of the man we now refer to as Trojan. In view of the way Trojan has helped in this investigation, his life would be in acute danger if he were in any way to be identified in this book.

So there was Ballantine in his study on February 6. It was nearly 4.45 in the afternoon. And there was still no call from Carmell.

Maybe, he thought, Carmell had been caught. Maybe he'd been caught and killed. It all bordered on being outrageously impossible but, after what he had seen at NASA, Ballantine no longer considered anything impossible.

Obviously he ought to contact the man in Switzerland. He'd promised Carmell that he would. Well, he'd more or less promised him. But even that wasn't as simple as it seemed. Carmell had given him no address or telephone number. Only a surname. And Geneva was rather a large place.

By 5.30 he was convinced that Carmell was dead. He was also convinced that there was serious danger for himself. Carmell's words kept running through his mind: 'I knew these bastards were evil but I never imagined ...' And now Ballantine's own imagination was churning over. They probably already knew about his tape and about what he intended doing with it ...

He took the tape from the drawer, knowing that he had to get it to somewhere safe. That was when he realised there was one friend who might be able to advise him – John Hendry, the London managing editor of an international news agency.

Hendry, to start with, had a staff reporter in Geneva – and he would almost certainly trace the man named by Carmell. Hendry would also be able to tell him the best way to break the news – for it was essential to make as big an initial impact as possible. He'd pull the whole bizarre business right into the eye of the public. He'd also force a thorough investigation into the disappearance of Harry Carmell.

He checked his watch again. Early Sunday evening. Chances were that John Hendry was still at his office. They worked odd hours in Fleet Street. It was worth trying.

He was lucky. He caught Hendry just as he was preparing to leave. Here, again with Lady Ballantine's permission, is a transcript of that telephone call:

BALLANTINE: John? ... This is William Ballantine ...

HENDRY: Well, what a happy surprise! How are things at Jodrell?

BALLANTINE: I've got a problem, John ... rather a serious problem ... and I need your help ...

HENDRY: Certainly, you know full well that any help I can give ... what sort of problem?

BALLANTINE: Can I meet you this evening?

HENDRY: You in London?

BALLANTINE: I'm calling from home ... but it wouldn't take me long to drive ...

HENDRY: Well ... I was just about wrapping up for the night ...

BALLANTINE: It is important, John ... and I promise you it's the biggest story you've seen this year ...

HENDRY: So how can I say 'no'? You want to come to the office?

BALLANTINE: I'll be with you as quickly as possible. Oh – and John – I'm also putting a package in the post to you ... but I'll explain that when I see you ...

HENDRY: I don't follow ... why not bring it with you ... ?

BALLANTINE: Because I've got a feeling ... a premonition if you like ... that events are starting to move rather fast ... and I want it safely out of my possession ...'

HENDRY: And that's supposed to be logic? William, what *is* all this about?

BALLANTINE: Just wait for me ... then you'll understand everything.

The sequence of events which immediately followed that conversation have been described by Lady Ballantine. We met her on July 27, 1977. Here is the statement she made then:

I entered the study just as my husband was replacing the receiver and I couldn't help noticing, right away, that he was in a state of agitation. This was unusual because he was normally a calm and extremely self-possessed man. He never allowed himself to get flustered. He had been behaving a little strangely, a little out-of-character, for about a week – ever since he had a phone call from some man in America. He wouldn't discuss it with me – which, again, was unusual – but he seemed to be very much on edge.

However, I'd never seen him quite as he looked when I went into his study. I had the distinct feeling – and I don't think I'm dramatising with hindsight – that he was frightened.

44

I asked him what was troubling him, for it was obvious that something was, but he kept shaking his head and saying there was nothing.

He told me that he had to drive to London immediately for a meeting . . .

Lady Ballantine became rather distressed during this part of the statement and we waited for a while until she had composed herself. She apologised for crying and said she was anxious to continue because she wanted to assist. Our investigation, she pointed out, would have had the fullest endorsement from her husband. She went on:

He took a package from the drawer of his desk and sealed it into a large envelope which he addressed to Mr. Hendry in London. He put stamps on it and asked me to take it straight away to the post box. He said it was most urgent and, although I pointed out that there was no collection that evening, he was quite adamant that I should take it then.

He said that he would probably be back from London in the early hours of the Monday morning but, as you know, I never saw him again.

Why did Ballantine act so strangely over that tape? It would have been more logical, surely, for him to have taken it with him to London. Getting his wife to post it — so ensuring it would be delayed before reaching Hendry — seems to make little sense. We confess we do not have the answer. Unless there is one to be found in that transcript of his conversation with Hendry . . .

'I've got a feeling . . . a premonition if you like . . .' That's what he said. And it could be the key. We now know that the tape would never have reached Hendry if it had gone into Ballantine's car. But then, borrowing an expression from Lady Ballantine, we do have the benefit of hindsight.

Ballantine's death, as you may recall, made all the front pages. The splash headline in one of the tabloids read FREAK SKID KILLS SCIENCE CHIEF – and that seemed to sum it up. There *was* no obvious explanation for his car having careered off the road on that journey to London. Ballantine was a competent and steady driver who had travelled that route often before. He would have known about that awkward bend and about that terrible drop beyond the protective fencing.

And, even in an agitated state, he would almost certainly have approached it with caution. A freak skid. Yes, that seemed to say it all.

Only one photograph of the crash was made available to the Press and television. A whole series were taken by agency cameraman George Green but only one was ever released. It showed part of the wreckage – and a blanket-covered shape on a stretcher.

We asked Green what was in the other pictures. Why had they been confiscated?

'I've been ordered to keep my trap shut,' he said. 'But I'll tell you this . . . you ought to ask that Professor Radwell why he lied at the inquest. Now I'm not saying any more . . . it'd be more than my job's worth. He's the boy you want to talk to.'

Professor Hubert Radwell was the pathologist who gave evidence at the Ballantine inquest. He had reported that the body had been 'extensively burned'. That in itself was puzzling for there had been no fire – and Radwell had not been pressed for an explanation.

We checked back on Trojan's transcript of the Policy Committee meeting – the one held only three days before Ballantine's death. And we studied the words used about Ballantine and Harry Carmell:

   R SEVEN: As you say then, there is no room for question . . . both of them have got to be expediencies.

   A EIGHT: All agreed? . . . Good . . . I suggest a couple of hot jobs . . . coroners always play them quiet . . .

46

'Hot jobs' and 'extensive' burns ... and coroners 'always playing them quiet'. And now this cryptic statement from cameraman George Green. It all had to add up to more than mere coincidence.

Professor Radwell, at first, refused to make any comment. 'The Ballantine business is in the past,' he said. 'Nothing can be gained by raking it all up.'

We formed the impression that he was under some pressure, that he had been given instructions to stay silent. And that he was uneasy about those instructions.

That impression proved right. We pressed him to specify the extent of the burning. And suddenly, to our surprise, it seemed as if he wanted to unburden himself. 'It was uncanny,' he said. 'Quite uncanny.' He paused before adding: 'They told me it would cause unnecessary alarm ... that there was no point in people knowing ... but now I'm not sure ... I've always regarded the truth as sacrosanct.' Another pause. Then, obviously having taken a big decision, he talked quickly and at length. His statement, which we will be presenting later, provides an astonishing insight into what really killed Sir William Ballantine. And into what the Policy Committee mean by a 'hot job'.

Harry Carmell first heard the news of Ballantine's death on a radio bulletin. He heard it early in the morning on February 7 and it hardly registered.

Very little was registering with Carmell at that time. The prolonged strain of dodging out of America, of knowing he was a target for execution, had pushed him back into a habit he thought he'd kicked for ever. He was back on drugs. Hard drugs.

He was in his mid-thirties but normally looked at least ten years younger. On this particular morning, in an hotel bedroom in London's Earls Court, he was more like a sick man of sixty or more. He lay fully dressed on the covers of the unmade bed, his bleached blue eyes fixed unseeingly on a crack in the ceiling. His skin, too

47

tight over his face, had the pallor of a shroud. And he felt as if he might once again start to vomit.

His girl, Wendy, was out getting the morning papers. He lit a cigarette, tried to will himself back to normality. But his head still seemed full of fog.

Ballantine. He could almost swear he'd heard that guy on the radio mention the name Ballantine. Or maybe it was a name very similar.

It made him remember, however, what he'd got to do. He'd got to contact Ballantine. He'd got to give him the juke-box. He checked the date on his watch and swore with quiet desperation. February 7. Jesus! That had to mean he'd been blown out of his mind for three whole days – ever since he'd got to England. Suddenly, recalling exactly what he'd said to Ballantine, he was in a panic. He'd told Ballantine, told him quite specifically, that he'd call by February 6 at the latest. And that if he didn't call by then, Ballantine could assume he was dead.

He scrambled off the bed, started fumbling through his wallet. Where the hell was that bloody number? He found it on a slip of card just as Wendy returned. He sat on his pillow to start dialling and she handed him one of the newspapers. One glance at the front page made him drop the receiver as if it was suddenly white-hot. That guy on the radio ... he *had* heard him properly. Ballantine had already been murdered.

Fear instantly cleared his brain. 'Throw your things together.' He was on his feet and his tone was decisive. 'We're pulling out – now.'

Wendy stared at him, bewildered. 'What's up?'

'I want to go on living – that's what's up.' Carmell was already bundling his clothes into a leather grip. 'Now come on – shift.'

Twelve minutes later they'd settled their bill and were out of the hotel. And, as they hurried away, he told her exactly why they were in England.

We should mention here that we are suppressing

48

Wendy's surname at her request. She fears retaliation from the Policy Committee and, although we consider those fears are not justified, we have agreed to respect her wishes.

We have interviewed her on three occasions and she has explained that she thought their furtive escape through Canada was somehow connected with Carmell having broken his contract with NASA.

She had not questioned him. And she certainly had no idea his life was in danger. Not until that morning in February. He told her everything that morning, as he bustled her along the pavements of Earls Court. He told her the lot.

'They'll start scouring the hotels now,' he said. 'So from here on we live rough. We find ourselves a squat somewhere and we live rough.'

And later, in the derelict house where they slept for the next two nights, he told her he was determined to go ahead with his plan. He was going to expose them and their atrocities. And he wasn't going to be stopped by Ballantine's death.

'Maybe I ought to go straight to the Press,' he said. 'That's the only way to play it now . . .'

'But what if they don't believe you?'

'Of course they'll believe me! It's the truth and I'll damned well make them believe me!'

'I was watching a programme on television the other night,' said Wendy. 'While you were . . . you know . . . asleep. I was watching a programme called *Science Report* . . .'

'So?'

'So it strikes me that a programme like that would have scientific advisers . . . and those advisers, dumbhead, might understand what you're talking about . . .'

Carmell immediately got enthusiastic. 'You're damned right they would . . . better than any newspaper reporter. Hey, I really think you've hit it. This *Science Report* . . . what station was it on?'

49

'I got the impression it goes out every week ... but I can't remember which station,' said Wendy. 'I do know it had a plug-spot in the middle so it couldn't have been the BBC ...'

'I'll find it,' interrupted Carmell. 'And I'll give them the most sensational science report they've ever had ...'

SECTION FOUR

Science Report had a very successful thirteen-week trial on ITV in 1975. Ratings were good, surprisingly good for such a serious project, and Sceptre Television had little difficulty persuading the network to take a twenty-six week run in 1976.

That was tremendous for Chris Clements and his ego, for *Science Today* was his baby. He produced it and directed it. And he claimed, not without justification, to have originated most of its brightest ideas.

So the network's decision was a great compliment to him. It was also an enormous challenge. Keeping up that standard for twenty-six weeks in a row — it really was quite an order. Clements had no doubts, however, about his ability to meet that order. It merely got his adrenalin going.

He was a wiry little man, who looked as if he might once have been a jockey, and he had sparse dark hair which always needed combing. He always spoke fast, in urgent staccato sentences, as if his tongue were in a permanent hurry. And he generated enthusiasm. Nobody could generate enthusiasm like Chris Clements.

They were going to stockpile at least a dozen programmes. That was the plan. Then they'd do the last fourteen during the run.

By the middle of December, 1975, they already had seven in the can — so they were comfortably ahead of schedule — and the production team was considering which subject to tackle next.

There were eight of them that day in Clements's office which was across the corridor behind Studio B. He'd often protested that the office was too small to hold proper meetings and also that he disliked the

51

cooking smells which drifted up from the canteen kitchen.

His protests had done no good. They'd merely brought curt little notes from Leonard Harman – Assistant Controller of Programmes (Admin) – pointing out that space was at a premium, that *Science Report* didn't qualify for its own Production Office. Harman, of course, had a far bigger office. One with proper air-conditioning.

So there they were, the eight of them, in the office which was really too small. Clements's production assistant, Jean Baker, was at the desk. She usually sat at the desk during these meetings because she did most of the note-taking and the referring to files and because Clements liked to think on his feet. He paced back and forth, his hands and arms dancing expressively, as they bounced ideas around.

The others included former ITN newscaster Simon Butler, the programme's anchor-man, and reporters Katherine White and Colin Benson. Opposite them were the scientific advisers, Professor David Cowie and Dr. Patrick Snow, and in the corner nearest the door was researcher Terry Dickson.

'Wave-power,' suggested Benson. 'Energy from waves . . .'

'Been flogged to death, love,' said Clements. 'Didn't you watch BBC-2 last Wednesday?'

Dickson felt disappointed. He hadn't seen the programme on BBC-2 either. And, reckoning it a good subject, he'd been quietly researching wave-power. He'd have to scrap that now. Clements, despite his habit of calling everybody 'love', was tough. When he said no he meant no.

'Newsweek have got an intriguing piece on robot servants,' said Cowie. 'They're now being built, it seems, to polish the floors and even make beds . . .'

'Now that I like!' said Clements gleefully. 'Mechanical maids! Yes, we could really have fun with

52

that one. Jean love ... put that down as a possible ... we'll come back on it.'

'I think it's time we took a really close look at the Brain Drain,' said Butler.

Clements stopped his pacing, looked at him doubtfully. 'I don't know, Simon ... strikes me as a bit heavy.' He cupped his chin in his right hand. 'Is it really us?'

'Well if it isn't, I think it ought to be,' said Butler. 'We are a science programme and you consider the number of scientists who are leaving ... and what it means to this country ...'

'Yes,' conceded Clements. 'Maybe if we dressed it up with some good human stories ...' He looked at Dickson. 'How about it, Terry? Reckon you could dig up a lively selection of case-histories?'

Dickson could see his work-load growing fast. 'It would take time,' he said guardedly.

'Of course it would, love. Getting the right people ... I can see that. But it doesn't have to be top priority. Say we were to think of it in terms of five programmes from now ... then you could plod along with it when you're not too hectic with the first four ...'

It was as simple and as casual as that. None of them at that meeting had the slightest inkling that they were about to embark on the most astonishing television documentary ever produced – the one which was to explode the secrecy of Alternative 3.

Dickson knew there was only one satisfactory way to tackle this sort of problem – dozens of telephone calls. Probably scores of them, even. It was no use hoping to rely on local stringers because they never really came up with the goods. Not on this type of job.

He'd have to call head-hunting firms and the major professional organisations ... universities and research establishments. He'd get told that people didn't want to appear on the programme or he'd find that they were too damned dull to be allowed on the programme. And if he worked at it hard enough – and had a bit of luck – he'd finish up with a good varied collection. Of people who mattered and who could talk.

He got lucky, as it happened, quite soon. One of his first telephone calls – made purely on spec – was to a complex of research laboratories. A helpful man in the Public Relations department told him that one of their solar-energy experts would soon be leaving for America. Her name was Ann Clark and she was aged 29.

The P.R. man pointed out that naturally he couldn't say if Dr. Clark would agree to take part in the programme. If she did agree, however, there would be no objection from the management. He also told Dickson that Dr. Clark was 'a real cracker' but quickly added that that was background information and that he did not wish to be quoted.

Ann Clark, to Dickson's relief, said she'd be pleased to appear in *Science Report*. In fact, she was delighted that a television company should be planning to show the disgusting conditions in which British scientists were expected to work. She was, quite obviously, a very fluent speaker.

Clements usually liked to see a photograph and a biographical breakdown of people before committing himself to putting them on his programme. He'd made that rule, years before, after blind-booking an expert on beauty aids – only to find that she looked and sounded like the worst of the *Macbeth* witches. He'd had to record her, of course, and they'd junked the recording after she'd left the studio. And Harman had raised hell about the waste of valuable studio time.

Now Clements played safe. He had this rule. So Dickson arranged for a Norwich news-agency to call on Ann Clark. This agency came back with the whisper that she wasn't going to America purely because of working conditions. The conditions were bad, very bad, but she'd also had some sort of romantic bust-up ...

Dickson decided to forget the whisper. It only complicated matters. Clements approved the photograph. And Colin Benson, the young coloured reporter, set off with a film unit for Norwich.

Later there were suspicions that the assignment was sabotaged by somebody at Sceptre. Those suspicions could never be proved. So we can merely record that *something* happened to the film after it was taken back for processing – and that only a fraction of it could be used in the transmitted programme.

At the time, however, it seemed like a routine job. Benson says: 'Dr. Clark was not only extremely articulate and eager to co-operate but she had obviously also done a great deal of useful home-work on emigration. She pointed out that, apart from the frustrations facing her at the laboratory, there were many ways in which initiative and flair were being stifled in Britain.

'I remember her talking about how a man called Marcus Samuel started the Shell organisation – in 1830, I think she said – as a small private company selling varnished sea-shells. Men of his calibre, she said, were now being positively discouraged in Britain – and that was another reason she was glad to be off to America.

'She was, in fact, a really good interviewee, a television natural. And I was delighted with what we'd got in the can.'

His delight died abruptly when they got back to the studios and the film was processed. Most of it – sound and vision – was completely blank. It had never happened before and there was no logical explanation for it having happened now. There had been more than forty-five minutes of interview which, after editing, would have provided about twelve minutes of screen time. All they could salvage was a fifteen-second segment.

Clements, naturally, was fuming. Sending a unit all the way to Norwich was damned expensive – and he knew how Harman would squeal about him going over budget. He quizzed Benson at length. 'You're really sure that she is that good? That it's really worth going there again?'

'It was a hell of a good interview,' insisted Benson. 'I say we should go back.'

He telephoned Ann Clark, explained the situation, and fixed a new appointment. He takes up the story from there: 'She was very sympathetic and she agreed quite willingly to see us again. But two days later, when we got to Norwich, it was all very different . . .

'She wasn't at her flat, where we'd arranged to meet her, but after quite a lot of trouble we did find her at another address. She looked flustered and — I don't think I was imagining this — a bit frightened. It seemed quite clear that, for some reason or another, she'd been hoping to give us the slip.

'She certainly didn't want to talk, didn't want to know at all. Later we discovered she'd even told the security people at the laboratories that we were pestering her and that they shouldn't let us in. It was just a crazy situation.

'I did manage to grab a few words with her at the gate the next morning — although she tried to duck away when she spotted us waiting there — and I asked her what was wrong.

'You know what she replied? She just looked at me sort of queer and said — "I'm sorry . . . I can't finish the film . . . I'm going away."

'Then she scuttled inside and that was the last we ever saw of her.'

Benson, although he did not realise it at that stage, was just starting to get enmeshed in Alternative 3 . . .

Benson and the film team were travelling dejectedly from Norwich when Terry Dickson noticed the paragraph about Robert Patterson in the *Guardian*.

Dickson knew that this time he wouldn't need to worry about getting a picture and a biography for Patterson, apart from being a leading mathematician, often appeared on television as a taxation expert. He was a fluent and impressive performer.

At first Patterson seemed uncharacteristically reluctant. He had a lot to do. He wasn't sure if he could spare time for an interview. But finally Dickson persuaded him. They agreed that the unit should be at Patterson's home at 11.0 a.m. the following Tuesday.

'Let's hope we have a bit more luck than at Norwich,' said Clements sourly. 'I've never known such a run of disaster...'

In fact, of course, it was even worse than at Norwich. Benson got no reply when he arrived at the house in Scotland. The downstairs curtains were partially-drawn and, peeping through the gaps, he could see that the rooms were untidy. There were bits of food and dirty dishes in the kitchen and on the dining-room table ... books and oddments of clothing strewn across the floors. There were six pints of milk outside the front door and the garage was empty. The whole place looked as if it had been abandoned in a hurry.

Benson checked with the neighbours. The Pattersons, he was told, had left three days earlier. They had driven off at speed on the Saturday and they had not been seen since.

Benson went to the University of St. Andrews and there he was told by the vice-chancellor that Patterson had already gone to America. He'd had to go, apparently, a little earlier than he'd originally intended.

'He told me that they wanted him more urgently than he'd realised,' said the vice-chancellor. 'I'm terribly sorry you've had this wasted journey ... and I must say it's not like him at all ... breaking an appointment like this. I can only assume that, in the rush, he completely forgot...'

They? Who were they?

The vice-chancellor shook his head apologetically. 'Can't help you there either, I'm afraid. Patterson was rather mysterious about what he was going to do – and

57

about exactly where he was going. Somewhere in America ... that's as much as he ever said.'

We have now checked with every university in America. Not one of them has any knowledge of any post having been offered to Robert Patterson. And no-one can suggest where he might possibly be.

We have also checked with the American company which Dr. Ann Clark was due to join – the one which was 'in a hurry to have her'.

They have confirmed that they did offer her a job at more than double her Norwich salary. They have also told us that they received a brief letter from her – regretting that, for personal reasons, she would not be able to go to America.

Simon Butler, you may recall, explained the next step in the mystery during that television documentary. He went with a camera-crew to the car park of Number Three Terminal, Heathrow Airport, and pointed out the car which had been hired in Norwich by Ann Clark.

We quote the exact words he used in that programme: 'Whatever was going on brought Ann Clark here ... she had told friends that she was flying to New York. And yet there is no record of Ann Clark leaving this airport on that or any other day. The only evidence that she was here at all is her abandoned car. Beyond that – nothing.'

There was another abandoned car nearby in the same park. A blue Rover. It belonged to Robert Patterson.

It was some time, however, before the television team found those cars. Months, in fact, after Benson's return from Scotland. They might never have found them – and the Alternative 3 programme might never have been produced – if it hadn't been for the bizarre business of Brian Pendlebury.

By April, 1976, the Brain Drain project had been almost completed. Dickson had found another batch of interviewees and work had progressed in double-harness with work on other subjects – including a revolutionary new method for 'stretching' petrol consumption and the Mechanical Maids.

Butler merely had to do a couple of final studio links and the Brain Drain would be ready for transmission.

They were, of course, baffled by the strange behaviour of Ann Clark and Robert Patterson – and there'd been some caustic memoranda from Harman about the 'reckless waste of film facilities' – but they were a science programme. And runaway people were hardly their concern.

So that's how it would have been ... if Chris Clements, in his local one evening, hadn't heard an oddly disturbing story from one of his neighbours ...

This neighbour had relatives called Pendlebury who lived in Manchester. And it appeared that the Pendleburys' son – an electronics expert – had completely vanished in Australia. And, even stranger, it seemed that he'd been writing to his parents for months – from an address where he was not even known.

'Brian always was a selfish little sod, only interested in what was in something for himself, but this is just plain daft, isn't it,' said the neighbour. 'You know, he even sent them pictures and everything but now it seems he wasn't even there ...'

It certainly didn't make sense to Clements. He mulled it over that night and mentioned it the next day to Colin Benson. 'Seems to be the season for disappearing boffins,' he said. 'Or, on the other hand, maybe he's just playing some prank on his folks.'

'What if he isn't?' Benson asked suddenly.

'Well what else could it be?'

'What if there's some pattern here? What if Clark and Patterson and now this Pendlebury ... what if they're all connected in some way?'

'I fail to see how they could be ...'

'Let me go up to Manchester and see the parents ...'

'Look, love, please ... we're already a week behind

schedule and we can't afford to go bouncing off at tangents . . .'

'Chris, I've got a feeling . . . don't ask me why . . . but I've got a feeling we're on the edge of something big here.'

Clements shook his head. 'We've got a show to do. I know you're still sore, Colin, over what happened in Norwich and Scotland . . . but nobody blamed you for those cock-ups . . . so do me a favour and relax.'

'Harman blamed me . . .'

'Harman blames everybody for everything. That's the way Harman's made. And, anyway, it was me that got the kicking – not you.'

'I'll go on my day off,' said Benson. 'And I'll pay my own damned expenses.'

'Waste of time, love,' said Clements. 'And don't imagine I m having the train fare swung on to my budget.'

'Couldn't I put it down as entertaining contacts?'

Clements grinned. 'I don't think I've ever met anybody quite as persistent as you. All right – go ahead and do a bit of entertaining.'

We have presented that conversation exactly as it took place, with the help of the two men, because it emphasises how there was nearly no further investigation . . . how Sceptre Television almost veered away from Alternative 3.

Benson's decision to go to Manchester was the turning-point. It culminated in Sceptre Television abandoning a thoughtfully-balanced but unspectacular programme on the Brain Drain – and replacing it with one which was to startle the world.

Dennis Pendlebury was a milkman until his retirement in 1976. He and his wife Alice live in a terraced house in one of the shabbier suburbs of Manchester. They are, as they say themselves, a very ordinary couple. They have never had much money and they made many sacrifices to get their son Brian through university.

60

Mrs. Pendlebury, in fact, worked as a charwoman – to help pay for extras – until Brian joined the RAF.

Benson was in their front room, the one reserved for visitors and special occasions, looking through the coloured photographs which appeared to show their son in Australia.

He recorded the entire conversation, with the Pendleburys' permission, and they have agreed to us making use of the transcript in this book.

The Pendleburys were together on the sofa, facing him over the tea-cups and cakes. 'So we were a bit disappointed, of course, when he stopped writing but we didn't give it too much thought at first,' said Mr. Pendlebury. He re-lit his pipe, took a couple of reflective puffs. 'Our Brian, he never was much of a one for writing.'

'So how did you find out?' asked Benson. 'I mean, about him not being there . . .'

'It was Mrs. Prescott over at number nine,' said Pendlebury. 'She was the one who found out. Her daughter Beryl emigrated out there . . . what would it be . . . five years ago now?'

'Six years,' said Mrs. Pendlebury. 'Seven come September.'

'Well, anyway, five or six . . . makes no odds. Her daughter's living out there . . . that's what I'm saying . . . and Mrs. Prescott was going to visit her, see. So we said to her . . . why don't you look up our Brian? We thought it would be a nice surprise for him. You know . . . someone from home. She'd known him, you see, since he was knee-high to that table . . .'

'Tell the man what she said . . .'

'That's what I'm doing, woman . . . I am telling him.' There was a trace of irritation in Pendlebury's tone. His pipe had gone out again and there was a pause while he struck another match. 'So she went to the address – the one on the letters and that – but the man there reckoned he'd never heard of him.'

61

'Who was this man?' asked Benson.

'What beats me is that we wrote to him there,' said Pendlebury. 'And we know he had the letters because we got replies.'

'This man,' persisted Benson. 'What did Mrs. Prescott say about him?'

'He was an American, I think she said,' said Pendlebury. 'I don't think she said any more than that.'

'Perhaps he was the new tenant? Perhaps your son had just moved out?'

'No, I don't think so. He'd been there for years, judging by what he said to Mrs. Prescott.'

'What about where he worked?'

'Well, that was it, wasn't it. They said exactly the same ... that they'd never heard of him.'

Mrs. Pendlebury prodded him with her elbow. 'Show the man the letter,' she said.

'Oh yes, you've got to see the letter,' said Pendlebury. 'It's in the other room, mother — behind the clock on the mantelpiece.' He leaned forward and lowered his voice confidentially as his wife left the room. 'It's getting her down something awful,' he said. 'The worry of not knowing.'

He offered Benson another cup of tea, which Benson refused, and poured one for himself. 'We wrote to this firm to try finding out what was going on and ... ah, here's their reply. You just take a look at that.'

Benson accepted the letter from Mrs. Pendlebury and saw from the letter-heading that it was from the Sydney office of an internationally-known electronics company. It was signed by the Personnel Director and it was addressed to Mr. Pendlebury. It read:

Thank you for your letter which has been passed to me by the Managing Director. I am afraid that you have been misinformed for I have checked our personnel records for the past five years and I have established that at no time has the company employed, nor offered employment to, anyone by the name of B. D. Pendlebury.

I can only suggest that you are confusing us with some other organisation and I regret that I cannot help you further in this matter.

Benson read the letter twice and frowned thoughtfully. 'And you're sure you're *not* confusing them with another outfit?'

'Positive,' said Pendlebury. 'Pass me that wallet, mother ...' From the wallet he took a slip of paper bearing the name and address of the firm in Sydney. 'See ... there it is ... in Brian's own writing.'

Mrs. Prescott from number nine, a widow with a shrewd and agile mind, confirmed their story but had little to add. She picked her words carefully, obviously not wishing to hurt the Pendleburys, but she gave Benson the impression that she'd never really approved of Brian. It was all in her tone rather than in what she actually said. Benson remembered what Clements had been told by his neighbour ... about Brian Pendlebury having been a 'selfish little sod' ... and he wondered if Brian might be playing some cruel trick on his parents. Then he dismissed the thought. It was too ridiculous.

Benson borrowed the letter from the electronics company, together with the photographs, and Mrs. Prescott offered to show him a short-cut to the stop for the station bus.

As they turned the corner she suddenly spoke with quiet vehemence: 'You see ... that's the thanks they get for spoiling him.'

He glanced at her in surprise. 'How do you mean?'

'He looks down on them, does Brian. Bit ashamed of them, if you ask me. Going to university ... it gave him big ideas ...'

'You surely don't think he's disappeared on purpose?'

She pursed her lips. 'Not my place to say,' she said.

'Look ... there's your bus coming ... you'll have to run if you're going to catch it.'

He didn't take her implied opinion at all seriously – not until months later. It seemed to him then, as the bus trundled through Manchester, that she'd merely been trying to squeeze the last ounce of drama from the situation.

He spent a long time on the train studying the photographs, particularly those taken in the open. There was one detail in them which intrigued him, which didn't seem quite right. And yet he could not be sure ...

Back at the studios he sought the help of a stills photographer who was attached to the graphics department. This man made copy-negatives of the outdoor photographs and then re-printed them as large blow-ups.

Benson was not concerned with the one which appeared to have been taken in a nightclub for that, he reasoned, could have been posed almost anywhere. In London. In Manchester even. And, anyway, it didn't contain that one off-key detail ...

He waited impatiently until the blow-ups were ready. Then he saw, quite clearly, that he'd been right. In every picture – including the one of Brian Pendlebury surfing and the one of him by the Sydney Harbour Bridge – there were three birds in the sky. Those birds were identical in every picture – and so were their positions.

There was also something else, something which had not struck him before: the pattern-formations of the wispy clouds were exactly the same in each picture.

The explanation was startlingly obvious: these 'Australian' snaps of Brian Pendlebury had been taken against a painted backdrop. They were, without question, 'studio jobs'.

He scooped them up, raced along to Clements's office behind Studio B. 'We've stumbled on one hell of a Brain Drain story here,' he said. 'I can't start to understand it yet but ... Chris ... we've just got to do some digging ...'

SECTION FIVE

This digging, as Simon Butler said on television, soon revealed one astonishing fact:

Twenty-one other people, mainly scientists and academics, had vanished in the same mysterious circumstances. They were among the 400 researched – ostensibly for an extended version of the Brain Drain programme – by the *Science Report* team.

Some, as Butler explained, had disappeared entirely on their own. Others, like Patterson, had gone with their families. All had told neighbours or colleagues that they were going to work abroad.

However, as we have already indicated, only part of the story was presented on television. Many facts were still not known at the time of transmission. And much material which *was* known was censored from the programme.

The principal censor was Leonard Harman, Assistant Controller of Programmes (Admin), who also tried to neuter this book.

Letter dated August 9, 1977, from Leonard Harman to Messrs. Ambrose and Watkins:

I have been given to understand that you propose writing a book based on one of the *Science Report* programmes produced by this company and that you plan to publish certain confidential memoranda concerning this programme which I originated or received.

You should know that I am not prepared to sanction such publication and that I would consider it a gross invasion of my privacy.

I suggest that the book you are apparently preparing would savour of irresponsibility for, as you are undoubtedly aware, my company has now formally denied the authenticity of much of the material presented in that programme.

It is to be hoped that you do not proceed with this project but, in any event, I look forward to receiving a written undertaking that no reference will be made to myself or the memoranda.

Letter dated August 12, 1977, from lawyer Edwin Greer to Leonard Harman:

I have been instructed by Mr. David Ambrose and Mr. Leslie Watkins and I refer to your letter of the 9th inst.

My clients are cognizant of the statement made by your company following the transmission of the Alternative 3 programme and, in conducting their own inquiries, they are mindful of the background to that statement.

They point out that any copies of memoranda now in their possession were supplied willingly by the persons who either received them or sent them and that they therefore feel under no obligation to give the undertaking you seek.

One of the first batches of memoranda we received related to a curious discovery made by researcher Terry Dickson in the middle of May, 1976. By that time, despite objections from Harman, the *Science Report* team had been enlarged and allocated its own production office. The Brain Drain programme had by then been withdrawn from the series – with the intention of the investigation being presented, as it eventually was, as a one-off special.

Memo dated May 17, 1976, from Terry Dickson to Chris Clements – c.c. (for info only) to Fergus Godwin, Controller of Programmes:

We have now established that relatives of at least two more of our missing people, Dr. Penelope Mortimer and Professor Michael Parsons, received letters which appeared to have come from them in Australia. In both cases the letters, which ceased after four or five months, bore the address used in the Pendlebury case.

Photographs of Dr. Mortimer and Professor Parsons, allegedly taken in Australia, show the backdrop used in the Pendlebury shots. The birds and clouds are all identical.

As you requested, I arranged for a Sydney freelance to check the address given in the letters. He reports that it is a two-bedroomed ground-floor flat near the waterfront which has now been empty for nearly a year. It was occupied, apparently, by a middle-aged American called Denton or Danton (he has been unable to verify spelling).

Neighbours say that Denton or Danton was remote and secretive. He was never known to have visitors. Our man says there are local rumours that he had connections with the CIA. Do you want him to pursue the Denton/Danton trail and do you want me to arrange still pix of the flat?

Memo dated May 18, 1976, from Leonard Harman to Mr. Chris Clements:

A copy of Dickson's note concerning inquiries made in Australia, without my authorisation, has been passed to me in the absence of the Controller of Programmes.

I have already issued specific instructions that I am to be kept fully informed on all aspects of this project. Please repeat those instructions to Dickson and all other members of the *Science Report* team — and ensure that they are fully understood.

I am surprised to learn that, despite my earlier warnings, you are apparently still determined to waste company time and money. Let me remind you that *Science Report* is regarded by the Network as a serious programme and that its credibility can only be damaged by this wild-goose course on which you are set.

The more I learn of this affair, the more obvious it becomes that you are losing your objectivity as an editor. Many people do disappear quite deliberately because, for personal reasons, they wish to break all contact with their pasts and make completely fresh starts. I will not tolerate this station turning that sort of situation into an excuse for silly sensationalism.

I had assumed that you were experienced enough to recognise that you are clearly being hoaxed over this business of the photographic backgrounds. Now, I gather from Dickson's note (which, I repeat, should *also* have been sent to me), that you are apparently getting involved in 'local rumours' — supplied by a freelance journalist we have never before used — about some man whose name you don't even know having 'connections with the CIA'.

Have you considered that some of your so-called mysteries might have been caused by incompetence on the part of your staff?

Did Dr. Ann Clark, for example, refuse to grant Benson a second interview because she found his manner offensive during the first one?

Did Dickson confuse the date fixed for the interview with Robert Patterson and so send an expensive unit on a fool's errand to Scotland?

These are the questions which should be occupying your attention, not some nonsense at the other end of the world. I am not prepared to sanction any further expenditure in Australia and I recommend, once again, that you resume the duties prescribed in your contract.

Memo dated May 19, 1976, from Chris Clements to Terry Dickson:

CONFIDENTIAL. I attach a copy of a rollicking I've just had from Harman. It's self-explanatory and, for the moment, I'd like you to keep it to yourself. In future don't send carbons to anyone before checking with me.

We'd better soft-pedal for the moment on Australia.

Will you line up Mortimer and Parsons parents to be interviewed by Simon or Colin?

Please ignore that snide comment about Robert Patterson. Not worth getting upset over. And *please* don't mention that crack about Ann Clark to Colin. He sometimes gets a colour-chip on his shoulder, as you know, and it isn't like that. This is just Harman being Harman.

Six days later, on May 25, Terry Dickson gave Clements the bad news. 'We're not going to get any interviews with the Mortimers or the Parsons,' he said. 'They've changed their minds and are refusing to have anything to do with the programme.'

'But why?' demanded Clements. 'They surely gave you a reason.'

'None at all,' said Dickson. 'They just say they'd sooner not.'

'You think they've been got at?'

Dickson shrugged, pulled a face. 'That's the impression I got but proving it . . . that's another matter.'

'They're important, love . . . have another go at them.'

Dickson did. But Mr. and Mrs. Mortimer were adamant. So were Mr. and Mrs. Parsons. Not one of them, despite having agreed earlier, would have anything further to do with *Science Report*. We tried to contact them in September, 1977, but we were too late. Neighbours said they had gone to live abroad. And they had left no forwarding addresses.

This whole question of the staged photographs – and of the forged letters – was deliberately omitted from the

69

television programme. Clements admits that he now regrets having left them out for, as he now realises, they were an intriguing feature of the Alternative 3 operation. He explains that he didn't use them because they baffled him and he didn't see what significance they could possibly have — and because of pressure from Harman.

He told us: 'At the time I thought Harman was nit-picking. They didn't seem important enough to merit all the aggro I was getting from him. Of course, if I'd known then what I know now . . .'

We were equally baffled by those photographs and letters. We intended to mention them, just as we have, simply so that you would know all the circumstances. But as for offering any explanation . . . we were prepared to recognise that would not be possible. That was how it seemed until January 3, 1978, when we received an envelope from Trojan. The contents provided an unexpected insight into what they call The Smoother Plan.

Trojan's covering note explained that he had discovered the attached document — an early directive to Alternative 3 cells in various parts of the world — in an otherwise empty archives file.

In fact, he had sent a Photostat copy of the document. It was dated November 24, 1971, and it had been issued by 'The Chairman, Policy Committee.' It was addressed to 'National Chief Executive Officers' and it read:

The recent publicity which followed the movement of Professor William Braishfield was unfortunate and potentially damaging. In order to avert any repetition, it has been agreed to adopt a new procedure in all cases where families or others are likely to provoke questions.

The procedure, to be known as The Smoother, is designed to allay fears or suspicions in the immediate post-movement period.

70

Department Seven will arrange for letters to be sent, in appropriate handwriting, to reassure those whose anxiety might constitute a security risk. It is usual for people to send home photographs of themselves in their new surroundings. Arrangements will therefore also be made for the dispatch of suitable photographs. These photographs will be taken immediately before embarkation.

A list of manned cover addresses will be circulated to National Chief Executive Officers by Department Seven. Officers will then allocate addresses to individual movers.

At least four addresses will be provided in each 'country of destination' — so enabling Officers to 'separate' any movers who may originate from the same area. There is, however, no limit to the number of movers who can be allocated to any of the addresses.

It may prove necessary to change the addresses from time to time and Department Seven will notify Officers of such changes.

The Smoother Plan will operate for a maximum of six months in respect of each individual, unless circumstances are exceptional, for that is considered long enough to provide a reasonable 'break-off period'.

It is emphasised that, because of the administration involved, The Smoother Plan is to be activated in selected cases only. The sole criterion will be if, in the opinion of the Officer responsible, there could be a publicity risk. Most movers, certainly all those taking families, will not merit this treatment. Components of Batch Consignments, obviously, will not be considered.

Suddenly it made sense. It was clinical and cruel. But it still made sense.

The Pendleburys idolised their son. That was why

they got those cheerful and gossipy letters – written by a stranger they would never meet.

Ann Clark had left no-one who'd been really close to her so there was no-one who would have expected letters. Friends might have been offended, perhaps, if they'd written but got no reply. But they would not have been sufficiently offended to have turned it into a great public issue.

As for Robert Patterson ... well, he took his family with him.

But these people, and others like them, had apparently all gone willingly. Where had they gone? And why?

It is now clear that Brian Pendlebury deliberately took part in the conspiracy to fool his own parents. Such behaviour might seem beyond any logical explanation. But we must point out, in fairness to Brian Pendlebury, that his actions must be measured against the nightmare background to Alternative 3. That background, you might feel, excuses them all. Well ... almost.

Thursday, March 3, 1977. Another submarine meeting of Policy Committee. Chairman: R EIGHT. Transcript section supplied by Trojan starts:

A TWO: Sure, Ballantine was neat enough ... nobody's bitching about Ballantine ... but what about Carmell?

A EIGHT: We'll find him ... he's still on the loose somewhere in London ... but we'll damned well find him ...

R SEVEN: A man like him being allowed out of America ... it was a bad, bad mistake ...

A EIGHT: For Chrissake ... please ... don't let's start that crap again ... I told you last month that our people goofed ... now didn't I tell you that?

R SEVEN: Yes, but it is particularly serious when ...

A EIGHT: Listen . . . there's no need to turn this into a Federal case. He hasn't got the tape and, as long as he hasn't got it, there's no great panic . . .

R THREE: Do we have any idea at all where the tape might be?

A EIGHT: No . . . that's just one hell of a mystery . . . we've turned Ballantine's place over but there's no sign . . .

R EIGHT: And it was not with him in the car when he died?

A EIGHT: No . . . definitely not. Our man was right there with him . . .

A TWO: So we don't know where Carmell is and we don't know where the tape is . . . what's to say they aren't already together?

A EIGHT: Because he wouldn't have waited, that's what . . . he'd have blown it already.

R ONE: Has there been any sighting of Carmell? Or are we merely assuming that he is in London?

A EIGHT: He was in an hotel in Earls Court . . . he was there with a girl . . . our people missed him by about an hour . . .

R TWO: And now?

A EIGHT: Our information is that they're probably living rough and keeping on the jump . . . couple of nights here, couple of nights there . . . but it's only a matter of time . . .

R EIGHT: Time is important . . . particularly with that tape still missing . . . perhaps we should put more operators into London . . .

A TWO: The guy's right . . . we ought to saturate the town . . . Jeez! With a character like Carmell at large . . .

A EIGHT: Okay, okay . . . so we'll step it up . . .

A THREE: We've got muscle to spare in Paris and . . .

A EIGHT: I *said* we'll step it up – all right? . . . so just let me handle the details . . . we'll get Carmell and that damned tape.

R EIGHT: I look forward to hearing of both achievements at our next meeting ... Now, you have all seen the expediency report on Peterson?

R TWO: Entirely satisfactory ...

A FIVE: I'm still not sure he deserved a hot job ...

R FOUR: Very few men deserve to die but for some it is necessary ... and Peterson was one of them ...

A ONE: That's right ... and, remember, people don't suffer long with a hot job ... it is instantaneous ...

R EIGHT: Dr. Carl Gerstein ... the old man ... it was agreed at the last meeting that he should be kept under surveillance ... what is the news on him?

A EIGHT: No news ... he's been laid up with bronchitis and, apart from his housekeeper, he's seen no-one for weeks ...

R EIGHT: So the situation, then, is unchanged ... I recommend that we maintain observation on the old man ... are we all agreed? ... Good ... Now, we have had a request from Geneva for more Batch Consignments of animals ...

A SEVEN: Yeah ... I've already got things shifting on that one ... we'll be taking cattle from Kansas and Texas and ponies from Dartmoor ... had a bit of a snarl-up over transport but lifts are now scheduled for the second week in July ...

R EIGHT: How many beasts will be in each Batch?

We never learned the reply to that last question. That was where the transcript section ended. We have no concrete evidence of cattle disappearing in *significant* numbers from either Kansas or Texas during the second week of July, 1977, although there were complaints of an increase in rustling at that time.

However, we do know — because it was published in the *Daily Mail* on July 15 — that the pony-lift from Dartmoor ended in disaster.

That section of transcript also emphasises how close Dr. Carl Gerstein — the person mentioned merely as 'the old man' in the February transcript – was unwittingly hovering near sudden death. If an Expediency order had been agreed by the Policy Committee – at either the February or the March meeting in 1977 – Simon Butler would never have been able to interview Gerstein at Cambridge. And Alternative 3 might never have been exposed.

How would Gerstein have died? Probably, like Ballantine and Professor Peterson, the aerospace expert, in what the Policy Committee call a 'hot job'. And, as was pointed out by the anonymous A ONE, a hot-job death is instantaneous. We have had that confirmed by pathologist Professor Hubert Radwell who gave evidence at the Ballantine inquest.

Professor Radwell, when pressed about the 'extensive' burns on Ballantine's body, eventually made this statement:

It was technically accurate to describe Ballantine's body as having been extensively burned although those words embrace only part of the truth. They represented an understatement. I was requested to make that understatement in order not to promote any unnecessary public alarm.

I was conscious, of course, that there had been some degree of public hysteria following earlier reported instances of spontaneous combustion and I agreed that it would be of no benefit for all the details to be described at that hearing.

I now regret having made that decision and I welcome this opportunity to correct the record.

Ballantine's body was not merely burned. It was reduced to little more than cinders and scorched bones. His skull had shrunk because of the intense heat to which he had been subjected and yet his clothing was hardly damaged.

There were small scorch marks on the leather cover of the steering wheel, obviously where Ballantine's hands had been gripping it at the time of the incident, but the rest of the vehicle showed no evidence of burning.

However, extensive damage was suffered by the vehicle, as the police stated at the inquest, and Ballantine's spine was severed by the engine which had been hurled backwards after breaking free.

This is the first occasion on which I have personally encountered spontaneous combustion in a human being but I have studied papers relating to twenty-three similar occurrences. The effect can be likened to that seen during the micro-wave cooking of a chicken, except, of course, that it is far more severe. The chicken flesh is roasted within seconds although the covering skin is not charred and any receptacle containing the chicken remains cold enough to be handled.

There is still no known explanation for this phenomenon.

We asked Professor Radwell if it were conceivable that spontaneous combustion could be deliberately induced. He replied: 'The Americans and the Russians have certainly been experimenting along those lines, with a view to developing spontaneous combustion as a remote-controlled weapon, but the results of those experiments have been kept secret. I would consider that the possibility of them having been successful is highly unlikely . . .'

Highly unlikely! Almost everything connected with Alternative 3 is highly unlikely. The super-powers furtively pooling scientific information – that is highly unlikely. So is the conspiracy of silence about the real achievements in space. But the terrifying truth is that it has been happening. And that it continues to happen.

On Wednesday, February 10, 1977 – three days after learning of Ballantine's death – the American, Harry Carmell, telephoned the *Science Report* office at Sceptre Television.

Colin Benson took the call and he thought, at first, that he'd got another crank on the line. The man was being so guarded and mysterious – refusing even to give his name. And, particularly since the transmission of the Mechanical Maids programme, there'd been a spate of crank callers.

It was strange, really, the way some viewers had reacted to the robot servants. One man had angrily accused anchor-man Simon Butler of having stolen his invention – claiming that he'd been working on an identical model for five years in his attic. Two women had wanted to know if there was a domestic agency where they could hire these maids. And an ardent trades-unionist had given a heated tirade about Sceptre encouraging 'cheap, scab labour'.

This peculiar American, it seemed to Benson, fitted right in the crank category – until he mentioned knowing about scientists who had disappeared. That was when Benson switched on the tape-recorder attached to the telephone. Here is the transcript of the rest of that conversation:

BENSON: Would you repeat that, please ... what you said about scientists ...

CARMELL: I said I know why they're vanishing ... and who's behind it ...

BENSON: So tell me then ... why and who?

CARMELL: Not on the telephone ... I can't talk on the telephone ...

BENSON: Well, really, this is a bit ...

CARMELL: Listen, I'm not bulling ... you know what they did to Ballantine ...

BENSON: Ballantine?

CARMELL: Sir William Ballantine the astronomer ....

BENSON: Oh yes, I read ... the car crash ...

CARMELL: I met him when he came to NASA HQ in Houston ... that's why he died ...

BENSON: I'm sorry ... this doesn't seem to be making much sense ...

CARMELL: Can we meet?

BENSON: What do you mean that's why Ballantine died?

CARMELL: No more on the wire ... either we meet or I go some place else ...

BENSON: Where are you calling from?

CARMELL: Public box ... about a mile north of your studios ...

BENSON: Then why not come here?

CARMELL: Too risky ... you know somewhere less obvious?

BENSON: Look ... Mister ... er ...

CARMELL: Harry. Just call me Harry.

BENSON: Fine. Now, Harry, you're not having me on, are you? ... I mean, you really were with NASA?

CARMELL: A busy street would be best ...

BENSON: All right ... we'll do it your way ... There's a big street market just around the corner from the studios ... you can't possibly miss it ... how's that sound?

CARMELL: Give me a spot in this market ... and how will I know you?

BENSON: There's a post-box outside a fruiterer's called Drages ... and you won't have any trouble identifying me. I'm wearing a dark-blue suit and I'll be carrying a red book ... and I happen to have been born in Jamaica ...

The appointment was fixed for one hour later. And if you saw that special edition of *Science Report* you will already know exactly what happened next. Simon Butler told viewers:

What you are about to see may be considered by many of you as unethical. However, we believe that in the light of subsequent developments our action

78

was justified. A hidden camera was positioned near the market. (*Authors' Note: The camera was actually installed in a Tourist Information Kiosk*). Benson was equipped with a miniaturised transmitter so that we could record the conversation between them.

We should point out that we have challenged Sceptre Television on the ethics of filming in that manner – particularly in view of Carmell's obvious anxiety for secrecy. Clements has defended his decision by claiming that the film would not have been transmitted if events had developed differently. It is a matter of record, however, that Clements and the company were subsequently reprimanded by the Independent Broadcasting Authority.

Here, verbatim from the transcript of that controversial piece of TV film, is the conversation which took place in the market:

BENSON: I think you're looking for me – Colin Benson.

CARMELL: Yes ... hello ... thanks for coming ... listen, something I have to know: how far are you willing to go with this thing? I mean, all the way?

BENSON: That's what I'm here for. Can you help?

CARMELL: I can help ... and if you want confirmation you'd better talk to Dr. Carl Gerstein.

BENSON: Gerstein?

CARMELL: Carl Gerstein ... he's at Cambridge. Ask him about Alternative 3.

BENSON: You're talking in riddles, Harry ... what's Alternative 3?

CARMELL: Later ... we do this my way – okay?

BENSON: Okay.

CARMELL: Let's ... let's walk on a little, hm?

BENSON: Fine.

Viewers will recall that the sound quality was poor during this interview, particularly during the section when they were discussing Carl Gerstein and Alternative 3. There was a great deal of static interference and Benson's radio microphone was also picking up the voices of passers-by and the sounds of traffic. Most of the words, however, were quite discernible.

CARMELL: I'm sorry if I seem a little nervous — it's mainly because I am.

BENSON: Nervous of what?

CARMELL: (Brief laugh) Of contracting a fatal case of measles ... you know what I mean? Like Ballantine?

BENSON: But surely that was an accident ... I remember reading in the papers that there was some sort of freak skid ...

CARMELL: Crap! There was no way for that to be an accident ... it was what they call an Expediency and I know why it happened ... and I've got to get it on record before they get to me ...

BENSON: They ...?

CARMELL: Listen, let's just stick to me telling you what I have to tell you — okay?

BENSON: If that's how you want it ...

CARMELL: Right! That's how I want it ... this address, tomorrow morning, ten-thirty. Bring everything you've got — camera, tape machines, witnesses — that's the kind of protection I need. I'll have all the answers for you there ...

BENSON: Hey! Hold on a minute ... come back ...

He grabbed at Carmell's sleeve, tried to stop him, but Carmell was too fast. He jerked his arm free, dashed through the narrow gap between two fruit stalls, and disappeared in the crowd thronging the centre of the road. Benson was disappointed. The whole elaborate set-up, it seemed to him then, had been a ridiculous waste of time. He looked at the scrap of paper which Carmell had pushed into his hand. On it was scrawled an address in Lambeth.

'Well, what do you think?' he said later to Clements.

'Follow through, love, of course. I'll fix for you to have a film-crew tomorrow morning.'

'And what about this Gerstein character?'

'I'll talk to Simon ... see if he fancies a trip to Cambridge.'

So that's how it was left on the evening of February 10, 1977. Simon Butler, who had interviewed Dr. Carl Gerstein years before for Independent Television News, was to go to the university. Colin Benson was to keep the Lambeth appointment.

Both were due for surprises. Particularly Colin Benson.

SECTION SIX

Benson arrived at the Lambeth address with a full camera crew shortly before 10.30 a.m. on February 11. It was a three-storeyed terraced house – dingy and claustrophobically gaunt – with rubbish mouldering in the narrow patch of front garden. Most of its windows, like those of its neighbours, had been boarded up but one on the first floor appeared to be screened with a dirty sheet. The garden gate had been ripped away and there were broken roof-tiles on the path leading to the front door.

Benson hurried up the steps, followed by the technicians, and rapped on the door. No reply. He tried again, harder. Still no response. The house appeared to be deserted. He shouted and started pummelling with both fists. Then there was a girl's voice from inside: 'Who is it?'

'My name's Benson. Colin Benson.'

On the other side of the shabby door, in the darkness of the hall, Wendy was frightened. She still didn't know exactly who *they* were or what they wanted but she did know that they could arrive at any time. And that they were likely to hurt Harry. She bit her bottom lip, regretting now that she'd betrayed her presence. 'Who?' she asked.

Benson shook his head in frustration. There was no number on the house. He stepped back along the path to double-check the numbers on either side, returned to the door. 'This is 88, isn't it?'

'Who did you say you are?' Wendy's American accent, now more obvious, was the confirmation Benson needed.

'Colin Benson,' he repeated. 'I'm here with a television film unit.'

82

Wendy, as she has since told us, was still suspicious. Still fearful. And, with the way things were that morning, she wasn't thinking too clearly. Maybe this was a trick. Harry had said *they* used all sorts of tricks. 'How can I be sure of that?' There was a tremble in her voice. 'What programme are you with?'

'*Science Report* . . . we were asked to come by a man called Harry.'

A short silence. Then the sound of heavy bolts being drawn back. The door was opened just a couple of inches.

Wendy, her hair unkempt and her eyes wide with anxiety, stared at Benson and then at the camera and the sound equipment. She seemed to be having difficulty making up her mind. 'So you really are the telly,' she said eventually.

Benson grinned, trying to reassure her. 'That's right,' he said cheerfully. 'I really am the telly. Is Harry in?'

She didn't respond to his friendliness, made no attempt to open the door wider. 'Not for talking,' she said.

This, Benson decided, was getting stupid. 'Can we come in and see him?' he said. 'He did invite us.'

Wendy shrugged with indifference. 'If you really want to.' She pulled the door wide open. 'But you won't get much out of him,' she said. 'Not this morning.'

They followed her through the mildewed hall and up a flight of naked stairs. Ancient paper decorated with roses was peeling away from the walls and the whole place smelled of dirt and of damp. Wendy stopped, suddenly remembering, at the landing and she shouted down to the soundman who was the last in: 'Bolt the door after you . . . we've got to keep it bolted.' And she waited, watching, while he did so.

'You know, this really is a waste of time,' she said quietly to Benson. 'Maybe it would be better, after all, if you just turned around right now and left.'

'He asked me to be here – so I'm here.'

83

She shrugged again. 'As you like.'

There were three doors leading off the landing. She opened the one at the front of the house. And there, in the room with the sheet-covered window, Benson saw Harry Carmell.

He didn't recognise Carmell, not at first, for what he saw was a haggard and vacant-eyed creature. It was shivering convulsively and its teeth were chattering and it was clutching a matted blanket to its naked shoulders – and it seemed impossible that this could be the man he'd met, only the day before, in the market.

But it was Carmell. It really was. He was hunched defensively, with his knees up to his chest, on an old sofa – the only bit of furniture in the room – and he was blinking rapidly as if trying to see more clearly.

Benson stepped forward tentatively. 'Harry?'

Carmell pressed himself back harder against the sofa. He'd stopped blinking now and was staring with mistrust and bewilderment. 'Who are you?' Even his voice was different. Like that of an old, old man.

'You remember me . . . Colin Benson.'

Wendy tried to help. 'It's all right, Harry . . . he's with the telly . . .'

Suddenly, horrifyingly, Carmell gave a howl of despairing terror. 'It's *them*!' he yelled. 'They've bloody tricked you and now they've found me . . .'

'What's he talking about?' demanded Benson. 'What is the matter with him?'

Wendy ignored him and hurried across to kneel by the sofa and cradle Carmell. 'Now, Harry . . .' she said soothingly. 'It's quite all right . . . and there's nothing to be frightened of.' She glanced up at Benson, jerked her head towards the door. 'You'd better go.'

'Is he on acid or something?'

'Just get out of here, will you!'

'But maybe we should get a doctor . . .'

That was when Carmell, in an unexpected burst of hysterical violence, flung Wendy aside and came hurtling off the sofa. 'So come on then, you bastards!'· he yelled. 'Come and kill me!' He waved his arms wildly and the blanket slipped to the bare boards. Now they could see that he was wearing no clothes apart from his socks.

Suddenly he was very still – half-crouched like an ape just a few feet in front of Benson. His fingers, rigid as metal rods, were spread wide and his hands were raised to the level of his hips. Now there was defiance smouldering in his eyes. 'But Harry Carmell don't die that easy.' His voice – contrasting disconcertingly with his grotesque appearance – now sounded normal. Just as Benson had heard it in the market. 'Harry Carmell's a fighter . . . and he'll bloody take you too.' As he spoke, he took one pace backwards to steady his balance and then, with an horrendous battle-scream, he sprang at Benson. Benson ducked, tried to dodge, but Carmell's nails raked down his face – narrowly missing his eyes – to make deep and symmetric furrows in the flesh of both cheeks.

The film technicians, wedged behind Benson in the doorway, were unable to help and Benson, now as terrified as Carmell had been, was lashing out wildly in an attempt to beat off the attack. One of his blows crunched sickeningly into Carmell's nose and suddenly the fight was over.

Blood spouted from Carmell's nose. He moaned, clutched his face with both hands and collapsed in surrender to the floor. He lay there with his face pressed hard against the dirty boards. And suddenly his puny naked body was racked with great juddering sobs.

Benson moved backwards, unsteadily, to the landing where the cameraman grabbed his arm to support him. 'I'm sorry,' he said to Wendy. 'I didn't expect . . .'

'I told you to go.' She was now again kneeling by Carmell, gently wiping his face with a handkerchief. 'Now for God's sake just leave us!'

They reported to Clements as soon as they got back

to the studios and it was Clements who decided to notify the police. 'We can't possibly leave him there like that,' he said. 'Sounds to me as if he needs hospital treatment.'

There was, however, no sign of Carmell or Wendy by the time the police got to the house. Wendy had gone out almost immediately after the TV team had left. We know that because she has told us.

She had gone out to buy antiseptic and a bandage from a nearby shop. When she returned, there was no Harry. There are reasons to suspect that he became a hot-job victim but we have been unable to find any proof. So we can merely record that Harry Carmell has never been seen since.

There were three of them — Clements, Benson and Dickson — clustered around one of the little editing machines in the Film Department. They were watching, yet again, the uncut film shot in the market.

'That's the spot!' said Clements. 'Go back on that!'

The technician sitting in front of them touched the rewind key and there were high-pitched Donald Duck noises from the sound-track as the film raced in reverse.

A flip on another key and the pictures stopped whirling in a backwards blur. Now there was silence and on the midget screen there was a frozen shot of Benson and Carmell.

'Right, love, shift it.'

The tiny black-and-white figures immediately became animated, walking away from the postbox in the background, and their voices could be heard. Benson was talking about Ballantine:

BENSON: But surely that was an accident ... I remember reading in the papers that there was some sort of freak skid ...

CARMELL: Crap! There was no way for that to be an

accident ... it was what they call an Expediency
and I know why it happened ... and I've got to get
it on record before they get to me ...

'Okay ... kill it there,' said Clements. The technician
stopped the film, switched off the machine. 'Well?'
asked Clements. 'What do you reckon?'

Dickson shook his head doubtfully. 'Acid-head,' he
said. 'Obviously he'd read about Ballantine in the
papers and he was living out some fantasy ...'

'I'm inclined to agree,' said Clements. 'I'm not sure
we should waste any more time on him. Colin?'

The marks on Benson's cheeks were now scarring
over. He rubbed them thoughtfully. 'Remember what he
said about vanishing scientists. So maybe you're right
... maybe he is an acid-head ... but it's a hell of a
coincidence, isn't it ... the way his fantasies spilled over
into our work. Did Ballantine go to America like Harry
said?'

'Yes, he did visit NASA but that was also in the
papers,' said Dickson. 'I checked the cutts.'

Benson looked at him sharply. 'There! Aren't you
missing the obvious? You know because you checked
the cutts. What're you saying? That this acid-head
also checked the cutts? Or was it that he really
knew?'

Clements stood up, glancing at his watch. 'So what
do you want to do, Colin?'

'Maybe talk to Lady Ballantine?'

'You can't go troubling her, man. It's the funeral
today.'

'So I'll be discreet,' said Benson. 'And I'll wait till
tomorrow.'

Friday, February 12, 1977. Lady Ballantine was
composed and hospitable when Benson arrived by
appointment at 3.30 p.m. She told him virtually what
she later told us on July 27. And he was particularly

interested in the large envelope which Ballantine had insisted on her posting. Did she know what it contained?

'I just can't imagine,' she said. 'I know it was a package that he took out of his desk but I have no idea what was in the package.'

Did he give any explanation for having it posted to London – although he was driving to London that same evening?

'That's what puzzled me most of all,' said Lady Ballantine. 'Particularly when I discovered later it was addressed to the man he was planning to meet.'

'I'm sorry,' said Benson. 'I don't follow . . .'

'The envelope . . . it was addressed to a journalist called John Hendry. He and William – they'd been friends for years. Well . . . late, very late, on Friday I got a call from Mr. Hendry. He was still in his office waiting for William and, well, you know the rest . . .'

'Have you spoken to Hendry since? Asked him about the package?'

'He rang again on Saturday . . . with his condolences . . . but I was far too upset to think about packages or anything like that . . .'

Four hours later Benson was in Hendry's office in Fleet Street.

'A premonition – that's the word he used,' said Hendry. 'Events were starting to move fast and he had a premonition – that's exactly what he said. Extraordinary, isn't it . . . when you think what happened.'

'The package,' persisted Benson. 'What was in the package?'

Hendry got up from his desk, crossed to a table by the window, took a spool of tape from a drawer. 'Just this,' he said. 'No message, no nothing.'

'But what's on it?'

'That's the oddest part of all. Not a damned thing as far as we can make out.'

'You've played it right through?'

'Sure ... we tried everything but there's nothing there. You know what I think? I think he sent the wrong one by mistake.'

'That hardly sounds likely, does it,' said Benson. 'A man like Ballantine — surely he'd be meticulously careful.'

Hendry went back to his desk, threw the tape on the desk, lit a cigar. 'Normally, yes ... but, as I told you, he wasn't himself on Friday. His voice on the telephone — I hardly recognised it. He was all strung-up and excited and — I hate to say this because he was a friend of mine — but he was talking the most incredible rubbish. Maybe he'd been over-working or something — who knows? — but I got the impression that he'd really flipped. And you know something? That could explain the accident. If his driving was half as wild as his words ... well, it's hardly surprising, is it?'

Benson picked up the tape. 'Could I borrow this?'

Hendry drew deeply on his cigar, making the end glow fiercely. 'Don't want to be personal,' he said. 'But those marks on your face ... how did you get them?'

Benson fingered his cheeks, grinned ruefully. 'It's all right, they're not tribal markings,' he said jokingly. 'I had to interview rather a rough character. I don't think he liked my questions.'

Hendry returned the grin. He'd been a reporter in Fleet Street during the 'heavy-mob' days — before the place had got so sedately respectable — and his nose was slightly lop-sided. 'It happens,' he said laconically. 'Why do you want the tape?'

'We've got some pretty sophisticated equipment at the studios. Maybe we can trace something on it.'

'No harm in you trying,' said Hendry. 'But I'll want it back afterwards and if you find anything interesting I'll expect to be told right away.'

There was nothing on the tape. Or, at least, there seemed to be nothing.

It was played in its virgin state, you may recall, in that television documentary. And, as Simon Butler pointed out then, it apparently held only 'the ceaseless noise of space – not much different from countless other tapes in the archives of radio astronomy'.

At that stage in the programme Butler told viewers: 'What it meant ... what the vital information was that Sir William Ballantine had deciphered out of this apparently random cacophony ... was something we would have to wait much longer to find out.'

They discovered later that the waiting time would have been far shorter if Harry Carmell had not been drugged out of his mind on that February morning in Lambeth. For Carmell, of course, had the de-coder – the one he'd stolen from NASA.

But they were steadily making progress. While Benson was in that derelict house, being attacked by the crazed Carmell, Butler was trying to fix an appointment with an old man at Cambridge – an old man who would eventually steer them closer to the astonishing truth about Alternative 3.

Dr. Carl Gerstein's housekeeper was possessively protective over him. She'd been bullying him for years over his pipe-smoking. It was a filthy and disgusting habit, in her opinion, and it was certainly bad for him with his weak chest.

There'd been a told-you-so tone in her voice when he developed a severe bout of bronchitis at the end of January, 1977. All she'd said about that pipe, she felt, was now vindicated. Maybe this time he'd listen and throw the dirty thing away. But Gerstein, of course, had no intention of throwing away his pipe. It was part of him.

She had her way, however, about visitors. There were to be none, absolutely none, until he was completely fit. He needed absolute rest – that's what the doctor had said – and she was going to make sure he got it. She refused to even allow him downstairs to speak on the telephone. 'It's draughty in that hall and if you need to speak on the phone you can do it through me,' she said. 'You're staying up here in the warm.'

That was why, on February 11, Butler found himself having to deal with her. She'd seen Butler often on television and she had a soft spot for him. But it wasn't soft enough for her to relax the rules.

'Not this month,' she said. 'Out of the question.'

'How about next month?' asked Butler. 'Isn't he expected to be better by then?'

We should mention here that Butler was later horrified when we showed him the relevant part of Trojan's transcript – dealing with Gerstein – of the Policy Committee meeting held on March 3, 1977:

A EIGHT: No news ... he's been laid up with bronchitis and, apart from his housekeeper, he's seen no-one for weeks ...

R EIGHT: So the situation, then, is unchanged ... I recommend that we maintain observation on the old man ...

Butler would have acted very differently if he had known that Gerstein was under surveillance. But he did not know and he persisted: 'It really is very important ... I wouldn't dream of troubling him if it were not ...'

She relented, said she would go upstairs and check with the doctor. Soon she was back on the line. 'I can only make a provisional arrangement, Mr. Butler,' she said. 'It'll have to depend on how he's feeling.'

'What date do you suggest?'

'It's not me suggesting – it's Dr. Gerstein. He says he's quite looking forward to meeting you again.' She was determined to keep things in proper perspective. 'March the fourth, about two o'clock – would that be suitable?'

91

Butler checked his desk diary. Tuesday, March 4, was completely clear. 'Thank you,' he said. 'Unless I hear to the contrary, I'll be there then.'

The investigation, although they still did not realise it, was soon to take an astonishing turn.

SECTION SEVEN

That interview, which was filmed, took place as planned on March 4, 1977, and it was an important feature of the programme transmitted on June 20. Here is how Simon Butler, in a voice-over link, introduced it to viewers:

Gerstein's theories, when he first put them forward over twenty years ago, had been almost universally dismissed. He was called an alarmist and a pessimist. Events proved him, on the contrary, to be something of an optimist.

By the late Sixties the earth was already so trapped within an envelope of its own pollution that heat was having increasing difficulty in escaping.

Ten years' earlier than Gerstein's prediction, the notorious 'greenhouse' effect — due to the eight-fold increase in the carbon dioxide levels last summer — had become a reality, threatening to double the average global temperature.

Gerstein's chest was still not clear at the time of that interview. He was still wheezing. And he was still smoking his pipe. 'This mysterious Harry of yours . . .' he said. 'I don't think I can place him.'

'He was very specific about you,' said Butler. 'He told us to ask you about something called Alternative 3.'

Gerstein stared down at his desk, pulled thoughtfully on his pipe. 'Did he now . . .' he said slowly. 'That was a rather curious thing for him to do.'

'This Alternative 3 — you know what it means?'

'Let me show you something,' said Gerstein. He rummaged through the bottom drawer of the desk, pulled out a buff folder, turned over half a dozen pages of typescript. 'The Americans, when it comes to public statements, have a remarkable talent for soft-pedalling the truth,' he said. 'Read that . . . it's a CIA report.'

Butler took the folder, read the passage which had been ringed around in red:

> In the poor and powerless areas, population would have to drop to levels that could be supported. Food subsidies and external aid, however generous the donors might be, would be inadequate. Unless or until the climate improved and agricultural techniques changed sufficiently, population levels now projected for the Less Developed Countries could not be reached. The population 'problem' would have solved itself in the most unpleasant fashion.

'What does this mean?' asked Butler. 'Unless or until the climate improved . . .'

'That's it!' said Gerstein. 'That's the key phrase! And that report, let me tell you, is about four years old. What it means is that at that time the Americans were prepared to reveal just a smidgeon of the truth. Not all the truth, of course, for that would be too frightening. But you can take it from me that they knew the whole truth. I told them. Back in 1957 – at the conference in Huntsville, Alabama – I explained it all to them. That's why they started giving serious thought to the three alternatives.'

'And what exactly did you tell them?' asked Butler.

'I told them that we were killing this planet.' Gerstein was stopped by a fit of coughing which shook his whole body, made his eyes water. He apologised. 'Through all the centuries man thought of the atmosphere surrounding us as being so vast that it could never possibly be damaged,' he said. 'So we've gone on abusing it and polluting it . . . and now it's too late.'

He shook his head sadly. 'We've created a greenhouse around this world of ours . . . a greenhouse made of carbon dioxide. Short-wave radiation from the sun passes straight through it, just as in any garden greenhouse, but it absorbs and holds the heat emitted from the surface of the earth.

'You know how much carbon dioxide we've thrown up there in the last hundred years? More than 360 billion tons! And once it's up there it stays there – and it's being added to every year.

'Human lemmings! That's what we are! Do you realise that we're even helping to destroy our world by trying to *smell* nice? No . . . I assure you . . . I'm perfectly serious. Those aerosol sprays that people use – they alone are still squirting nearly half a million metric tonnes of fluorocarbons into the atmosphere every year.'

He delved in the desk again, produced another folder. 'A British Royal Commission on environmental pollution was shocked by the sheer volume of this filth. Listen to what they said in their report.' He opened the folder, thumbed over a few pages and began reading:

'If the worst fears about the extent of damage by fluorocarbons to the ozone layer were realised, and if no means of combating this threat could be devised, the consequences to mankind and, indeed, to most of life on Earth could be calamitous.'

He snapped the folder shut, dropped it contemptuously on the desk. 'There!' he said. 'That's their word – calamitous! And that report, I should point out, was written by people who probably weren't aware of the full seriousness of the situation. They almost certainly still don't know of the need for one of the three alternatives.

'Yet people go on using these things . . . to clean their ovens and spray their hair . . . to kill flies and smells and pains in the back. Good God, we've even got spray-on instant snack food! We're conveniencing ourselves to death, Mr. Butler, that's what we're doing – and now it's all become irretrievably lethal.

'Some belated attempts have been made, of course, to scratch at the problem. Last year, for example, the United States Food and Drug Administration banned fluorocarbons from American aerosol sprays – and that, I can tell you, was a devil of a jolt for an industry with a $9,000 million turnover in America alone.

'But other countries, including Britain – which, by the way, is Europe's principal producer of aerosols – decided not to follow the American initiative. Close your eyes to the dangers and pretend they don't exist – that seems to be the line. You see . . . there are jobs at stake . . . about 10,000 in Britain alone . . . and there's also big money. Still, not that it makes any difference any longer. It's so late now that it's all become completely academic.'

Gerstein was seized by another bout of coughing. He looked accusingly at his pipe which had gone out. And he re-lit it. 'You hear people talking glibly about the concrete jungle, Mr. Butler. What they should be talking about is the concrete storage heater. That's what we're turning this world into – a gigantic storage heater. Concrete . . . asphalt roads . . . brick buildings . . . they're all retaining the heat and they're helping to ferment the disaster.

'Then there's all that waste heat from industry, power stations, cars and central-heating systems. Do you realise that New York city generates seven times more heat than it gets from the rays of the sun? That, Mr. Butler, is a fact. And you just imagine that sort of heat – from all over the world – being trapped in our great atmospheric greenhouse!'

'Yes,' said Butler. 'But this Alternative 3 . . .'

Gerstein ignored the interruption, got up from the desk, walked to the study window. He stood there, hands clasped behind his back, contemplating the wide expanse of neat lawn. 'I'll tell you what's going to happen,' he said. 'This world's going to get hotter and hotter until it gets like Venus. I can't tell you when this will finally happen . . . not to the nearest hundred years . . . but I can assure you that it will happen.

'When that time comes the North Pole and the South Pole will be as hot as the tropics are today. And as for the rest of the world . . . well, it won't be able to support any life apart from insects and cold-blooded creatures like lizards.'

He turned to face Butler, gestured over his shoulder. 'All that out there, all that greenery and beauty, will be a burnt wilderness.

'There won't be any people at all then, not in countries like this. There'll probably still be survivors at the Poles but then it won't be long before they're also killed by the heat – and that will be that.'

He sat down, looked sombrely at Butler. 'So, as you can see, that CIA report you're holding – with that stuff about the climate possibly improving – is just so much public-relations twaddle.'

He sighed resignedly, took the file from Butler, replaced it in the drawer. 'That, I suppose, is the technique. They make a big display of showing part of the truth – which is precisely what they did in that report – to make people believe they're being shown the whole truth.'

'But you mentioned three alternatives,' said Butler. 'You said they considered them at the Huntsville conference...'

'That was a long time ago,' said Gerstein evasively. 'Twenty years ago. And it was all very theoretical...'

'I realise that some of the discussions at Huntsville were held in secret and so, naturally, I can understand your reluctance,' said Butler. 'But this is clearly a matter of immense public concern and, as you say, Huntsville was a long time ago. So wouldn't it be possible for you to say...'

Gerstein held up a hand to stop him. 'Alternative 1 and Alternative 2 were quite crazy,' he said. 'They're not worth even talking about...'

'I'd still like to know about them,' said Butler. 'Couldn't you give me just a brief outline?'

Gerstein was silent, thinking, for a while. Eventually he shrugged. 'Well ... they were abandoned so I suppose it can do no harm,' he said. 'The basic idea of Alternative

1 was rather like throwing a few stones at a conventional greenhouse — making holes in the glass to let the heat escape. The suggestion was that a series of strategically-positioned nuclear devices should be detonated high in the atmosphere — to punch holes in that envelope of carbon dioxide. Then we'd have chimneys in the sky, if you like. That would have eased the immediate problem and then, as a follow-up programme, there would have had to be a dramatic reappraisal of the way life is lived on this earth.

'Men would have had to start living more primitively to prevent another build-up. For example, there'd have had to be international agreements, stringently enforced, to make all motor vehicles illegal — except for the most essential purposes.

'You could almost draw up your own list of things which would have to be sacrificed to stop carbon dioxide being pumped into the air in such quantities.

'Then there would have to be a great co-ordinated effort to give the world back its lungs — by getting rid of every unnecessary bit of concrete and by seeding vast tracts with plants and trees which could absorb the gas.

'That, in essence, was Alternative 1 ...'

'Well, I can see it would be an incredibly complex project ...' said Butler. 'But it would seem to make sense ... if the situation is as desperate as you say ...'

'It was crazy,' said Gerstein curtly. 'Knocking holes in a garden greenhouse is one thing. Doing the same with Earth's atmosphere is a very different proposition. Oh, they could do it all right ... they've got the technology to do it, but what they haven't got is the technology to patch up the holes after they've made them ...'

'I'm sorry ... I don't quite follow ...'

'The ozone layer!' said Gerstein impatiently. 'Don't you see? It would mean punching great gaps in the ozone layer and it's that layer, as you must know, which screens us from the full effects of the ultra-violet rays from the sun.

98

'Without the protection of that ozone layer, Mr. Butler, we'd be bombarded with far more radiation and that would immediately bring all sorts of horrors – such as an increase in the incidence of skin cancers.

'No, there were too many hazards involved. Alternative 1 was rightly rejected.'

'And Alternative 2?'

Gerstein was having more trouble with his pipe. Re-lighting it was a major job which required all his attention. It made him cough and splutter but, after using three matches, he won. And, once again, he was contentedly wreathed in smoke. 'Can you imagine yourself living like a troglodyte, Mr. Butler?'

It was obviously a rhetorical question. Butler waited, knowing he was not expected to reply.

'Alternative 2, in my view, was even crazier than Alternative 1,' continued Gerstein. 'I recognise, of course, that there is enough atmosphere locked in the soil to support life but . . . no, this was the most unrealistic of all the alternatives.'

'Troglodyte,' prompted Butler. 'Why troglodyte?'

'There is good reason to believe that this world was once more civilised and far more scientifically advanced than it is today,' said Gerstein. 'Our really distant ancestors, living millennia before what we call Prehistoric Man, had progressed far beyond our present stage of knowledge.

'Then, it is argued, there was some cataclysmic disaster – maybe one comparable with that facing us now – and these highly-sophisticated people built completely new civilisations deep beneath the surface of the earth . . .'

'But,' said Butler, 'I don't see how . . . .'

'Please!' Gerstein was in no mood to be interrupted. 'There is evidence, quite considerable evidence, to suggest that there were once whole cities – linked by an elaborate complex of tunnels – far below the surface. Remains of them have been found under many parts of

99

the world. Under South America ... China ... Russia ... oh, all over the place. And in this subterranean world, so it is said, there is a green luminescence which replaces the sun as a source of energy – and which makes it possible for crops to be grown.

'So they evacuated down there and very likely thrived for some time ...'

'Then what?' asked Butler.

Gerstein shrugged. 'After all this time ... who can tell? Maybe there's historical truth in the Biblical story of the great Flood. Maybe the disaster which drove them there in the first place was followed by the Flood – and they were all trapped and drowned down there. Maybe that's how their civilisations ended ...'

He paused, sucked reflectively on his pipe. 'And it could follow that the people we think of as Prehistoric Men were merely the descendants of a handful of survivors – the real children of Noah, if you accept the Bible version – who had to start from scratch in a world which had been utterly devastated. Is that why they took so naturally – instinctively, if you like – to living in caves? Then the agonisingly slow process of rebuilding the world started all over again until now we find ourselves in a similar position ...'

'So Alternative 2, then, would involve transporting everybody down into the bowels of the earth?'

'Not everybody,' said Gerstein. 'That would be hopelessly impracticable. There'd be selected people, people chosen for their special skills or talents, people who'd be regarded as vital to the future of the human race.

'There were, I have to tell you, many people at Huntsville in favour of Alternative 2. They pointed out that there would never be another flood, not with the entire planet drying up, so it would not all end as it apparently did once before.'

He took the pipe from his mouth and pointed its stem at Butler. 'You know ... there was one very prominent man – died a couple of years ago now – who even put forward a plan for using ordinary people . . . superfluous people, he called them . . . as slave labour.

'It was quite startling, the way he had it all worked out. These gangs of slaves, who'd do all the heavy work down there, would be treated – either surgically or chemically – so that they would just complacently accept their new roles. They'd be rounded up, as he put it, in Batch Consignments. Yes, that was the expression he used – Batch Consignments . . .'

Butler shook his head in disbelief. 'But that's unthinkable . . . quite inhuman. And, anyway, an operation on that scale . . . it could be mounted only with the closest co-operation between the super-powers. America and Russia would have to pool their resources and scientific know-how and that in itself, surely, would be out of the question . . .'

'Allies are united by the need to fight a common enemy or to combat a universal danger,' said Gerstein. 'Think of the Second World War. Britain, America, Russia – they were all partners in the mutual struggle for survival. It didn't seem so strange then, did it, that they should co-operate. And this present threat, Mr. Butler, is far greater than the world was facing then . . .'

'Is the technology available to do all this?' asked Butler.

'Technology, yes. Cash would obviously be the problem. Countless billions of pounds would be needed but, in extremity, it could be raised.'

'In that case, why did you consider Alternative 2 to be the most unrealistic of them all?'

'Because, at best, it would be no more than a stop-gap solution. As I told you . . . the carbon dioxide, once it's up there, stays there. We're trapped inside the great greenhouse and it will be only a matter of time before the effects permeate down into the earth. Things down there, really deep down, will eventually wither and start to smoulder.'

He paused, gave a brief humourless laugh. 'Maybe our legends and superstitions about Hades — with the demonic stoker down there in the bowels of blackness — are merely unconscious visions of the future. How about that for a thought?'

He stared hard at Butler and, getting no reply, he continued: 'The situation, you see, isn't just irretrievable — it has now reached the stage where it can do nothing but deteriorate. That was why Alternative 2, in my opinion, was ridiculous.'

Outside the study window there were the bird noises of early Spring. Butler looked over Gerstein's shoulder and saw an old woman sedately walking her dog around the perimeter of the lawn.

Out there it was so peaceful, so normal. And that made their conversation all the more bizarre. Here, in this book-lined and sunlit room, they were talking about Armageddon. They were talking about it in measured and cultivated tones as if it were no more than a matter of academic interest. It was hard, very hard, to grasp that the subject really was the approaching end of the world.

This was the strangest interview Butler had ever conducted. But, as a professional, he pushed ahead with his questions.

'And Alternative 3?'

Gerstein shook his head. 'I don't know . . .' he said. 'Maybe I've been too indiscreet already. I've been out of touch with things for rather a long time now and it's hardly my place to talk about Alternative 3. They may have abandoned it for all I know . . . decided that it simply couldn't be done. You'd have to talk to someone connected with the Space Programme because the truth is that I just don't know . . .'

'Well, give me a pointer . . .' persisted Butler.

'I'll give you a sherry,' said Gerstein. And that was where the interview ended.

During the following months public fear continued to mount over the weather – and over the effect it was likely to have on the future of the world. On August 28, 1977, the *Sunday Telegraph* carried a major article headlined: WEATHER MEN AT A LOSS. It was written by a member of the newspaper's 'Close-Up' investigative team and it said:

What is happening to the British weather? That seemingly innocuous question has suddenly become a major subject for research.

Even the meteorologists are cautiously echoing the man in the street's opinion that something distinctly odd has been affecting our climate to give us the extremes of the past two years ... Many countries have experienced strange weather phenomena over the same period. Mr. Edwin P. Weigel of the United States Weather Bureau in Washington told me:

'We don't know what's hit us. California and other western states have had two years of drought which have smashed all-time records. Water is being rationed in some parts...'

There are several shades of opinion on how ominous it all is and there is only a very shaky consensus on how unusual such extremities really are...

The official attitude, however, was still guarded. Experts who knew the real truth were anxious not to provoke mass panic. Kevin Miles of the Meteorological Office's 40-strong climatic research team at Bracknell, Berkshire, was quoted in this *Sunday Telegraph* article as saying: 'We must agree that what we have been experiencing is unusual. Reports from all over the world have confirmed our own picture of increased variability. But we have learned not to over-react to what might be seen as odd in several small parts of the globe.'

Mr. Miles went on to admit that he and his team would 'dearly love to understand what has been going on recently'.

So, on orders from the highest level, the charade was maintained — with weathermen on both sides of the Atlantic insisting that they still did not know the truth, that they were still investigating the disturbing mystery.

The *Sunday Telegraph* article continued:

> The Bracknell meteorologists are enlarging their research programme to investigate every hypothesis that might give a correlation with the fluctuating weather. Oceans, clouds, land forms and the Earth's surface are all being scanned with the help of one of the world's fastest computers.
>
> While such sophistication is being perfected, the American experts are flying as many scientific kites as their British counterparts. The Washington bureau is currently looking at possible effects of volcanic eruptions and changes in the movements of the sun. 'Some of it comes excitingly close, some is clutching at straws,' said Mr. Weigel.
>
> Amateur weather-watchers, who blame everything from Concorde to the atom bomb for the climatic unrest, will not be appeased by the promise of more and better research.

Those 'amateurs' certainly would not have been appeased if they had been told the full story. They would have been terrified.

'Talk to someone connected with the Space Programme.' That's what Gerstein had suggested. But it wasn't easy to follow his advice. Not when *real* information was needed.

Of course, there were people at NASA who were prepared to talk to Sceptre Television. But they were the public-relations specialists, the glib front-men, who could be charming and convincing. And who could say a great deal without saying anything.

Clements knew that he had to get more. Far more. The project, by this time, had become almost an obsession

104

with him. He was determined, somehow, to find someone who really knew about this Alternative 3 – and who would be prepared to explain it.

'We'll obviously get nothing out of anybody still with NASA,' he said to Terry Dickson. 'They'd be too scared of losing their jobs and I can't say I blame them. So see if you can track down someone who's already quit. One of the moon-walkers, perhaps, They may know something or they may have seen something.'

'One or two of them, from what I gather, are rather bitter about the way they've been treated. I was reading – in the *Daily Express*, I believe it was – about Buzz Aldrin complaining that he'd been used as a travelling salesman. Try to get hold of him or one of the others. At the very least, they might point us in the right direction . . .'

Dickson rubbed his chin, pulled a rueful face. 'And how do I start doing that?' he demanded. 'I don't know where any of them are these days . , .'

'I don't ask you how to point the cameras, love . . . you're the researcher . . .'

'Yes, but . . .'

'And make it a priority job, Terry.'

'It'll cost,' persisted Dickson. 'I'll have to hire someone in America and that could cost real money. Harman's not going to like it. Remember what he said about Australia . . .'

'Never mind about Harman.' Clements was being crisply executive. 'You do your job and leave Harman to me.' He grinned suddenly and added: 'Anyway, he's a busy man and I don't think we ought to trouble him with such small details.'

A freelance journalist in America was commissioned by Dickson. Three former astronauts refused to co-operate. A fourth said he would need time to consider his position. That fourth man was Bob Grodin.

The American freelance also supplied Dickson with a tape containing a conversation which had taken place between Grodin – during his first moon walk – and

105

Mission Control. Here is the transcript of the relevant section:

GRODIN: Hey, Houston . . . d'you hear this constant bleep we have here now?

MISSION CONTROL: Affirmative. We have it.

GRODIN: What is it? D'you have some explanation for that?

MISSION CONTROL: We have none. Can you see anything? Can you tell us what you see?

GRODIN: Oh boy, it's really . . . really something super-fantastic here. You couldn't ever imagine this . . .

MISSION CONTROL: O.K. . . . could you take a look out over that flat area there? Do you see anything beyond?

GRODIN: There's a kind of a ridge with a pretty spectacular . . . oh my God! What *is* that there? That's all I want to know! What the hell is that?

MISSION CONTROL: Roger. Interesting. Go Tango . . . immediately . . . go Tango . . .

GRODIN: There's a kind of a light now . . .

MISSION CONTROL (hurriedly): Roger. We got it, we've marked it. Lose a little communication, huh? Bravo Tango . . . Bravo Tango . . . select Jezebel, Jezebel . . .

GRODIN: Yeah . . . yeah . . . but this is unbelievable . . . recorder off, Bravo Tango, Bravo Tango.

No more speech could be heard. Grodin, at that point, had switched to another frequency. On the tape there was only static . . .

Simon Butler, you may recall, underlined that point when the television documentary was transmitted. He said: 'Bravo Tango? Jezebel? A form of code? Almost certainly. But what did it mean? Absolutely nothing to the estimated six hundred million people listening in on earth . . .'

Remember the allegations, which we outlined in

106

section one of this book, made by former NASA man Otto Binder?

'Certain sources with their own VHF receiving facilities that by-passed NASA broadcast outlets claim there was a portion of Earth-Moon dialogue that was quickly cut off by the NASA monitoring staff.'

That censored portion, according to Binder, included these words from Apollo 11: 'These babies were huge, sir ... enormous ... Oh, God you wouldn't believe it! ... I'm telling you there are other space-craft out there ... lined up on the far side of the crater edge ...'

Could that have a direct link with the exchange heard on the Grodin tape? Had Grodin, like the men of the Apollo 11 mission, seen something too startling to be revealed to ordinary people?

Or were these moon-explorers all mistaken? Was there something in outer space which induced hallucinations?

The idea of unknown and unidentified space-craft being 'lined up' on the moon — to the astonishment of human astronauts — was surely too ridiculous. And yet ...

Grodin agreed to be interviewed by Sceptre Television, via satellite, from a studio in Boston, Massachusetts. The plan was to tape the entire interview and edit it later. In fact, as viewers will probably remember, the interview ended abruptly and in the oddest possible way. And it placed an even bigger question mark on the whole subject of Alternative 3.

There was, right from the start, something slightly manic in Grodin's expression and he showed a tendency to laugh nervously for no apparent reason. But he talked fluently and he displayed no reluctance about discussing the breakdown he had suffered after his final return from space. Nothing remarkable happened, or seemed likely to happen, until Simon Butler asked a question which we present verbatim from the programme which was transmitted:

Now it has been suggested, among others, by some very responsible people that you — that all of you on the Apollo programme — saw far more out there than you have been allowed to admit publicly. What comment do you have to make on that suggestion?

The immediate effect on Grodin was electrifying. His face suffused with anger and he shouted: 'What are you trying to do, man? Just tell me that! What are you trying to do?'

Butler apologised. 'I was only . . .'

'You trying to screw me?' demanded Grodin. He leaned forward in his chair, glowering into the Boston camera. 'That what you want? You want to screw me real good?'

'Of course not,' said Butler quickly. 'And I'm sorry if . . .'

'Like that dumb bastard Ballantine? Is that what you want to . . .'

He got no further. His voice was chopped in mid-sentence, his picture on the monitor screen vanished in a haze of white static.

'What *is* going on?' asked Butler. 'Hell's teeth . . . what's the matter with this . . .'

He was interrupted by Clements's voice from the studio control-room. 'We've lost it — and it's not this end. Looks like somebody's pulled a plug somewhere.'

It took Clements nearly half-an-hour to get through to the Boston studios on the telephone. 'Sorry,' said a curt voice. 'Mr. Grodin is no longer available.'

'But we were in the middle of an interview! Where is he?'

'He left the studio,' said the voice. 'We don't know where he's gone.'

Like that dumb bastard Ballantine! That's the line which grabbed their attention. It had to fit in, somehow, with the mystery of the meaningless tape received by Hendry — and with the strange circumstances leading up to Ballantine's death. It just had to be connected with what the man Harry had said: 'There was no way for that to be an accident ... it was what they called an Expediency and I know why it happened.'

'We've got to find Grodin again,' said Clements. 'We've got to find him and talk to him face-to-face. Terry, love ... see what your lad in America can come up with.' He turned to Colin Benson. 'I'll probably be sending you over there,' he said.

Benson beamed. 'Great!' he said. 'But isn't Harman going to raise stink?'

'Probably,' said Clements. 'But leave that to me.'

Harman did 'raise stink'. He raised it more vehemently than Clements anticipated. We have the memoranda which reveal the strength of Harman's feelings. In our view they show a strength bordering on fanaticism ...

Wednesday, July 13, 1977. Another submarine meeting of Policy Committee. Chairman: A EIGHT. Transcript section supplied by Trojan starts:

R TWO: This Princeton man ... Dr. Gerard O'Neill ... appears to have a disturbing lack of discretion ...

(*Authors' note:* This meeting, being held a little later in the month than was customary, was exactly two days after the *Los Angeles Times* published the controversial interview — detailed in Section One of this book — in which Dr. O'Neill outlined the solution he called 'Island 3'. He said in that interview — 'There's really no debate about the technology involved in doing it. That's been confirmed by NASA's top people.')

The Trojan transcript continued:

A FOUR: Sure ... he shouldn't have shot his mouth off in that way ... but I don't see there's any real harm done ... people will assume he's just talking theory ...

A EIGHT: It *is* just theory, for Chrissakes, as far as he is

109

concerned. He knows the technology but beyond that he knows nothing ...

R FIVE: He is a respected man ... a man whose words mould public opinion ... and he should be discouraged from making such stupid statements ...

A EIGHT: That's already been done ... for him and for others like him ...

R TWO: What is this you are saying? An unauthorised Expediency?

A EIGHT: Hell, no! That's not necessary. Like I said ... Gerard O'Neill doesn't know enough, not about the politics ... he doesn't even have any idea that we meet this way ...

R SIX: Then what has been done?

A EIGHT: Let's keep this in perspective, shall we ... Washington doesn't want publicly to pinpoint the O'Neill thing because that would make it seem too important ... best to ignore it ... that's the official attitude and I'm damned sure that attitude is right ...

R SEVEN: But when O'Neill talked about Island 3 ...

A EIGHT: Hold on ... let me finish. Something is being done but it's being done as a blanket operation ... Right now there's a secrecy Bill being scrambled on to the Statute Book and I promise you that'll close every worrying mouth ...

Fourteen days after this meeting of the Policy Committee, as we mentioned earlier, columnist Jeremy Campbell broke the news of the 'suppression' Bill in the London *Evening Standard*. Campbell is a highly experienced journalist with a deserved reputation for knowing the background to the published news. Here, we are confident, is one of the rare instances where he did not know the real background.

The rest of the transcript supplied by Trojan was brief:

R SEVEN: That may well be but I have to tell you that our people in Moscow are becoming increasingly

110

worried about the level of security in America . . .
there was that bad business of Carmell . . .

A EIGHT: Oh no! . . . not Carmell again! Carmell's
settled . . . that's all over, okay?

R SEVEN: And Carl Gerstein?

There was no reply to that question. The meeting had
obviously continued but that was the end of the transcript.

The end of August and the beginning of September,
1977 — only days before the 'Suppression' Bill reached
the Statute Book — brought more curious evidence of the
treatment which had been given to Batch Consignment
victims. It gave a deeper insight into the work which had
been continuing in America and Russia. And in Britain.

This evidence is now public knowledge for, as library
files show, it has appeared in reputable newspapers. But,
because of its special significance, we consider it worth
repeating here.

On August 27, William Lowther, the distinguished
Washington correspondent of the *Daily Mail*, wrote an
article which was headlined THE SPY WHO CAME IN
FROM THE BATHROOM.

It said:

Morgan Hall was a spy. He always kept a jug of
martinis in the refrigerator. He had a two-way mirror
in the bathroom.

But Morgan's life was full of woe. His masters were
slow in sending money. His assignment was awful
sleazy. The code name for his project was 'Operation
Midnight Climax'. It was meant to be a perpetual
secret. And no wonder.

For two full years Morgan spent his working hours
sitting on a portable toilet watching through his mirror
drinking his martinis while a prostitute entertained
men in the adjoining bedroom.

Her job was to persuade clients to drink cocktails.

What they didn't know was that the drinks had been mixed by the mysterious Morgan. They were more chemical than alcohol.

Morgan had to record the results. We still don't know just what they were, or how they worked. But some of the drinks gave instant headaches, others made you dizzy or drunk or forgetful or just plain frantic. The effects were only temporary and nobody was harmed, much.

Morgan was employed by the Central Intelligence Agency and it was America's top spy bosses who sent him out from headquarters near Washington to set up the 'laboratory' in a luxury apartment overlooking San Francisco Bay.

Now 1,647 pages of financial records dealing with the operation have been made public as part of a Congressional investigation.

(*Authors' note:* That was the Congressional investigation provoked by the information supplied to us by Trojan.) Lowther's article continued:

It was all part of the agency's MK-ultra mind control experimental programme ... it was reasoned that a prostitute's clients wouldn't complain.

The financial records released yesterday show that Morgan was always writing to headquarters. Says a typical letter — 'Money urgently needed to pay September rent.'

His bills for the flat include Toulouse-Lautrec posters, a picture of a French can-can dancer and one marked: 'Portable toilet for observation post.'

Says the CIA: 'Morgan Hall died two years ago. We have no idea where he is buried.'

Here we must ignore suspicions and accept the official word of the CIA. Our own inquiries in America have yielded nothing further about Morgan Hall and we must state, quite categorically, that we have found no evidence to support any suggestion of his having been an Expediency victim.

Lowther's story was quickly followed by two more reports which confirmed something we had already been told by Trojan – a series of secret experiments in behaviour control had also been conducted in Russia and in Britain.

On September 2 *The Times* gave front-page prominence to a report supplied from Honolulu by Reuter and UPI. It was headlined 'PSYCHIATRISTS CONDEMN SOVIET UNION' and it said:

> The general assembly of the World Psychiatric Association, meeting behind closed doors, has adopted a resolution condemning the Soviet Union for abusing psychiatry for political purposes, conference sources said today.
>
> The conference, which has brought together 4,000 delegates from 60 countries, last night also unanimously approved of an international code of ethics after the Soviet delegation withdrew objections which had delayed a vote. The code forbids psychiatric treatment in the absence of illness...
>
> The resolution called on the WPA to look at the 'extensive evidence of the systematic abuse of psychiatry for "political purposes" in the Soviet Union...'
>
> The international code of ethics, called the 'Declaration of Hawaii', adopted by the congress follows years of criticism against the WPA for not taking action on ethical standards.

Other newspapers claimed that 'scores of mentally healthy Soviet citizens are forcibly interned in mental hospitals'. This is unquestionably true but the facts need to be seen in their proper perspective. The vast majority are detained because of their stand on human rights. They are sane people who are considered enemies of the State. Only a small percentage are there purely because they are needed as guinea-pigs. These are the ones who have been detained because of Alternative 3.

A story which was more surprising — certainly to people in Britain — appeared on August 28 in the *Sunday Telegraph:*

> Hospitals for the mentally ill and mentally handicapped have been instructed by the Health Department to collect statistics on operations being carried out to change personality.

> For the first time, ministers have acknowledged that there is growing concern. The operations, known as psychosurgery, are carried out to remove or destroy portions of brain tissue to change the behaviour of severely depressed or exceptionally aggressive patients who do not respond to drugs or electric shock treatment.

The *Sunday Telegraph* said that 'the change was irreversible' and quoted a prominent consultant psychiatrist as saying: 'My hospital is littered with the wrecks of humanity who have undergone psychosurgery.'

However, the newspaper did not point out that these operations can also be performed to control the behaviour pattern of men and women who are completely sane. Or that, in fact, they *have* been performed on such people.

Dr. Randolph Crepson-White spoke to us about these operations when we met him in the Somerset village to which he retired in 1975. He talked frankly on the strict understanding that we would not divulge his name. However, as he died of natural causes on October 19, 1977, we do not consider ourselves to be now bound by our undertaking.

Dr. Crepson-White told us: 'I performed five of these operations on people — four young men and one young woman — who appeared to be completely sane. There were two objects. The patients had to be completely

114

de-sexed, to have their natural biological urges taken away, and they also had to have their individuality removed. They would, after being discharged, obey any order without question. In fact, they would virtually be thinking robots.

'I recognised that what I was doing was most unethical, and I did protest that very strongly, but I was told that the operations were vital to the security of the country.

'Nobody actually told me that those patients had been involved in espionage but that was the impression I was given. I was ordered to sign the Official Secrets form and that is why you must not mention my name – apart from the fact that I'm frightened, there'd be repercussions of a violent nature if certain people realised I'd been talking to you.'

We should point out that, in order to protect Dr. Crepson-White's anonymity, we had agreed not to be so specific about the number of operations he had performed. That agreement, of course, is now unnecessary.

He continued: 'I still had distinct reservations about this aspect of my work. Soon it became apparent that I would be required to do more operations involving sane people ... possibly many more ... and that was when I decided to get right out.

'I had not intended to retire for another three years but, under the circumstances, I considered it impossible to go on.'

Dr. Crepson-White, we are certain, knew nothing about people being collected into Batch Consignments. He knew nothing about Alternative 3. But a complete insight into the use being made of his work was eventually supplied to us by Trojan. It was supplied in an astounding document which we will be presenting later.

SECTION EIGHT

Leonard Harman was far from happy with the letter sent to him on August 12, 1977, by our lawyer Edwin Greer.

Letter dated August 15, 1977, from Harman to lawyer Greer:

I am surprised by the contents of your letter and I must *insist* on receiving an undertaking from Messrs. Ambrose and Watkins to the effect that I will not be mentioned in their projected book. I note that your clients are aware that Sceptre Television has admitted that the Alternative 3 programme was an unfortunate hoax and I am puzzled by the apparent evasiveness of your second paragraph.

You state that your clients are 'mindful of the background to that statement'. What, if anything, does that mean?

I repeat that it would be extremely wrong to perpetuate in book form what has already become a public misconception. There is absolutely no truth in the suggestion of any East-West covert action such as that described in the programme and your clients apparently intend to compound what has already been admitted as a serious error of judgement.

If your clients persist in their attitude, particularly in respect to my privacy, I will have to seek legal advice and/or redress.

Letter dated August 18 from Edwin Greer to Leonard Harman:

There was no evasiveness in my letter of the 12th inst.

I merely pointed out that my clients have conducted their own investigations in Britain and America into the subject of their projected book. Indeed, that investigation is still continuing. Any decisions taken by Mr. Ambrose and Mr. Watkins, in consultation with their publishers, will depend on their eventual findings and I am instructed to inform you that it is not possible for them to give you any undertaking.

Six days later Greer received a letter from a well-known Member of Parliament who had been lobbied for support by Harman. We included the name of that MP — and of one other who tried to suppress this book — in our original manuscript but, because of Britain's restrictive libel laws, we have been advised to delete those names from the published version.

This particular MP was taking the same line as Harmán. His letter said:

In common with a number of my colleagues in the House of Commons, I have already deplored the misguided motives which resulted in the television programme about the so-called Alternative 3.

Letters from many of my constituents demonstrate the alarm which was engendered and which, despite the subsequent statement by the television company, still lingers.

The fact that your clients should apparently be determined to capitalise on that alarm is, to my mind, quite scandalous. I intend to seek an injunction to prevent the publication of this book . . .

He did try for that injunction. The fact that you are reading this book at this moment is the proof that it was refused to him — and to one of his colleagues in the House of Commons. As we will explain later, however, these MPs did force us into a reluctant compromise.

However, they did not succeed in preventing us from

using more of the memoranda which circulated inside Sceptre Television.

Memo dated April 12, 1977, from Chris Clements to Fergus Godwin, Controller of Programmes – c.c. to Leonard Harman, Colin Benson, Terry Dickson:

Through contacts in America we have now traced former astronaut Bob Grodin to a new address. He is living with a girl and is not aware he has been located. I have instructed the American freelance to make no direct approach for, in view of the way Grodin went into hiding after the break-down of that Boston interview, he would almost certainly try to dodge us again.

I want to send Benson to America to quiz Grodin in greater depth for, particularly considering his reference to Ballantine, I am certain he holds the key to an immensely important story.

It would be essential, of course, for Benson to arrive without prior warning. May I have your authorisation to make the necessary arrangements?

Memo dated April 12, 1977, from Leonard Harman to Mr. Fergus Godwin, Controller of Programmes:

CONFIDENTIAL. The note from Clements, bearing today's date and relating to his interest in America, is clear confirmation of what I have already indicated to you and the Managing Director.

Clements has become unprofessionally obsessed with this ridiculous investigation with which he is persisting and I recommend that he be replaced immediately as producer of *Science Report*. I have studied his contract and we would be within our rights to transfer him to some area of our output where he would not be such an expensive liability – possibly the gardening series or the God Spot.

I have on several occasions had to warn him about squandering company time, money and resources –

remember those abortive film unit journeys to
Norwich and Scotland? – but he has defiantly persisted in doing so.

I was told nothing of the inquiries which have
apparently been commissioned on our behalf in
America although, as I mentioned again at the Senior
Executives' Meeting on Friday, it is company policy
for matters of that nature to be channelled through me.
It would be utterly wrong to sanction Benson's
going to America. Nothing can possibly be gained by
talking to this man Grodin – even allowing for what
Clements admits is the unlikely chance of him agree-
ing to talk. I have formed the impression from
newspaper accounts that Grodin is unstable and
probably unbalanced and it is no part of our function
as a reputable television company to hound such a
man – particularly for such a ridiculous reason.

We should, I suggest, instruct Clements to
abandon this fool-hardy exercise and we should also
give priority consideration to replacing him.

*Memo dated April 13, 1977, from Fergus Godwin to
Leonard Harman:*

CONFIDENTIAL. Let us not forget that *Science
Report* is a Network success purely because of
Clements. However, I note your objections and I
must confess that I have also been concerned about
the amount of money which has gone into this
particular project. I have arranged for Clements to
see me today and, naturally, I will keep you informed.

The meeting between Clements and Godwin – on
Tuesday, April 13 – did not go well. Godwin had seen the
unedited version of the interview filmed at Cambridge
with Gerstein and he had not been impressed. The way
the old man had veered away from any discussion of
Alternative 3 had made him suspect that there was no
Alternative 3 – that the dangers and the solutions were

119

probably all theoretical. *Science Report* was already well over budget and Godwin knew how that would incense certain men on the Board. One of the Board members was an accountant, with the creative imagination of a retarded Polar Bear, and he was an apoplectic little man. Godwin didn't fancy another row with him – not on an issue where his own ground was so uncertain.

'Let me think it over,' he said to Clements. 'I'll let you know.'

Memo dated April 14, 1977, from Fergus Godwin to Chris Clements – c.c. to Leonard Harman:

> Further to our talk yesterday, I feel we would not be justified in sending Benson to America. If the situation should change as a result of any further information you may get, I will be prepared to discuss the matter with you again. For the moment, however, it's not on.

Clements read the note, pushed it across his desk to Dickson. 'That bloody Harman!' he said. 'This is his doing.'

'Now what?' asked Dickson.

'We are going to do it, Terry. We are *definitely* going to do it. What we need now is some further information.'

'Like what?'

'I don't know, love ... you're the researcher ... the sort of information that'll swing it with Fergus.' He frowned, got up, started pacing the room. 'What was it Gerstein said about co-operation between the super-powers?'

'He seemed to have the idea that they were working together on the Alternative 3 thing ...'

'That could be it!' said Clements excitedly. 'Do we know anyone who might develop that thought for us? It'd have to be somebody with real prestige ...'

'Broadbent?'

'Who's Broadbent?'

'Great expert on East-West diplomacy ... runs the Institute of International Political Studies in St. James's ...'

'Hm ... well there's no harm in trying. Is Colin around?'

Dickson shook his head. 'His day off.'

'It's always his day off when I need him,' said Clements unfairly. 'Ask Kate to pop in and see me, will you? She can start sounding out Broadbent ...'

At 5.15 p.m. that day reporter Katherine White started her interview with Professor G. Gordon Broadbent – parts of which, as you may recall, were eventually used in the transmitted programme.

It took her some time to get Broadbent really talking. He was cautious, suspicious of her motives, anxious not to become involved in any sensationalism.

That was understandable for, after all, he is a man who is internationally respected. After a while, however, he was more forthcoming and we now print the significant part of that interview – verbatim from the transcript – as it was presented in the televised documentary:

BROADBENT: On the broader issue of Soviet-US relations I must admit there is an element of mystery which troubles many people in my field. To put it at its simplest, none of us can understand how it is that the peace has been kept over these past twenty-five years.

WHITE: You mean the experts are baffled?

BROADBENT (with a smile): But also, for once, in agreement. The popular myth that it's been proof of the balance of nuclear power frankly doesn't entirely stand up. And the more you look at it, the less sense it makes. There are too many imbalances – especially when you put it in the perspective of history.

WHITE: So what is your explanation?

121

BROADBENT: Essentially what we're suggesting is that, at the very highest levels of East-West diplomacy, there has been operating a factor of which we know nothing. Now it could just be — and I stress the word 'could' — that this unknown factor is some kind of massive but covert operation in space. But as for the reasons behind it . . . we are not in the business of speculation.

Clements went barging into the Controller's office without waiting for any response to his token tap. 'You read the Broadbent transcript?' he asked.

Godwin, busy at his desk, sat back and smiled resignedly. 'Yes — and your covering note.'

'Well?'

'Well, what?'

Clements groaned, exasperated. 'Surely that clinches it.'

Godwin slowly shook his head. 'No, Chris, not as far as I'm concerned. It's just more theory . . . that's all it is.'

'But Fergus, it all fits! Gerstein and Broadbent — each a top man in his own field — both suggesting some sort of secret co-operation in space between the super-powers.

'That man Harry, the American who claimed to know why scientists keep disappearing, and the links he seemed to have with Ballantine and with NASA. Then there was Grodin who, without any shadow of doubt, saw something really incredible up there on the moon . . . we can't just leave the whole damned thing now and forget it!'

'Stop bouncing around, Chris, and sit down.' Godwin gestured to a chair. 'Go on . . . sit down.' He waited until Clements had done so. 'Now, for the last time, let's get this clear. I realise that something odd may be going on but I can't start to understand it and I don't consider it's any of our concern . . .'

Clements started to jerk angrily out of the chair, bursting to interrupt, but Godwin stopped him: 'You've done a tremendous job with *Science Report*, Chris. Everybody thinks so and the ratings have proved it. So I want you to get back just to doing what you do so well...'

'That means you're still saying "no" to America?'

'That's exactly what it does mean.'

'If it's on grounds of cost, can I point out how much profit this company made last year ...'

Godwin has since told us ruefully that he dislikes only one aspect of his job – that of being the chief buffer between his editors and the money men above him. One lot inevitably think he's mean and the others suspect him of being a spendthrift. Being wedged in the middle ... it's not much fun. That's why his reply to Clements was uncharacteristically sharp:

'It's hardly your place to point that out but, as you've done so, let me tell you something. The company does make profits and it makes good ones but it does not do so by sending teams gallivanting around the world on fool's errands ... so, please, let it rest ...'

Clements got up, prepared to leave. 'How about if I fixed a facility trip?'

'Airlines aren't throwing many free flights around these days – not across the Atlantic.'

'Benson could do a piece for the holiday series while he's over there. I've spoken to Simon Shaw who's taken over the holiday programmes and he's quite keen ... and I know an airline who'll play ball.'

'God ... you don't give up, do you!' Godwin grinned. 'All right ... tell Benson to go to America.'

'Why did you disappear that night?' asked Benson. 'That night of the interview ... why did you run out like that?'

'Have another beer,' said Grodin. He pushed a fresh can across the low table and poured another for himself. 'The bastard was trying to screw me. Did I see more than I've been allowed to admit publicly! Jesus ... what sort of fool question was that?'

123

Benson forced a grin, tried to relieve the tension. He felt like an angler playing a difficult fish. Gently ... gently ... that was the only way. He took a long drink, sighing with satisfaction as he put down the empty glass. 'I needed that beer,' he said. 'Had myself a real thirst.'

'You planning on doing the same?' Grodin was glowering suspiciously. 'You aiming to screw me as well?'

He was frightened. That was quite obvious. And he was trying to hide his fears under aggressiveness. Benson felt a twinge of pity. The man seemed so pathetically vulnerable and Benson was reminded of what Harman had said in that memo: 'Grodin is unstable and probably unbalanced and it is no part of our function as a reputable television company to hound such a man.'

Maybe, after all, there'd been something in what Harman had said. Grodin clearly wasn't normal. It was all very well to be ruthlessly professional but would anything really be gained by pushing Grodin any further? Wouldn't it be fairer to drop the whole thing, to get back into the car and forget about Grodin? Benson hesitated. It would be so easy to tell Clements that Grodin had simply refused to talk, that there was no way for him to be persuaded. Clements wouldn't like it – in fact, he'd be bloody furious – but he'd have to accept it, particularly after the fiasco of that chopped-off interview.

Then he remembered the man called Harry. He remembered him at Lambeth – naked and terrified in that crumbling house. And he wondered how many more there were like him. And how many there would be in the future if the truth were not revealed.

'Camera, tape machines, witnesses – that's the kind of protection I need.' That's what Harry had said. And they had failed him. They had arrived too late.

Protection from what? That was still a mystery. But it tied in somehow with the disappearance of Ann

Clark. And with those of at least twenty other people including Brian Pendlebury and Robert Patterson.

Grodin had the key to at least part of the answer and Benson knew there was no choice. He had to get answers. Somehow he had to squeeze every bit of information out of this man ...

'Well?' persisted Grodin. 'You aiming to screw me as well?'

Benson shook his head, opened his next can of beer. 'I'm just hoping for a few answers,' he said.

They were in canvas chairs, just the two of them, on the green-slabbed patio behind the ranch-style bungalow which Grodin was renting in a lonely corner of New England. It was peaceful there. No neighbours. No town or community of any sort for fifteen miles. Far in the distance, beyond the vast spread of scrub, they could see the toy-like sprawl of the smoke-blue mountains. And the top of those mountains seemed to dissolve into the sky. Tranquillity. Only them and the drowsy-soft sound of insects.

There were no noises from the bungalow behind them but Benson knew that the girl called Annie was probably busy in the kitchen. Grodin had said they'd soon be having a meal so that's where Annie had to be. Benson had been introduced to her, very briefly, when he'd arrived and then she'd scuttled shyly out of sight. Annie, he felt, wasn't at all happy about this intrusion. She looked young, far too young for Grodin, with straight hair, no make-up and gold-rimmed granny-glasses. The sort of earnest girl who should be reading psychology somewhere. It wasn't hard to guess her main function. Benson hoped she was also a good cook.

On the far side of the bungalow, at the top of the winding drive, Benson's technician-partner, Jack Dale, was still in the car checking and preparing his equipment. He had a small sound-camera but he knew better than to produce it until he got the nod. It had to be kept out of sight until Benson got Grodin into the right mood ...

Grodin drained his glass. 'Owned a place like this myself once,' he said. 'Not just rented it like this one but really owned it. Thought I was putting down roots, y'know? Used to go up there in the summer with the family. Ah, it was all different then. We had a few horses and . . .' He stopped, pulled a face, smiled ironically. 'Guess you can say I'm not much into planning for the future any more.'

He studied his glass as if trying to puzzle why it was suddenly empty. He held the can upside-down over it and one small glob of beer fell out. 'I swear they only half-fill the cans these days,' he said bitterly. 'That's how they make their money — y'know that? — by half-filling the cans.' He threw the can away disgustedly and it clattered to the edge of the patio.

'That's how it is these days. Everybody screwing everybody else for all they can get. No ethics left, not nowhere.' His speech was slightly slurred and Benson wondered how much drinking he'd done before their arrival.

'Cheap-jack booze-peddlers!' shouted Grodin. 'Short-changing bastards!' He turned in his chair, called over his shoulder. 'Annie! We're right out of beer! Bring a couple more, will you . . .'

He glanced at Benson. 'Or you want a *real* drink?'

'Beer's fine,' said Benson.

Grodin grunted and shrugged. 'Annie!' he shouted again. 'There are two men out here dying of thirst . . .'

She came out with two more cans of beer and shook her head smilingly, her expression implying that she saw him as an adorably mischievous small boy. As someone who needed mothering. Grodin squeezed her hand. 'Thanks baby.' He seemed to feel some explanation was necessary. 'They don't fill them like they used to . . .'

She smiled again. 'They never did,' she said.

'Great kid, that,' said Grodin as she returned to the bungalow. 'And she ain't my daughter! Right? I want that on record!'

126

'How about getting something else on record?' suggested Benson quietly.

'Like what?'

'Like what you know about Ballantine ...'

The guarded expression was back on Grodin's face. 'I never knew the guy.'

'That time he went to NASA HQ ... didn't you meet him then?'

'Drop it, kid, will you! I told you, for Chrissake. I never knew him ... I never met him ...'

'But you know what happened to him – and why.'

Grodin stood up. 'Time to eat,' he said. 'Let's give your pal a shout.'

Towards the end of the meal Grodin switched to drinking bourbon on the rocks. He tried to persuade the others to join him but Benson and Jack Dale stuck with beer. So did Annie. And later, while she was sorting out the dirty dishes, Grodin agreed to be interviewed. By that time he was a little bleary but he was still thinking coherently. That interview, filmed by Dale, was presented in the famous *Science Report* programme on June 20, 1977. We now quote direct from the transcript:

GRODIN: All I know about Ballantine is that he showed up at NASA with some tape he'd made, and got pretty damn excited when he played it back on their juke box.

BENSON: Juke box?

GRODIN: De-coder. You can pick up a signal if you have the equipment, but you can't unscramble it ...

BENSON: ... without NASA's equipment?

GRODIN: Right. Some young guy helped him do it. Say, now *he* should've known better.

BENSON: This man?

Benson then showed Grodin a postcard-sized photograph of Harry Carmell – blown-up from a frame of the film taken in the street. Grodin frowned, trying to remember.

127

GRODIN: Could be. Yeah, that looks like him. Sure you don't want a bourbon?

BENSON: Beer's fine.

GRODIN: Bourbon's better for you.

BENSON: No, thanks ... are you saying Ballantine was killed because of what he discovered on that tape?

GRODIN: I'm saying nothing. I just saw the way those guys were looking at him. But I knew those looks ... I've seen them looking at me that way.

BENSON: 'Them'?

GRODIN: Oh, c'mon ...! Have a proper drink, for God's sake.

At that stage there was a break in the interview. Viewers saw Grodin empty his glass and shamble across the room to refill it at the bar in the corner. They did not see Annie come back from the kitchen. Nor did they hear the argument between her and Grodin. She was, as Benson has told us, frightened that Grodin was saying too much, that he was being dangerously indiscreet. But by then Grodin had enough drink in him to make him reckless – and to make him resent getting orders from a girl. He yelled at her, cruelly and crudely, telling her that she didn't have 'no nagging rights' because she wasn't his goddamned wife and so would she start minding her own goddamned business. She went on arguing, trying to persuade him, and he got still madder. He threw a tumbler of bourbon at the wall and the glass exploded all over the place. Then she left in tears and he apologised for her behaviour. 'Women!' he said. 'Think they goddamn own you!'

For the next hour he drank. He drank heavily. And Benson was starting to worry that he would soon be unable to speak but, surprisingly, Grodin was still making sense. At one time he seemed to hover on the edge of being hopelessly drunk, of collapsing across the bar, but then he had another drink and, in some strange

128

way, that seemed to pull him through. It was, in Benson's words, as if he was 'starting to drink himself sober'.

Grodin was having problems forming certain words – 'as if his tongue was slipping out of gear' – but his mind seemed clear enough. And eventually he agreed to continue with the interview:

BENSON: Bob ... what did happen out there ... the moon landing?

GRODIN: Well ... I don't know how best to put this ... but we had kind of a big disappointment ... the truth is we didn't get there first.

BENSON: What d'you mean?

GRODIN: The later Apollos were a smoke-screen ... to cover up what's really going on out there ... and the bastards didn't even tell us ... not a damned thing!

BENSON: What *is* going on?

GRODIN: Man, how the hell do I know? Ask the Pentagon! Call the Kremlin – after all, they were in space first. You don't think they just gave up, do you ... oh Christ, I need a drink ...

Here, as viewers will recall, there was another break. It lasted only a split second on the screen but, in fact, filming stopped for more than half-an-hour. When they resumed Grodin was sweating heavily. He was sweating because of the alcohol and because of his excitement over what he was saying.

They'd said he wasn't to talk about it. That's what the bastards had said. Well, he'd show them Bob Grodin wasn't the sort of guy to be scared into silence. They didn't own him. He was out of the service now and, anyway, maybe it was time for *someone* to talk. He was holding yet another drink as he waited for Benson's first question ...

129

BENSON: Bob, you've got to tell me . . . what did you see?

GRODIN: We came down in the wrong place . . . it was crawling . . . made what we were on look like a milk run . . .

BENSON: Are you talking about men . . . from Earth?

GRODIN: You think they need all that crap down in Florida just to put two guys up there on a . . . on a bicycle? The hell they do! . . . You know why they need us? So they've got a P.R. story for all that hardware they've been firing into space . . . We're nothing, man! Nothing! We're just there to keep you bums happy . . . to keep you from asking dumb questions about what's *really* going on! . . . O.K., that's it, end of story. Finish. Lots o' luck, kid.

And that was it. End of interview. Grodin finished his drink in one great gulp and then he fell. Right there on the carpet. Annie heard the thump, came running into the room, told the pair of them to get out. They suggested helping her get Grodin into bed but she refused the offer. She just wanted them out. So there it was. They left.

In November, 1977, we visited that bungalow in the hope of getting Grodin to elaborate. We were certain there was far more he could tell. And we felt he might talk more freely without the presence of a film-camera.

The bungalow was empty. It had been empty, as far as we could tell, for weeks or possibly months. We have been unable to find the girl Annie. She appears to have completely disappeared. But we did trace Grodin. We traced him to a mental hospital on the outskirts of Philadelphia. He was allowed no visitors. At least, that's what we were told. We tried to insist on seeing him but they were emphatic. Quite out of the question, they said. His condition was too severe. And, anyway, a visit would be quite pointless. Grodin couldn't string together two consecutive words. His mind was completely gone . . .

130

Grodin's death was reported in the newspapers in January, 1978. Suicide. That's what the world was told. Grodin had knotted pyjama trousers around his neck and hanged himself from a hot-water pipe fixed high on the wall of his room. We have suspicions that he may have been the victim of an Expediency but, without evidence, they can be no more than suspicions.

Another intriguing piece of the jigsaw was supplied by the American freelance hired by Dickson. It was a copy of a tape containing dialogue between NASA Mission Control at Houston and the Lunar Command Module Pilot during a 1972 moon mission. And Clements puzzled over it when he first played it at the Sceptre studios:

> MISSION CONTROL: More detail, please. Can you give more detail of what you are seeing?
> LUNAR MODULE PILOT: It's ... something flashing. That's all so far. Just a light going on and off by the edge of the crater.
> MC: Can you give the co-ordinates?
> LMP: There's *something* down there ... Maybe a little further down.
> MC: It couldn't be a Vostok, could it?
> LMP: I can't be sure ... it's possible.

All this fitted logically with the content of the taped conversation between Mission Control and Grodin — during Grodin's first moon walk:

> MISSION CONTROL: Can you see anything? Can you tell us what you see?
> GRODIN: Oh boy, it's really ... really something super-fantastic here. You couldn't ever imagine this ...
> MC: O.K. .... could you take a look out over that flat area there? Do you see anything beyond?
> GRODIN: There's a kind of a ridge with a pretty

spectacular ... oh my God! What *is* that there?
That's all I want to know! What the hell is that?

It also fitted with the exchange — reported by former
NASA man Otto Binder — between Mission Control
and Apollo 11 during the Aldrin-Armstrong moon
walk:

MISSION CONTROL: What's there? ... malfunction
(garble) ... Mission Control calling Apollo 11 ...
APOLLO 11: These babies were huge, sir ... enormous
... Oh, God you wouldn't believe it! ... I'm telling
you there are other space-craft out there ... lined
up on the far side of the crater edge ... they're on
the moon watching us ...

There was, however, one reference in the latest tape
which made it startlingly different — the reference to a
Vostok. Russia's Vostok flights took place in the early
Sixties. According to the information made public, they
were not designed to reach the moon but were merely
Earth-orbiting spaceships.

So what could be made of the casual suggestion by
Houston Mission Control — and an equally casual
acceptance by the Lunar Module Pilot — that an
obsolete Russian craft might be sitting on a crater on
the moon flashing its lights in 1972?

We now know that, for many years, the super-powers
have taken immense trouble to hide the extent of
advances made in space technology. Remember, for
example, how people were encouraged to believe that
the first living creature to be sent into space was a dog
in 1958?

Yet that dog mission was seven years after the four
Albert monkeys were hurtled into the stratosphere in a
V2 rocket. And there are sound reasons for doubting
that those monkeys were the first.

So was the *official* objective of the Vostok flights also
a blind? Were they, to paraphrase the words of Bob

Grodin, also a P.R. job for all the hardware that had been fired into space?

One dominant question develops automatically from all the others: Was the first publicly-announced moon walk in 1969 no more than a cynical charade – played by agreement between the super-powers – because by then men had really been on the moon for the best part of a decade?

If that was the truth, and all the evidence points to it being so, what was the purpose of that charade? And why has it been perpetuated? The answer to both those questions is Alternative 3.

The all-embracing threat to this planet, described by Dr. Carl Gerstein, is horrifying enough to make America and Russia kill their comparatively petty rivalries – and their archaic concepts of pride in national achievement – in a desperate bid to snatch some sort of future for mankind.

Simon Butler put the known situation into clear perspective in that *Science Report* programme. He told viewers: 'The drive to make the first man on the moon an American was launched by President Kennedy – in competitive terms. By the late Sixties it appeared that the race had been conclusively won. The Russians, it seemed, had simply dropped out and stopped trying. America had won.

'Yet today Cape Canaveral is a desert of reinforced concrete and steel. The most ambitious project in the history of mankind is apparently over.

'More and more, however, we hear talk of Skylab and a space shuttle. But shuttling what? And to where?'

All of us have seen on television the phenomenal amount of power required simply to pull a space-rocket clear of the earth's gravitational field. But suppose that power did not have to be consumed principally in merely getting into space. Suppose the rocket could start *from* space. What kind of travel would that bring within our grasp?

133

Technical journalist Charles Welbourne, author of three highly-acclaimed books on aerospace, was questioned on that tack by Butler. Here is a transcript of the key section of that interview:

WELBOURNE: Obviously we could go further with less power, or send a much larger craft. In fact, the only way we're going to see space travel on any scale is by this kind of extra-terrestrial launching – for instance from a space platform orbiting the Earth.

BUTLER: Or from the moon?

WELBOURNE: Sure ... if we could get the material there to build the craft, it'd make real good sense.

BUTLER: Could we transport the materials there?

WELBOURNE: It'd take one hell of a shuttle ... but, sure, we have the machines now ... in theory we could do it ... especially with some kind of international co-operation.

'International co-operation.' Welbourne's tone suggested that he considered such a likelihood rather remote. Certainly on the scale being discussed. But at the time of that interview, it must be remembered, Welbourne knew nothing about the Policy Committee and its submarine meetings. Nor did Butler.

Through the summer of 1976, while the Sceptre team continued its investigation, there was dramatic evidence to show how this planet was experiencing traumatic changes – the sort of changes which later were to be explained to Butler by Dr. Gerstein.

The great drought of that year was unequalled in recorded history. And Butler eventually told viewers: 'There was no panic ... only a growing unease that what we were experiencing was unnatural and that the Earth's climate was moving towards a radical change.

'The earthquake barrage in China and the Far East has done more damage and killed more people than several nuclear attacks. Meanwhile, on the other side of the Pacific, it seemed as if the whole Caribbean was about to blow up.

'Also in Italy and Central Europe the Earth's crust was undergoing dramatic changes.

'For the first time scientists are beginning to see glimmerings of the workings of spaceship Earth, a huge but delicate machine buffeted by the forces of the interplanetary ocean.'

At the height of the drought British government scientists contemplated trying to meddle with the weather. They decided not to do so – pointing out that Common Market countries might accuse Britain of stealing their rain. So Britain, like the rest of the world, went on suffering. Roads buckled in the intense heat. Firemen could hardly contain the infernos which raged through forests and across moors. And there was an astonishing range of unexpected casualties. Bees starved because there was not enough nectar or pollen in the parched flowers ... thousands of racing pigeons, unable to sweat like humans, collapsed with heat exhaustion.

On September 27, 1976, one of the authors of this book – Leslie Watkins – wrote a major article in the *Daily Mail* which started:

Houses which have stood solidly for a hundred years or more – together with modern ones and impressive blocks of flats – are today unexpectedly splitting and threatening to collapse. Our long summer of drought has brought acute anxiety to the insurance companies – and the prospect of financial disaster to many families. Damage estimated at nearly £60 million has been caused by subsidence. Homes in many parts of the country, but particularly in London and the South East, have been slowly sinking at crazy angles into the parched and contracting ground.

Britain has, in effect, been ravaged by a slow-motion earthquake.

However, few people then suspected that the drought was merely the start of a cataclysmic change in the world's weather. But soon it became apparent that the pattern was beginning to go berserk — lurching from one disastrous extreme to the other — like the frantic flailings of some gigantic, doomed creature.

On June 15, 1977, the main feature article in the *Daily Mail* — also written by Watkins — said:

No man in the world gambles more heavily on dry weather than 54-year-old Peter Chase.

That was why, early yesterday, every flash of lightning showed the misery etched on his face.

His wife Phoebe was urging him to get back into bed, to ignore the torrential rain and forget about business. But he stayed at the window, trying to calculate the cost.

Mr. Chase has good cause to be horrified by the violent electric storm which brought such devastation to many parts of Britain. He is the pluvius underwriter for Eagle Star — the leaders in rain insurance.

This has been a bad year for Mr. Chase. Jubilee celebrations, with street parties and other festivities almost drowned by deluges, were particularly disastrous . . .

We have, in fact, been experiencing the second heaviest spell of sustained wet weather since records were first kept in 1727. And the outlook for the rest of the week is 'showery' . . .

Most people have assumed that this sequence of drought followed by heavy rain was, in some mysterious and providential way, Nature trying to compensate and restore the balance — that the downpours have nullified the facts which have now been outlined by Gerstein.

That assumption, unfortunately, is incorrect. Meteorologist Adrian Lerman explains that the excessive rains were *produced* by the excessive heat, that they are not a pointer to long-term cooler weather.

136

He says: 'There is far more evaporation during periods of intense heat, with water vapour being drawn in great quantities from oceans, lakes, reservoirs and rivers, because warm air absorbs that vapour more efficiently than cold air.

'This inevitably results in an eventual increase in precipitation.

'Gerstein is undeniably right in anticipating that the greenhouse syndrome will continue to produce a great increase in global temperatures but I consider he has not laid sufficient stress on the most immediate threat to humanity – the threat of world-wide flooding.

'I am certain that Gerstein is wrong when he predicts that countries like England and America will become scorched wildernesses. They'll be destroyed all right . . . and they won't support life . . . but they'll be drowned rather than burned.

'Extreme heat, such as that which is now inevitable, will melt land glaciers. That will result in a marked rise in sea level and then there'll be the start of the extensive flooding – with London and New York among the first cities to be affected.'

So Lerman, having studied the situation with scientific precision, expects a replay of the global disaster described in the Bible.

'*Genesis*' *6-17:* 'And, behold, I, even I, do bring a flood of waters upon the earth, to destroy all flesh, wherein is the breath of life, from under heaven; and everything that is in the earth shall die.'

So there is a conflict of opinion between those experts who agree with Gerstein and those who agree with Lerman. They are, however, in total and terrible agreement on the key issue – that this world, because of man's stupidity, is now irrevocably doomed. Flame or flood . . . one of them, in the comparatively near future, will bring the agonising end.

And what of the men behind Alternative 3?

They, presumably, have also studied the Bible version

137

of the horrendous mass-death. *'Genesis' 7-21, 22, 23:*
'And all flesh that moved upon the earth died, both of fowl, and of cattle, and of beast, and of every creeping thing that creepeth upon the earth, and every man: All in whose nostrils was the breath of life, of all that was in the dry land, died. And every living substance was destroyed which was upon the face of the ground, both man, and cattle, and the creeping things, and the fowl of the heaven; and they were destroyed from the earth: and Noah only remained alive, and they that were with him in the ark.'

There can now be no doubt that those men, the ones who have supervised the mechanics of Alternative 3, have cast themselves jointly in the role of God – taking their cue from other verses in that chapter of Genesis.

The Lord instructed Noah to collect the people and the creatures destined to board the ark, the ones to be lifted clear of the global devastation.

Technology has made space-craft the modern equivalent of that ark. Who, then, decides which people shall be evacuated in the arks of the twentieth century?

These anonymous men have assumed the right to decide who shall live and who shall die. Their decisions are based, in the main, on information supplied by an elaborate international network of computers – an aspect of the operation which we will later examine in more detail.

They have also assumed a prerogative which many will consider far more obscene: that of deciding which people should be plucked away from their homes – to be mutilated and moulded into slaves. These people, these tragic victims, are those who – together with disappearing cattle and horses and other creatures – become part of Batch Consignments.

Tuesday, January 10, 1978. Another envelope from Trojan. This one, arriving exactly a week after that

Photostat copy of The Smoother Plan, contained the most serious indictment yet of the men behind Alternative 3. Trojan had again been scouring the archives and, as a result, had secured two documents – one dated Wednesday, August 27, 1958, and the other dated Friday, October 1, 1971. Both had been issued by 'The Chairman, Policy Committee'. Both were addressed to 'National Chief Executive Officers' and both were headed 'Batch Consignments'.

The covering note from Trojan was tersely triumphant. It said:

'Maybe now you'll *really* believe me! This is what made me decide I wanted out – and it's the only reason I'm working with you.'

The 1958 document said:

Each designated mover will, it is estimated, require back-up labour support of five bodies. These bodies, which will be transported in cargo batch consignments, will be programmed to obey legitimate orders without question and their principal initial duties will be in construction.

Priority will naturally be given to the building of accommodation for the designated movers.

However, it is stressed that, in the interests of good husbandry, accommodation will also be provided for the human components of batch consignments – as well as for relocated animals – as a matter of urgency. The completion of this accommodation, which will be of a more basic and utilitarian nature than that allocated to designated movers, will in normal circumstances take precedence over the erection of laboratories, offices, other places of work, and recreational centres. All exceptions to this rule will require written authorisation from the Chairman of the Committee in Residence.

It is estimated that the average working life-span

139

of human batch-consignment components will be fifteen years and, in view of high transportation costs, every effort will be made to prolong that period of usefulness.

At the end of that life-span they are to be considered disposable for, although this is recognised as regrettable, there will be no place for low-grade passengers in the new territory. They would merely consume resources required to sustain the continuing influx of designated movers and would so undermine the success potential of the operation.

Preliminary work is now progressing to adapt batch-consignment components, mentally and physically, for their projected rôles and the scope of this experimental work is to be widened. Further details will be provided, when appropriate, by Department Seven.

Pre-transportation collection of batch-consignment components will be organised by National Chief Executive Officers who will be supplied with details of categories and quantities required. No collection is to be arranged without specific instructions from Department Seven.

The 1971 document said:

Experimental processing of batch-consignment components is now producing a 96 per cent success rate. This is considered not unsatisfactory.

The Policy Committee briefing circulated on September 7, 1965, explained the necessity for all components to be de-sexed: 1) To eliminate the possibility of them forming traditional mating relationships which could detract from the efficiency of their sole-function performance. 2) To ensure components do not procreate and so haphazardly perpetuate a substandard species. This second consideration is of particular importance for the products of such procreation, during their initial years of growth and development, would have no operational value and would merely be a liability on the resources of the new territory.

The permanent elimination of self-will and self-interest has presented great difficulties. Long-term laboratory tests have revealed that an unacceptably high percentage of components eventually regress towards their pre-processing 'attitudes, so rendering themselves unreliable and unsuitable for the envisaged role.

Advanced work, conducted principally in America, Britain, Japan and Russia, has now resulted in a substantial reduction of the 'component-personality' failure ratio. However, this branch of research is now to be intensified.

The Policy Committee has given careful consideration to suitable means of jettisoning rejected potential components. It has been agreed that they are not to be considered responsible for their unsuitability and that there is nothing to be gained by killing them. Such a solution, although simple enough to implement, would be unnecessarily harsh. They are therefore to have their memories destroyed – a process for so doing has now been perfected at Dnepropetrovsk and details are being circulated to all A-3 laboratories – and then they will be permitted to resume their lives.

In future no de-sexing will be done until after the personality-adjustment of the projected component, male or female, has been assessed and approved. This will ensure that those which eventually return to their homes as rejects will betray no evidence of laboratory work.

On August 22, 1977, this story appeared in the London *Evening News:*

A mystery girl who baffled Scotland Yard for two weeks has discharged herself from hospital.

141

And the Yard said today it still does not know who she is or where she has gone.

The girl, aged between sixteen and twenty, was admitted to Whittington Hospital, Holloway, after wandering into a hospital building late one night.

She appeared to have lost her memory and, despite intensive efforts by doctors and detectives, her background remains a mystery.

One week before that story appeared, Hertfordshire police were appealing for help in identifying another amnesia victim – a man in his mid-thirties – found wandering on a golf-course near Harpenden. So were police in Manchester. Their memory-blank case was a man aged about twenty.

That particular section of August, 1977, produced a great rash of people with the same problem. They turned up in Germany and in France, in Italy and in Canada. They were all physically fit and apparently normal – apart from having no idea who they were or where they had been.

What produced that extraordinary epidemic of amnesia? Far too many cases were reported for the global outbreak to be dismissed as coincidence. Had something gone dramatically wrong with a complete batch of 'projected components' . . . something so severe that it had been necessary to return them to their old surroundings?

For instance, that man found wandering on the golf-course near Harpenden . . . was he there simply because the Alternative 3 planners had rejected him as a slave?

We do not claim to know. And although we have interviewed him – in addition to twenty-three other amnesia victims who appeared at about the same time – we see little hope of conclusively establishing that these people had been part of a 'pre-transportation collection'. However, in view of the 1971 document supplied by Trojan, we do consider that to be a distinct possibility.

SECTION NINE

Monday, May 2, 1977. Clements was now spending as little time as possible in his own office. The smells from the canteen below, he swore, were getting stronger every month. Nothing could be worse than a floating reminder of yesterday's unwanted cabbage . . .

He operated, most days, from a desk in the big open-plan office which had been allocated to *Science Report.* At times, however, it tended to be too noisy — with too many telephones and too many people — and occasionally he was forced to retreat to his own tiny room behind Studio B. This Monday morning was one of those occasions. Clements and Benson were closeted there together — studying a transcript of the final interview with Grodin.

Clements marked a section with a red pencil. 'There, love,' he said. 'That's the bit that really intrigues me. What exactly did he mean?'

Benson read the lines again: 'We're just there to keep you bums happy . . . to keep you from asking dumb questions about what's *really* going on!'

'I just don't know,' he said. 'That's where he dried up. I couldn't get another damned thing out of him.'

'Well that still leaves us with a load of questions, doesn't it?' said Clements. 'And what I need now, Colin, is answers.'

'Yes, but . . .'

'No "buts", love, please. I'm getting all of those I need from Harman. He's raising hell, y'know, about this American trip of yours . . .'

'Chris, I promise you, no-one could have got more out of Grodin . . .'

'He's put in a complaint about you to Fergus Godwin

143

'... says it was unethical of you to persist in questioning a man when he was drunk – particularly, as he puts it, when that man has a history of instability ... He's even suggested that we should junk the film because Grodin was talking nonsense ...'

'It wasn't nonsense, Chris. All right, so he was a bit smashed, particularly towards the end ... I'm prepared to admit that ... but I'm certain that he knew what he was saying and that he was telling the truth ...'

'I know – and then he fell flat on his face.' Clements chuckled. 'You stick with your version, love, because the Controller wants to see both of us this afternoon.'

'You're serious, then? Harman really is trying to kill it?'

'Believe me, I was never more serious. Let's face it, Colin ... we've put two fingers up at him all along the line on this investigation and he's out to make all the trouble he can. You might like to know, by the way, that he's complaining you didn't bother to do the other job in America ...'

'What other job?'

Clements grinned. 'The piece you were meant to do for the holiday series, the one we promised Simon Shaw he'd get for his next run. The airline are going to be narked when they find they've thrown away a facility – and young Master Shaw's not too happy either ...'

'Oh, come on ...'

Clements stopped him. 'He can fill in with the Isle of Man – that's the least of our troubles,' he said. 'We still need answers.'

'Then maybe we should be searching harder for Harry.'

'That crazy American! The one who attacked you!'

'He's got answers,' said Benson. 'Remember what he said on the telephone ... about knowing why scientists keep disappearing and about knowing who's behind it...'

Clements sniffed, frowned with disgust, got up to close the window. 'So where do you start searching?'

'Could try the police again.'

'Be back by mid-afternoon,' said Clements. 'We've got that session with the Controller.'

The desk sergeant was polite but unhelpful. 'You any idea how many people get reported missing in Britain every year?' he asked. 'About five thousand. And they're the ones officially reported. God only knows how many more never get reported . . .'

Benson handed him the photograph he had shown Grodin. 'That's him,' he said. 'Last seen on February 11 at that address in Lambeth.'

The sergeant glanced casually at the picture. 'And you don't even know his surname.' He snorted. 'Gives us plenty to go on, doesn't it? Anyway . . . what makes you think he is missing? Maybe he just doesn't want to see you any more . . .'

'He was frightened, very frightened, and he got me confused with somebody else,' said Benson. 'He seemed to think that somebody was planning to kill him.'

'You think that he's been killed? That he's been murdered? Is that what you're trying to say?'

'I don't know,' said Benson miserably. 'I don't think so but I don't know.'

'Why should he confuse you with somebody else?'

'Because he wasn't normal that morning. He was . . . well . . . bombed out of his mind.'

'Drugs?'

'That's right.'

They were short-handed at the police station and it was a busy morning. The sergeant decided he'd already wasted too much time. He pressed the picture back into Benson's hand, made a big play of putting his pen down firmly on the counter, sighed patiently. 'So what have we got, sir? An alien of uncertain age and of unknown name who uses drugs and who was last seen by you, briefly, nearly three months ago in a condemned house where he was apparently squatting.

'He imagined you were somebody who, for a reason we can't establish, wanted to murder him. Now, although he may have gone back to America for all you know, you want us to find him for you.

'Would you say that was a fair summing-up of the situation?'

Benson shuffled his feet and looked sheepish. 'Sounds a bit daft, doesn't it?'

'I've got your name and address,' said the sergeant politely. 'If Mr. Anonymous does turn up, I'll mention you were asking after him.'

The afternoon meeting with Fergus Godwin was also a rough one. The Controller had already been worked on vigorously by Harman and he was in a foul mood. He saw trouble looming with the Board over this particular *Science Report* project, especially with that apoplectic accountant, and he bitterly regretted having authorised Benson's trip to America.

Harman's words kept niggling at the back of his mind. Maybe Harman was right. Maybe Clements was becoming 'unprofessionally obsessed'. Godwin certainly had doubts about allowing the transmission of such a curious interview with a man who was patently drunk. There could be all sorts of repercussions . . .

'But Fergus . . . it could prove to be an invaluable part of the programme,' argued Clements. 'It's just that, at the moment, there are still some missing links.'

'Come back to me when and if you find those links.' Godwin glowered balefully at the pair of them. 'Until then that film gets locked away — and I can't see much chance of us ever using it.'

They returned to the small office. Clements sat at the desk and sniffed. 'Thank God there's no fish on Mondays,' he said. 'Fish days are always the worst.'

'Now what?' asked Benson.

'Gerstein — he's all we've got left. If only we could get him to open up on this Alternative 3 . . .'

'You want me to try him?'

146

Clements shook his head, picked up the grey internal telephone, dialled a number in the main *Science Report* office. 'Is Simon Butler there?'

In May, 1971, the authoritative publication *Computers and Automation* carried an article by Edward Yourdon which said:

'It seems, then, that computers could bring about a tremendous improvement in various phases of Government ... if one has faith: faith that the computers will work properly ... men had lost faith in their human leaders, and now ... things will be better if they have faith in a cold-blooded mechanical computing machine.'

Only a few months earlier, at the end of 1970, the staff magazine of Barclays Bank, *Spread Eagle*, had contained an article which read:

Computers have given birth to the Technological Era, have ushered in the Space Age, have begun to play such a dominating role in fields as diverse as military science, weather forecasting, medicine, industrial design and production, communications, commerce, business and banking that the question is seriously being asked whether they are beginning to dominate man himself.

Some even hold the view that in the foreseeable future we shall be stripped of our individual privacy and reduced to a string of meaningless dots stored in the magnetic bowels of some giant Government computer – a sort of Big Brother whose prying gaze will have us constantly under his attentive scrutiny.

Neither of those writers realised he was anticipating a situation which was by then firmly established. 'Individual privacy' had been scrapped years earlier because of covert decisions made within governments and between governments.

This was a fact that many people vaguely realised. Few people, however, guessed the extent of the intimate information — relating to ordinary men, women and children — which was being meticulously analysed and stored.

Details of achievements and personality flaws ... of career potential and sexual attitudes ... of health patterns and of religious beliefs ... these, and so many more, were regularly fed into the computer networks. And those networks, linked by long-distance telephone wires and satellites, were designed to speak to each other in code — to compare and assess their combined material.

In 1973, for example, about £20 million was spent linking all universities in America — including the University of Hawaii — to a gigantic central computer called Illiac 4. The potential academic value of this link seemed unlikely to justify the spending of £20 million. Yet this scheme has been mirrored by similar ones in other parts of the world. And, as we have now discovered, most of the major networks, on both sides of the Iron Curtain, have a direct feed into a central source in Geneva. And Geneva, of course, is the operations centre for Alternative 3.

Information about individuals is harvested in many ways. It comes from employers and university administrators. It comes, even, from teachers in primary schools. You may recall that during 1977 there were public protests from certain teachers in Britain about the 'intrusive details' they were required to supply on their pupils' 'confidential record cards' — details about the children's home-life, about the behaviour and personalities of the parents.

At many schools very young children are being encouraged to maintain weekly diaries about their home-life and are required to write essays entitled 'My Mother' or 'My Father'. All this, of course, sounds innocuous, tritely innocent and unimportant. But there

148

is an official and sinister motive behind these apparently harmless exercises. History is littered with examples of totalitarian states which have used children to spy on their own parents — and, perhaps unwittingly, to denounce their parents. Governments know that out of the mouths of babes . . .

Teachers have been told that it is imperative that all possible details be supplied regularly to the local authorities.

Other information is gleaned from official forms which individuals are required by law to complete, from apparently trivial 'survey questionnaires' conducted as doorstep interviews.

Newspapers occasionally snipe at the volume of 'official bumph' which comes deluging our homes and businesses from central government and local government. But it is no accident that our lives, and the lives of those in other countries, are becoming increasingly bounded by form-filling. Officialdom's voracious appetite for facts is not, as some have suggested, merely an excuse to maintain establishment levels in the Civil Service. It is an integral part of the great design — although, it must be stressed, the vast majority of officials paid to help process this information know absolutely nothing about Alternative 3.

So there are mountains of facts. Many mountains. And, despite denials from Westminster and Whitehall, these mountains are crunched together by computers which are officially autonomous.

For example, that monstrous driving-licence computer at Swansea . . . do you *really* believe it is not linked to those serving organisations such as the Inland Revenue and the Department of Health and Social Security?

Facts *are* cross-checked and cross-indexed. The result provides the basis for selecting those who, in the jargon of Alternative 3, are likely to become 'designated movers'.

Some of this background, just occasionally, spills into the open.

On September 9, 1977, *The Times* published a front-page story, by Home Affairs Reporter Stewart Tendler, which had a headline reading: NATIONAL SECURITY CITED BY POLICE AS REASON FOR MAINTAINING SILENCE ON USE OF RECORDS.

Tendler's story said:

> The names and personal details of tens of thousands of people scrutinized by the Special Branch for reasons of national security are to be fed into a new criminal intelligence computer bought by Scotland Yard and shrouded in mystery.

Note those last three words. 'Shrouded in mystery.' *The Times* is not a newspaper which would lightly use a phrase of that nature. The story continued:

> When plans for the computer were drawn up two years ago it is understood that the Special Branch was allocated space on it for up to 600,000 names out of the system's total capacity of 1,300,000 names by 1985 ...

Census projections have indicated that Britain's population will not increase in the next decade. So that figure of 600,000 means that the Special Branch was preparing to feed details of one person out of every ninety-five in the entire population into that computer. But that is merely the start ...

Discount from the total population all geriatrics, young children, and those who have been adjudged incurably insane ... and the ratio under surveillance comes down to about one person in fifty.

Take that one step further and the implications are startling ...

If the average household comprises two adults – and that is pitching it at its most conservative – the ratio is reduced to one household in twenty-five.

That means there can hardly be a street or road in Britain where at least one household — and probably far more — is not considered to merit computer-monitoring by the Special Branch.

Can you now be confident that you or your immediate neighbours are not being studied by the Special Branch? You can be absolutely certain that people you know, probably people very close to you, are getting this particular treatment.

And the figures we have given, astonishing as they may seem, do not allow for those people programmed into other Special Branch computers — computers which so far have remained hidden on the classified list.

Does all this savour of normal Special Branch work? Or does it indicate an operation on a far bigger scale? One, possibly, as enormous as Alternative 3?

The Home Office was clearly embarrassed by Tendler's discovery and sought to 'play it down'. His story went on:

Yesterday a police source said that the Special Branch had yet to decide how many names would be placed on the computer and denied that anything like 600,000 would eventually be filed.

Scotland Yard said last night: 'The question of the involvement of the Special Branch in the project to computerize sections of the records of C Department (the department covering CID and specialist detective squads) is not one we are prepared to discuss, since most of the work of the Special Branch is in the field of national security.

'The publication of any figures purporting to indicate the total number of records in any part of the project would amount to speculation' . . .

It (the Special Branch) is still surrounded by a certain amount of mystique and the same is true of the new computer. The Metropolitan Police and the

Home Office have made few public statements about the nature of its use.

Tendler also said in that story that the activities of the Special Branch were 'a closely guarded secret' and he added: 'It is not known whose names and details have been gathered by the officers.'

We cannot prove that this particular computer has been used to sift 'designated movers' for Alternative 3. However, because of information from Trojan, we are able to state categorically that similar computers are used for this purpose. We know of six – apart from the master one at the operation-control centre in Geneva. They are located in America, Britain, Germany, Japan, Poland and Russia.

There may be others. In fact, there almost certainly are. However, we have no information about them and, as we have already said, we have no intention of making statements which cannot be substantiated.

Britain's principal Alternative 3 computer is officially used exclusively by a local authority in the north-east and, as a cover, a small percentage of routine local-authority work is processed by it. The main one in America, installed and maintained at the expense of the Federal Government, is officially owned by a manu-facturing company in Detroit. The Polish one is in the Academy of Sciences in Warsaw's Plac Defilad.

Comparatively little trouble is taken over the selection of 'components' for Batch Consignments. They need to be strong, to have years of physical labour left in them. That is the prime criterion. Their personalities, back-grounds, mental agilities ... these are of secondary importance, for they will be scientifically moulded into the approved pattern. And, after all, they are expendable.

But what of the 'designated movers'? How is their value measured? And this mysterious 'new territory' in which they are apparently destined to live – what sort of society is being created there?

152

Trojan has supplied partial answers. He found them in a 1972 document – addressed to National Chief Executive Officers – from the Chairman of the Policy Committee:

Standing Instructions relating to the recruitment of designated movers have already been circulated by this Committee. However, recent reports from the Chairman of the Committee in Residence indicate that there have been certain failures in the execution of those instructions.

These failures have produced unwarranted problems in the new territory and have resulted in an unacceptably high wastage of post-transportation designated movers.

This situation cannot be tolerated and the Policy Committee therefore requires me, once again, to specify the aims and the requirements of the Committee in Residence.

Every effort is to be made to eliminate the problems which men have become conditioned into accepting as inevitable in the old territory.

Alternative 3 participants have evolved, or must be taught to evolve, away from the concepts of national or tribal interests which have traditionally resulted in warfare. This will become of increasing importance when the new territory becomes more intensively populated. National Chief Executive Officers will therefore give priority attention to this aspect of the operation and ensure it is fully understood by their regional subordinates.

No person is to be nominated as a potential designated mover if there is any doubt about him or her having the potential to evolve in this manner.

This requirement over-rides all other considerations of skills and training.

As this particular personality trait still cannot be assessed from a computer print-out, it is imperative that judgements be based on individual interviews. This puts the onus on regional officials for, in view of the size of the operation, it is not possible for this aspect to be handled centrally or even nationally.

There was more in this vein. Much more. This was by far the most comprehensive document obtained by Trojan. It stressed the need for an even mix of nationalities and colours among the designated movers for, although they were to be 'integrated into a new conception of a family community', it was considered that all ethnic groups should be represented in the new territory. That was emphasised in one particular sentence: 'The object of Alternative 3 is to ensure the survival of all strains of the human race and not merely those from the more advanced and privileged backgrounds.'

That sounds fine and noble — until one considers the nightmare treatment of those regarded contemptuously as 'components.' They have been pitilessly shanghaied from their families and reduced to sub-humans. They now labour as mindless beasts of burden. And their only escape from degradation lies in death. That is the true and unforgivable obscenity of Alternative 3.

The document continued:

Representatives of all aspects of human culture will eventually be transported to the new territory. Therefore, in time, designated movers will also be recruited from the arts. They will include writers, painters, sculptors and musicians.

In the early stages, however, only those with skills essential to the foundation of the new society are required. Approved category lists have already been circulated.

Explorations in the new territory have revealed certain factors which had not been entirely anticipated and, principally for this reason, amendments have been necessitated to category quotas.

154

The Committee in Residence particularly requests more intensive recruitment of doctors, chemists, neurologists and bacteriologists.

The new territory, for the moment, has a satisfactory complement of computer specialists, mining technicians, and agricultural overseers. Recruitment of these categories is to cease until further instructions.

Expansions and wastages will inevitably result in changes and monthly lists of personnel requirements will in future be circulated to National Chief Executive Officers by Department Seven.

The document then detailed the Alternative 3 attitude to children. They were to be introduced into the new territory for it was considered that their presence would have 'the beneficial effect of adding an additional dimension of social-structure familiarity'. That, when the jargon is stripped away, means that the emigrants would appreciate having them there, that children would help them feel more 'at home'.

However, children were not considered productive — not in the way required in the new territory — and so the quotá was to be severely restricted. Only those with 'key parents' were to be transported — and then only if the parents could not be persuaded to make other custodial arrangements for them in the old territory:

There may be instances in which vital personnel can be persuaded that their children can be left with relatives in the knowledge that they will be reunited with them at a reasonably early date and, where applicable, every reasonable effort should be made to secure the success of such persuasion.

No figures or percentages were given in that document but it would appear that mathematician Robert Patterson's children — sixteen-year-old Julian and fourteen-year-old Kate — are part of a very small minority. Unless, of course, there was a change of attitude towards 'the child quota' between 1972 and the time of their disappearance from Scotland in February, 1976.

Ann Clark, on the evidence of that document, is also part of a minority. All women are, in Alternative 3. The ratio among designated movers is apparently three males to each female. Unless, again, there has been a policy change since the document was circulated in 1972.

No facilities can yet be spared for maternity care, although naturally there are plans for the future, and so pregnancies are outlawed in the new territory. The Committee in Residence will provide notification of when this ruling is rescinded.

Accidental pregnancies will be automatically aborted and parties to the offence will be arraigned before the Committee in Residence.

The rest of the document dealt mainly with the provision of recreational and entertainment facilities. There is, apparently, a cinema. There are also a number of communal television-viewing rooms into which flow programmes transmitted from many parts of the world.

It is intriguing to realise that designated movers, including men like Brian Pendlebury from Manchester, were very likely watching that sensational edition of *Science Report*.

We have already mentioned how, in the course of that programme in June, 1977, Simon Butler told viewers that twenty-four people were then known to have vanished in mysterious circumstances – circumstances which pointed to their having been recruited into Alternative 3.

Three of those people, of course, were Ann Clark, Robert Patterson and Brian Pendlebury. Here we intended to give details of the other twenty-one – based on information collated for Sceptre Television by Terry

156

Dickson. In eighteen of those cases, however, we have received family requests for anonymity and, in deference to those requests, we are restricting ourselves to three examples:

Richard Tuffley, 27, endocrinologist. Born in Sidmouth, Devon, but living and working in Swansea, South Wales. Orphaned when young and brought up by mother's sister, now deceased. Unmarried and no known relatives. Lived alone in small rented flat near university. Disappeared Monday, January 5, 1976. Last seen driving light-blue mini-van in direction of Cardiff. Van has still not been located.

Statement from his departmental chief: 'He was a first-class and highly-conscientious colleague – certainly not the sort one would expect to let the team down as it now seems he did.

'He was rather introverted and made few friends but I had no indication that he was in any way unhappy here.'

Gordon Balcombe, 36, senior administrator with multi-national manufacturing conglomerate. Living in Bromley, Kent, and working in central London. Divorced in 1969. Father of three children, living with ex-wife, whom he did not see after divorce. Lived alone in former family home – detached house backing on to park – but said to have many women visitors. Some, according to neighbours, often stayed overnight. Disappeared Thursday, February 5, 1976. Last seen leaving his office in a taxi. Taxi-driver never traced.

Statement from his managing director: 'We were completely bewildered by his disappearance for he was a man with a tremendous future in this organisation. Plans were being mooted for him to move to a more senior position in our base at Chicago and he seemed genuinely excited by the prospect.

'We regard his disappearance as a great loss.'

Statement from Mrs. Marjorie Balcombe:

'Gordon, for all I know, could be anywhere. I suspect that he is probably somewhere in America.

'He is the sort of man that executive head-hunters do try to entice to new posts and it is quite possible that he would not bother to tell his old firm if he decided to accept a better offer. He would just go if it suited his purpose. That's the sort of person Gordon is. Self-centred.

'And I shouldn't be in the slightest surprised to learn that he has some woman in tow. Women are his great weakness.

'The only thing that really puzzles me is the way he left so many of his clothes and other personal possessions in the house. That does strike me as being out-of-character.'

Sidney Dilworth, 32, meteorologist. Living and working in Reading, Berkshire. Widower. Wife died in car crash in October, 1975. No children. lived alone in terraced house being bought on mortgage. Disappeared Friday, April 16, 1976.

Last seen driving hired car in direction of London. Vehicle later found in car-park at Number Three Terminal, Heathrow Airport.

Statement from his father, Wilfred Dilworth: 'I keep telling the police that something really bad has happened to our Sidney but, although they're very sympathetic, they don't seem to be doing much about it. I've got a nasty feeling he's been murdered or something. He was always a very considerate lad and he'd never want me and his mother to have this sort of worry hanging over us.

'He was very upset after his wife was killed and he talked about trying to start a new life in Canada. In fact, in the January before he disappeared he said he thought he had a job lined up there but, as far as I could gather, that just fizzled out. At the research station they say he never mentioned anything about leaving but I suppose he wouldn't want to tell them until it was all settled.

'Now we've reached the stage where I dread opening the newspaper in the morning for I'm sure that one
day I'll be reading that they've found his body.'

Now we know that this pattern has been repeated in
country after country. Right across the world.

Andrew Nisbett, 39, aerospace technician, born
Tulsa, Oklahoma. Disappeared on Tuesday, October 5,
1976, from Houston, Texas — together with his wife,
Rita, and their only son.

Pavel Garmanas, 42, physicist, born in Usachevka,
USSR. Disappeared on Thursday, July 14, 1977, from
his new home in Jerusalem, Israel.

Marcel Rouffanche, 35, nutrition specialist, born in
the suburb of Saint-Ruff near Avignon. Disappeared on
Wednesday, November 16, 1977, from his apartment in
Paris.

Eric Hillier, 27, constructional engineer, born
Melbourne, Australia. Disappeared on Thursday,
December 29, 1977.

Intensive investigation has shown that the figures
given by Butler in that television programme represented only a fraction of the true total. And that total
is still mounting.

The explosion of fear provoked by the *Science Report*
programme resulted, as we said earlier, in the company's being required to deny formally the truth of the
material which had been presented.

The wording of that statement had been prepared by
Leonard Harman and, despite violent opposition from
Clements, it was released by the Press Office. Most
newspapers accepted the denial — apparently making no
attempt to verify the curious background stories of
people like Robert Patterson.

The *Daily Express*, to Harman's relief, devoted most
of its front page the following day to a splash story
headlined: STORM OVER TV'S SPOOF.

The *Express* story started:

Thousands of viewers all over the country protested in shock and anger over a science fiction 'documentary' put out by ITV last night.

From the moment that 'Alternative 3' ended at 10 p.m. irate watchers jammed the switchboards of the *Daily Express* and ITV companies to complain.

This story made no mention of the evidence which had been given on screen by Dr. Carl Gerstein or by other respected authorities such as Professor G. Gordon Broadbent. Grodin's important contribution was also ignored. However, the story did indicate that the 'hour-long spoof' — transmitted at peak viewing time — 'purported' to show a version of the scientific brain-drain. It continued:

The programme was introduced by former newscaster Simon Butler as a serious investigation into a disturbing trend of scientific discovery.

American and Russian spacemen were seen collaborating to set up the 'new colony' ... while viewers were left to suppose that the reason for the exploration was the end of life on Earth.

TV advertised the show by saying: 'What this programme shows may be considered unethical ...'

Viewers taken unawares protested their shock immediately. Others, realising the programme was a spoof, complained of ITV's 'irresponsibility'.

Early today, a spokesman for the Independent Broadcasting Authority said it had thought long and hard before allowing the documentary to be shown.

But Mrs. Denise Ball of Camberley, Surrey, said: 'I was scared out of my wits. It was all so real.'

Mrs. Mary Whitehouse, the renowned Clean-Up-TV campaigner, was another who completely believed the 'Harman denial'. She was quoted in another newspaper as saying: 'I had hundreds of calls. The film was brilliantly done to deceive.'

So that was the immediate reaction. And that was entirely understandable. The facts assembled by Clements and his team were so stupefyingly frightening that people were eager to believe they were not true.

People were delighted to accept Harman's denial because it drew a comforting veil over the unacceptable.

All this put men like Terry Dickson in a most invidious position. Over Robert Patterson, for example. Had Patterson ever really existed? That question, together with others like it, was implicit in the attitude of most newspapers. And, for some unfathomable reason, officials at the University of St. Andrews refused to make any comment. The vice-chancellor there who had explained about Patterson going prematurely to America, who had apologised so courteously for the resulting waste of time ... he was on protracted leave somewhere in Europe and could not be contacted.

So was Patterson merely a figment of Dickson's imagination? Was that why Benson had been unable to interview him?

The questions were piling up. And they were getting crazier and crazier.

During the following few days, however, Fleet Street had time to make inquiries and certain journalists began to consider the television investigation in a rather different perspective.

Terry Dickson has told us that the biggest moment of relief for him came on June 26 when he opened his copy of the *Sunday Telegraph*. Columnist Philip Purser, respected as one of the most perceptive commentators in Britain, pointed out that 'a number of mysteries within the mystery posed by Alternative 3 remain unsolved'.

The first of those 'mysteries' detailed by Purser related to 'Dr. Robert Paterson (sic), one of the savants whose disappearance prompted this disturbing investigation'.

Purser had a special reason for being interested in

161

Patterson for, as he told his readers, he had indirect knowledge of the man:

The son of a friend of mine who lectures in the same department at St. Andrews tells me that Paterson, though an able mathematician and specialist in Boolian geometry, was also a true Scot, notoriously careful with his bawbees.

Those final five words are clearly a reference to the Patterson characteristic we described in Section Two – that of resenting having so much of his money taken in taxation. He tended to be such a bombastic bore on the subject that, as we said, many of his university colleagues were relieved when he announced he was leaving. Purser's contact at St. Andrews was probably one of those colleagues.

Philip Purser made it abundantly clear that he was too shrewd to be fooled by the Harman denial. He concluded his *Sunday Telegraph* article with these thoughts:

It would be a mistake to file 'Alternative 3' away too cosily with *Panorama*'s spaghetti harvest and other hoaxes. Suppose it were fiendish double bluff inspired by the very agencies identified in the programme and that the super-powers really are setting up an extra-terrestrial colony of outstanding human beings to safeguard the species?

Letters flowing into the studios showed there was also a significant proportion of thinking viewers who recognised the truth. One of the first received by Simon Butler was from the President of the European Space Association who wrote: 'I must congratulate you and Colin Benson on your assiduous research.'

Here are extracts from other typical letters:

I am a recently-retired aerospace technician and your investigation explained certain factors which I

162

discovered in the course of my duties and which have been puzzling me for some years. Thank God someone has at last had the initiative and the tenacity to present the unpalatable truth — E.M., Filton, Bristol.

Congratulations on not allowing the politicians to muzzle you! Your *Science Report* was absolutely terrifying but, of course, the truth so often is and surely we have a right to know what is really happening. The subsequent back-pedalling by official spokesmen for your company, which appears to have been blandly accepted by most newspapers, does not surprise me. Most of my professional life has been spent in the Civil Service and I am only too aware of how pressures can be applied, particularly when it comes to so-called Official Secrets. Please maintain your vigilance — J.N., London NW1.

Yet newspapers still showed an extraordinary reluctance to pursue the subject of Alternative 3.

Why? Why did they not question people like Wilfred Dilworth and Marjorie Balcombe? Why did they not contact Dennis Pendlebury in Manchester ... or Richard Tuffley's former colleagues in Swansea? These people were available for interview. They still are available.

Many attempts have been made, as we explained earlier, to prevent the publication of this book — and, because of action by those two MPs, *we* have been forced into a reluctant compromise. So is it possible that newspapers have been subjected to similar pressures? And that they, in 'the interests of national security', have yielded to those pressures? That, in a free society, may seem incredible. But the world has never before known anything as incredible as Alternative 3.

A key to the truth was provided by Kenneth Hughes in the *Daily Mirror* on June 20, 1977 — the day the programme was actually transmitted. He had secured

163

advance access to some of the material gathered by Clements and his team and his article was headlined: WHAT ON EARTH IS GOING ON? He wrote:

A science programme is likely to keep millions of Britons glued to their armchairs.

ALTERNATIVE 3 (ITV 9.0) is an investigation into the disappearance of several scientists.

They seem simply to have vanished from the face of the Earth.

Chilling news is read by former ITV newscaster Simon Butler who gives a gloomy report on the future.

Then came the truly telling paragraph:

The programme will be screened in several other countries — but not America. Network bosses there want to assess its effect on British viewers.

That is what columnist Hughes had been told. That is what he believed. The truth was, however, that television network bosses in America were permitted no discretion in the matter. Any screening of that *Science Report* programme was forbidden in that country by higher authority.

It was no mere coincidence that two of the countries where the documentary was banned were America and Russia — the two principal partners in this amazing conspiracy. Security forces in each of those countries were particularly alert to the nuances of public reaction...

The backlash of embarrassment which followed the transmission produced an immediate clamp-down of information in Britain. Even Professor G. Gordon Broadbent, a man noted for his independent attitudes, was reluctant to become more deeply involved. We wanted him to enlarge on the theories he had outlined in the programme, to elaborate on the theme of covert co-operation between the super-powers, and so Watkins

164

visited him at the Institute of International Political Studies in London. Here is a transcript from the tape of that interview which took place on July 7, 1977:

WATKINS: You are naturally aware of the statement which claimed that the Alternative 3 programme was a hoax. What is your reaction to that statement?

BROADBENT: It would be wrong, in the present political climate, for me to make any comment.

WATKINS: You suggested that co-operation between East and West could involve some 'massive but covert operation in space'. Would you give your reasons for that suggestion?

BROADBENT: You may recall that I stressed that this *could* be the situation but I did not state categorically that it was. In fact, as I remember, I explained that I was not in the business of speculation and I see nothing to be gained by enlarging on what I have already said.

WATKINS: You took part in that programme as an expert commentator. What are your feelings about this entire exercise now being dismissed as a hoax?

BROADBENT: Shall we say that the programme was of a more sensational nature than I had anticipated when I agreed to participate? I was surprised by some of its findings.

WATKINS: But do you feel those findings accurately reflected what is really happening?

BROADBENT: I'm sorry . . . I'd prefer to say no more.

The interview was extremely unsatisfactory. However, only a few weeks later, we received more information which provided a deeper insight into the workings of Alternative 3 . . .

Thursday, August 4, 1977. Another submarine meeting of Policy Committee. Chairman: R EIGHT. Transcript section supplied by Trojan starts:

A TWO: But losing a whole Batch Consignment just like that! . . . I mean, hell, surely we take precautions against that sort of thing?

A EIGHT: We had bum luck . . . that's all there is to it . . .

A TWO: Three hundred bodies smashed to bits . . . a complete write-off and that's all you can say! We had bum luck! Look, I'm not a technical man and I tend to get lost with some of this technical talk . . . so will someone please explain just how a thing like this can happen . . . because, I tell you, I've got a gut feeling there's been carelessness.

R FIVE: It is not possible to legislate against accidents of this nature . . . they are part of the hazards of transportation to the new territory . . .

A TWO: Yes, but . . .

R FIVE: Please . . . I will explain. Meteors are very common, far more common than people realise, and about a million of them enter the earth's atmosphere every day. Nearly all are very tiny, not more than about a gram in weight, but some are considerably bigger . . .

A EIGHT: That's right . . . some are too big to evaporate completely on their journey through the earth's atmosphere so they land as solid lumps. We reckon that about 500 kilogrammes arrive this way from outer space every year . . .

R FIVE: Sometimes these lumps are gigantic. There was one in 1919, for example, which landed in Siberia. It devastated about 100 square miles of countryside . . .

A EIGHT: Then there's that classic meteor crater in Arizona . . .

R FIVE: It is the same in and around the new territory . . . millions of meteors are bombarding its atmosphere and our craft have to travel through that bombardment . . .

A TWO: But our pilots . . . don't they take avoiding action?

166

A EIGHT: Imagine yourself on a bicycle ... trying to
dodge an avalanche that's rolling right on top of
you ... that's how it was with this lot ...

A TWO: And you're saying this one which hit the
Batch Consignment craft was maybe as big as that
Siberian one?

R FIVE: Possibly ... but we have no means of telling
... anyway, it wouldn't be necessary for it to be
that big ... one a hundredth that size would have
completely destroyed the craft ...

R EIGHT: This discussion, I feel, is leading us nowhere. Our scientific people at Archimedes Base
have assured us that this disaster − our first, I must
emphasise − could not possibly have been avoided.
And that has been confirmed by the Committee in
Residence. It is hardly our function to hold
another post-mortem.

A ONE: That's right. We ought to be thankful there
were no designated movers on board. So we lost
300 components ... is that so desperately serious?
All we've got to do is fix for another collection.

(*Authors' note:* The following month, you may recall,
brtught reports of mass disappearances in Australia. By
the end of September many of those who had disappeared were found by chance in what was apparently
a slave-labour camp − possibly in readiness for clinical
processing and transportation. Many others have never
been seen since. The discovery of those 'slave-labour'
men, coming so soon after that meeting of the Policy
Committee, might, of course, have been merely a
coincidence. However, we consider *that* to be highly
unlikely).

R EIGHT: The legacy of that unfortunate television
programme is of far more immediate importance
...

A FIVE: Listen ... that programme has been completely discredited. People have accepted it wasn't

167

meant to be taken seriously, that it was no more than an elaborate joke ... we don't need to sweat blood over it ...

R EIGHT: *Most* people have accepted the official statements but there are those who cannot be so easily convinced. We must not under-estimate the damage that has been done by that programme. It has made certain people think and wonder and that can be dangerous. We must make certain that its credibility is completely eradicated.

A TWO: I told you we should have killed that guy Gerstein ... way back in February ... I said then he was dangerous ...

R FOUR: My friend is right ... he did say that. And I pointed out then that Gerstein's talk could start a panic among the masses ...

A FIVE: So what are you saying? An Expediency?

R ONE: What value would that be now? He has said all he can possibly say. There is nothing he can add ... and now people are laughing at him. They say he is a crank. So what would be gained by an Expediency?

A TWO: He should never have co-operated with those television guys ... he deserves to die and ...

A EIGHT: I told you all before ... we don't use Expediencies for punishment purposes ... we use them only in the furtherance of the operation. So maybe we were wrong before ... maybe we should have had Gerstein killed ... but, now, I see no point ...

R EIGHT: We will vote. Those in favour of an Expediency? ... thank you ... And against? ... Good ... I entirely agree. Gerstein did behave in a most foolhardy manner but we have nothing to gain by his death ...

A TWO: But what about the regional officer concerned?

A EIGHT: You're right there. He should have stopped

168

that television crap. He's proved himself to be utterly unreliable. He failed and failed badly and, what's worse, he could let us down again. The man, without any question, is a liability and I propose an Expediency.

R TWO: Seconded.

R EIGHT: Those in favour? ... Then that is unanimous. The method?

A THREE: How about a telepathic sleep-job ... maybe with a gun ...

R EIGHT: That seems sensible ... it's too soon after Ballantine for another hot-job ...

That was where the transcript section ended. What had Gerstein said to cause such consternation? Those who saw the television programme will already know. In the next section, for the benefit of others, we will be giving full details of his interview with Simon Butler.

But what of the final part of that transcript: 'telepathic sleep-job with a gun'? That was gibberish to us – at that stage. It was not until later that we got a possible explanation from Dr. Hugo Danningham. We were accustomed by that stage to surprises. But Dr. Danningham's explanation came as one of the most startling surprises yet.

SECTION TEN

Dr. Hugo Danningham lectures regularly on parapsychology at three British universities and is a committee member of the European Institute for Brain Research. He was interviewed on our behalf by Colin Benson in Brussels on September 23, 1977. That interview, which Benson taped, provided an insight into the possible meaning of the phrase 'telepathic sleep-job'.

In the early 1960s, he explained, significant advances were made in the study of parapsychology at the University of Kharkov and at the University of Leningrad — advances which many experts feared were to be adapted for use in any future conflict between East and West.

They involved telepathy and, more specifically, the long-distance invasion and manipulation of minds. The potential military advantages were patently obvious. Enemies could be attacked and suborned literally from within. If the telepathic power were strong enough, they could be compelled to ignore the orders of their commanders in preference to those being beamed directly into their minds. They would, in fact, respond like remote-controlled puppets.

Military authorities in the West, fearful of the advantages this could yield to the Russians, initiated intensive research into this new style of weapon. And, as a result, it had been perfected by both super-powers.

'Experiments have proved that children, like birds and beasts and people in primitive tribes, are usually more receptive to telepathic messages and instructions than most adults in a civilised society,' said Dr. Danningham. 'This is because once intelligence has been fully developed, and once a tremendous amount of

170

education has been absorbed, information received on a major scale directly from other minds could easily result in mental confusion.

'As a result, the mind of civilised man has developed a protective barrier against telepathy. This barrier can be penetrated most easily when the defences are down – such as when a person is extremely fatigued or is going through a period of great emotional stress. And the defences of the mind, of course, are never more relaxed than during sleep. That is when a person is most vulnerable to telepathic invasion – particularly if such an invasion was being controlled by experienced professionals.

'That, I suspect, is the explanation behind that "sleep-job" expression.'

Benson frowned, shook his head in perplexity. 'I'm sorry ... I don't quite follow ...'

'A sleeping man can be given instructions and, if the circumstances are propitious, he will obey those instructions – even if they are that he should kill himself ...'

'Good God!' said Benson. 'You're suggesting, then, a sort of somnambulistic suicide! But this is quite fantastic! These circumstances you mention ... what exactly would they be?'

'For any action as dramatic as self-destruction there would almost certainly have to be a synchronization of many factors,' said Dr. Danningham. 'For example, it would be easier if the intended victim were at precisely the right period of his biorhythmic psi sensitivity cycle and ...'

'But surely the instinct for self-preservation would countermand any instructions calculated to result in suicide ... unless the sleeper wanted to kill himself anyway ...'

'Not if the telepathic instructions were cleverly presented,' said Danningham. 'Let me give you an illustration:

'Imagine you want to kill a man who, let's say, lives high

171

up in a skyscraper block. Now you're not going to tell that man to kill himself by jumping out of his bedroom window because – as you so rightly say – his instinct for survival would very likely intervene and reject the order.

'So what you do is feed him false information. You tell him telepathically that there is some wild beast rampaging around his room or that the building has caught fire. You tell him there is a safety net spread under the window and that, to save himself, he must jump. So, in a desperate bid to stay alive, he jumps – and breaks his neck.

'It is possible, of course, to play all sorts of permutations on this tack. You might persuade your sleeping victim, for instance, into believing there is some venomous spider attached to his chest, that he must stab it and kill it before it kills him. And so, in his sleep, he stabs himself.

'The variations, my dear Mr. Benson, are almost limitless. If the telepathic messages convinced your sleeper that he had accidentally drunk some corrosive poison and that the only antidote was in a bottle marked cyanide . . . well, I'm sure you see what I mean.'

'And you're saying that this sort of thing actually happens?'

Danningham shook his head. 'No, I'm not saying that at all. I'm merely telling you what is possible. Men in my field have the knowledge required to make those things happen but I cannot visualise anyone actually using that knowledge . . .'

Maybe Dr. Danningham was right. Maybe, at that time, the men behind Alternative 3 had not used somnambulistic suicide as a method of murder. However, we spent weeks researching newspaper archives in America and Britain and we discovered three cases which, to say the least, appear to merit a question mark.

Monday, February 2, 1976. James Riggerford, 42, happily married with three children, walked from his beachside home south-west of Houston, Texas, some time shortly after 3.0 a.m. – two days after resigning as an Operations Administrator with NASA. His body, still clad in pyjamas, was later recovered from the Gulf of Mexico.

Tuesday, September 7, 1976. Rodger Marshall-Smith, a 31-year-old physicist who had recently returned from temporary attachment to NASA in America, was living with his parents in Winchester, Hampshire. They found him just after 1.0 a.m. – two hours after they had all gone to sleep – in flames at the bottom of the stairs. He had apparently, while still asleep, doused his clothing with turpentine and then set fire to himself. The agony of burning had awakened him but it was then too late to save his life.

Saturday, January 15, 1977. James Arthur Carmichael, 35, aerospace technician, hurtled inexplicably to his death at 4.35 a.m. from a sixteenth-floor hotel bedroom window in Washington. Friends said that he had seemed happy and in normal spirits the previous evening and had gone to bed alone at about midnight. He, too, was wearing pyjamas.

Were these three men victims of 'telepathic sleep-jobs'? We do not claim to know but we consider it reasonable to suggest that the possibility cannot now be discounted. And what of the 'regional officer' mentioned in the transcript? The answer to that question was to come, eventually, in the most unexpected way.

Benson returned to the production office and Simon Butler joined Clements in the little room behind Studio B. 'How were things with Fergus?' he asked.

'Not good,' said Clements miserably. 'He wants to junk Colin's interview with Grodin. Quite frankly, Simon, the whole thing looks like getting screwed up ... unless, maybe, you can squeeze more out of Gerstein.'

'You mean Alternative 3?'

Clements nodded. 'That's what it all seems to hinge on,' he said. 'Gerstein obviously knows about it. Or, at least, he knows the theory ...'

173

'There's a big difference between knowing and talking.' Butler was remembering how he'd been given a sherry when what he'd really wanted was an answer. 'When I saw him in March he was quite definite. He simply didn't want to know . . .'

'Try him again,' urged Clements. 'Tell him everything you know . . . what we've got from Grodin and Broadbent . . . tell him the lot . . : and then see if you can't persuade him.'

'Well,' said Butler. 'I'm prepared to try . . .'

Two days later he was back in that book-lined study in Cambridge. And, to his surprise, Gerstein eventually agreed to talk about Alternative 3. At first Gerstein was very much on his guard, very reluctant to be drawn, but he listened courteously to all Butler had to say. 'You people have done your homework pretty thoroughly,' he acknowledged. He re-lit his dead pipe and stared thoughtfully at the desk. 'There doesn't seem any point now in me not telling you what I know . . .'

Here is a transcript of the interview which followed – as it was presented on television:

GERSTEIN: You already know about Alternatives 1 and 2 – and why they were rejected. Well . . . Alternative 3 offered a more limited option – an attempt to ensure the survival of at least a small proportion of the human race. We were theorists, remember, not technicians . . . but we realised we were talking about the kind of space travel that – twenty years ago – seemed no more than science fiction.

BUTLER: You mean . . . go to some other planet?

GERSTEIN: I mean get the hell off this one – while there was still time! I had no idea whether it would, or could, be done. And I still don't.

BUTLER: Did you have any ideas about who might go?

GERSTEIN: I remember we discussed the kind of

174

cross-section we'd like to see get away ... a
balance of the sciences and the arts, of course, and,
indeed, all aspects, as far as possible, of human
culture ... The list would never be complete – but
it would be better than nothing.

BUTLER: And these people ... where was it visualised
they might go?

GERSTEIN: Ah, now that was the big question. There
are about 100,000 million stars in the Milky Way
– about equal to the number of people who have
ever walked this earth – and as long ago as 1950
Fred Hoyle was estimating that more than a
million of those stars had planets which could
support human life ...

BUTLER: So it really was as vague and theoretical as
that?

GERSTEIN: In 1957 ... at the time of the Huntsville
Conference ... yes. But the situation has changed
quite considerably since then. Now the most
distinct possibility seems to be Mars ...

BUTLER: Mars!

GERSTEIN: Yes, I can imagine your viewers raising
their eyebrows because most people think of Mars
in terms of little green men with aerials sticking
out of their heads ... but, scientifically, our
attitude to Mars has had to be amended more than
once.

In the early days of astronomy Mars was
believed to have artificially-constructed canals –
which was taken as evidence of intelligent life on
the planet. Later this theory was discredited. In its
place we had a picture of a barren, inhospitable
planet, inimical to the survival of any form of life.

Then, more recently, an interesting idea was put
forward: Suppose life did at one time exist on
Mars ...

As the climate and conditions worsened, any
surviving life may have evolved into a state of

175

hibernation, awaiting the return of more favourable conditions. It has even been suggested that the actual atmosphere which used to support life may have become locked up in the planet's surface soil.

There was an occurrence several years ago which made this theory very persuasive. Mars has always had a covering of cloud, varying in density at different times, until the time of which I speak, when the cloud thickened to a degree never previously observed. This happened, and was scientifically recorded, in 1961.

It was obvious that storms of colossal proportions were taking place on Mars. Now ... this is the really interesting bit ... when the clouds eventually cleared, some remarkable changes were seen. The polar ice caps had substantially decreased in size, and around the equatorial regions a broad band of darker colouring had appeared. This, it has been suggested, was vegetation.

BUTLER: Has anyone explained this happening?

GERSTEIN: At a conference shortly before it happened, I put forward a theoretical suggestion. I said that if the atmosphere of Mars *was* in fact locked into the surface soil, then a controlled nuclear explosion might be able to release it – and, of course, revive whatever life was in hibernation. I made a little joke ... about how the only problem was to deliver the explosion well in advance of arriving there ourselves. That same year the Russians had a great space disaster. Yes, that was in 1959. Only the barest facts are recorded, the rest was kept secret. A rocket blew up at its launching. Numbers of people were killed and the area was devastated ... *what* were they trying to launch? And did they finally succeed?

Was that rocket carrying a nuclear device which accounted for the devastation it caused? A nuclear device which, on a second attempt, could

176

have reached the surface of Mars to cause the dynamic changes recorded in 1961?

The sudden outbreaks of storms on Mars, the dwindling of the ice caps, the growth of what appears to be vegetation in the tropical zone ... all that is recorded scientific fact.

The interview, as transmitted, ended at that point. The original version, before being edited, contained this additional exchange:

BUTLER: But I don't understand ... the pictures relayed from Viking 2 on Mars ... they showed little more than a plateau of red rock ... the sort of terrain that seemed to offer little prospect of survival ...

GERSTEIN: I don't pretend to understand that either. But, as you've already told me, there does seem to be some sort of cover-up going on. Maybe you should take that up with someone more up-to-date in these matters ... someone who is abreast of modern developments in aerospace ...

BUTLER: Yes ... maybe Charles Welbourne can help us there. But there's one other aspect I'd like to discuss with you, Dr. Gerstein, and that's to do with animals, birds, insects and so on. It's all very well talking about transporting man off to a new life on a different planet but how much of his environment could he, or should he, take with him?

GERSTEIN: That's one you ought to put to a biologist. Stephen Manderson ... Professor Stephen Manderson ... was also at Huntsville and he's a singularly pleasant man ... very approachable.

Butler telephoned Clements from Cambridge and Clements instructed Terry Dickson to make the necessary arrangements with Manderson. Kate White interviewed him the following day at his home in Reigate,

177

Surrey. The interview went well but, as you may remember, it was not included in the transmitted programme. Clements has explained that he was forced to omit it because, despite his pleas, his screen time was severely limited. ITN's *News at Ten*, scheduled to follow that edition of *Science Report*, could not be delayed. And, Harman had told him, he could not continue after the news because the rest of the evening had been allocated to programmes from other companies.

We consider that, in this instance, an exception should have been made to the rigid pattern of ITV's programme-planning. Manderson's views were fascinating. They were also extremely pertinent.

'The Bible concept of taking two of every type of creature into the ark ... that, in this context, would be impossible and quite irrational,' he said. 'Man, basically, is a selfish creature. There's nothing much wrong in that because a certain degree of selfishness is necessary for survival.

'We eat other creatures and make clothes and cosmetics out of them and, in fact, we use them in all sorts of ways. So in this Alternative 3 operation – if, indeed, there is such an operation – it would surely be logical to select only those we wanted to take with us.

'Would we want to take rats and mosquitoes, for instance? Of course not! We'd be given the opportunity to create the ideal environment for ourselves and, for the very first time, we'd be able to choose which creatures should share that environment. It would be a most marvellous opportunity.

'Don't be fooled by the conservationists because they sometimes talk the most abject twaddle. Endangered species! That's a phrase they love to use, isn't it? They faithfully trot it out emotively as if they'd lifted it straight out of one of the Gospels.

'But think of the species we could happily do without.

Starlings ... rooks ... pea-moths ... eelworms which do such damage to crops like potatoes and sugar-beet ... what possible use are any of them to us?

'Do you realise that three million species of insects have already been taxonomically classified and that, because of the present rate of insect evolution, the total classification will never be completed!

'And consider the damage they do! In India alone insects consume more food every year than nine million human beings — and that's in a country where there's widespread starvation.

'No ... leave them here and let them perish. Man doesn't need them ...'

Kate White interrupted: 'But surely some of the most humble creatures are useful to man. Earthworms, for instance, aerate the soil and ...'

'Earthworms, like every other species, would have to be properly assessed for usefulness,' said Manderson briskly. 'Gophers, for example, might prove to be more efficient. In the Canadian plains they perform exactly the same function as earthworms. Vast tracts there have no worms and it's the gopher which turns vegetable mould into rich loam ... no, as I said, each case would have to be scientifically assessed.'

'But what about the sort of creatures we now keep in zoos? Creatures like lions and giraffes and elephants?'

Manderson seemed surprised by her naivety. 'Well, what about them? It wouldn't be good economics to shuttle them off to another planet — even if sufficient transport were available. They'd have to die and, quite frankly, it wouldn't make one iota of difference.

'I beg you, Miss White, not to get bogged down in sentimentality. It's fashionable but it really is quite pointless.

'The dinosaurs lasted on this earth for a hundred million years — fifty times as long as man has been around — but the world goes on very well without them. And it's been the same with so many other creatures.

179

How many people, would you say, have ever been in mourning for the dinomys?'

'Dinomys? I'm sorry ... I don't quite follow ...'

'Precisely! You're an educated young lady but you've never even heard of them, have you? Dinomys ... rat-like creatures which grew as big as calves ... used to flourish in South America. Polar bears and ostriches ... they'll be the same one day ... people will look blank, just as you did a moment ago, when their names are mentioned.'

He smiled, and ruffled his fingers through his hair. 'I could give you example after example – just to show how narrow the conventional view-point really is ...'

'But creatures like bears ... they seem so, well, so *permanent* ...'

'So did the onactornis.'

'Onactornis?'

'Carnivorous bird ... eight feet tall ... couldn't fly but terrorised smaller creatures for millions of years.'

Kate White was anxious to divert the interview into more positive channels. Clements, she knew, would hardly thank her for wasting so much film footage on a philosophical discussion about prehistoric monsters. That, in her experience, was one of the troubles with experts. They often got carried away with their own cleverness. They liked, in fact, to show off. 'But if one assumes that the basic premise is correct, that men are colonising Mars, wouldn't they have to start from scratch with stocking an entire new world? And wouldn't that be an almost insuperable task?'

'Not when you understand the facts of life,' said Manderson. 'You've heard, of course, about the experiments which have resulted in the creation of test-tube babies ...'

'Yes, but ...'

'But do you realise that enough female eggs to produce the entire next generation of the human race could be packed into the shell of a single chicken's egg?'

'Goodness! I'd no idea.'

'And the same convenient compactness, Miss White, applies to other creatures. A mother cod, for example, can lay up to six million eggs at a single spawning. Fortunately most of those eggs are destroyed before they develop into fish . . . or else there'd be no room for people to paddle off our beaches. If they all survived the seas of our world would be solid masses of cod by now – and they *could* all survive if nurtured in the right conditions.

'There was a ling caught, not so long ago, which was carrying more than 28 million eggs! So you can see right away how easy it would be to stock any seas there may be on Mars . . .'

'That's assuming there's nothing already in those seas.'

'Granted – and there may well be for all we know.'

'But what if tiny things in the Martian seas – or on the Martian land for that matter – were harmful to man or were a nuisance to man?'

'Then we'd have to use our initiative to balance the ecology in our favour. It's been done often enough before, y'know. Sparrows, for instance, were first imported into New York in the middle of the nineteenth century – simply to attack tree-worms . . .'

'But wouldn't that automatically bring other problems? What about the creatures that live on the creatures you'd have to introduce to strike this ecological balance?' She paused, trying to grasp for a good example. Manderson, she'd decided by this time, was a cold and unlikeable man. He seemed to lack *soul* and she couldn't resist the temptation to bait him just a little. 'Like hedgehogs?' she said triumphantly.

'I beg your pardon?'

'Hedgehogs,' she repeated. 'I heard somewhere that they get withdrawal symptoms and become quite neurotic if they are deprived of their fleas . . .'

Manderson smiled indulgently. 'I'm sorry,' he said. 'I don't pretend to be an authority on neurotic hedgehogs

181

and I do feel we're starting to get in rather deep. Can I help you in any other way?'

'Just one last question. In this new world – as you see it, Professor Manderson – is there any room for creatures that people simply enjoy ... creatures like squirrels and nightingales?'

'Not unless their productivity value were proved,' said Manderson. 'No room at all.'

'You know something,' said Kate. 'I find that very, very sad.'

Charles Welbourne, interviewed on screen by Colin Benson, agreed that there was an obvious conflict between the description of Mars offered by Gerstein and the pictures which had been released by NASA.

'Many people have also wondered why NASA should apparently have been so stingy on its photographic budget,' he said. 'Particularly when you consider how important the pictures are supposed to be.'

'Why should people wonder in that way?' prompted Benson.

Welbourne pointed to a blow-up photograph of 'familiar' Martian terrain which was mounted on a board in the studio. 'That picture there almost says it for me,' he said. 'We're told that they spent all that money putting that probe on Mars and then what do they do? They equip it, if you please, with a camera which can focus only up to one hundred metres. And *that*, as somebody observed, is about the size of a large film studio.

'It doesn't start to add up. If they'd really wanted good pictures of Mars they would have fitted a vastly superior camera system. Better cameras *are* available – make no mistake about that – but the one they used ... well, it was almost as if they'd deliberately fitted blinkers to the whole mission.'

'You mean they were determined that we should see only what they wanted us to see?'

182

'That could well be. You've got to remember that all these pictures we get come in through NASA – they're simply passed on to the rest of us. So if they tell us it's Mars . . . well, we have to believe them.

'It's exactly the same soundwise, of course. I mean, we don't hear everything that's said between Mission Control and the spacecraft. There's a second channel. They call it the biological channel . . .'

'We did learn a little about that from Otto Binder,' said Benson.

'Sure, Binder the former NASA man . . . I remember he did blow the gaff on that after Apollo 11 . . . well, this biological channel is officially just for reporting on medical details. In fact, though, they switch to it whenever they have something to say they don't want the whole world listening in on . . .'

Welbourne paused, looked thoughtfully at the Martian picture. 'I've just had a crazy thought,' he said. 'How about if that picture *wasn't* taken on Mars? Look at it closely . . . don't you agree that *could* have been shot in some studio in Burbank?'

We should stress that Welbourne had been told nothing of the other pictures which we know *were* 'dummied-up' in a studio – the ones of people like Brian Pendlebury which were an integral part of The Smoother Plan.

He had no idea then how near the mark he was with his 'crazy thought'.

The proof came unexpectedly. It came from Harry Carmell's girlfriend Wendy – the one who had ordered Benson and his crew out of that derelict house in Lambeth.

And Wendy was very frightened.

SECTION ELEVEN

Wendy had not gone back to that house in Lambeth — not since the day Harry had disappeared. She had returned on that morning with the bandage and anti-septic and, realising that Harry had gone, she had panicked and fled. He couldn't have managed to get out on his own, not in the state he was in, so someone must have taken him.

Obviously he had been found by *them* — those mysterious men he'd sworn were determined to kill him — and she knew then, deep down, that she'd never see him again.

She had to get away. Far away. She had to hide. Or they might find her and kill her too. An hour later she was thumbing a lift to Birmingham. There was no special attraction in Birmingham. It just so happened that that's where the lorry was going. And it seemed a long way from London. *They* would not find her in Birmingham.

However, she had taken no chances there. She had kept on the move, rarely staying in one place for more than a couple of nights, for she had a frightening feeling that, somehow, they might catch her just as they had caught Harry. She also, as she has since told us, felt guilty. She felt she had let Harry down. For she kept remembering that small box which he had considered so important, the one he had hidden under floorboards in the derelict house, and she knew that she should have retrieved it. She'd forgotten all about it in the flurry of leaving but Harry had wanted so desperately to get it to the television people. It held the key, he'd told her, to something important ... to some tape which had been made by the dead man Ballantine. She felt she ought to

184

get that box to that coloured chap Benson. She ought to do that because Harry had been good to her and she owed him that much. But now it would mean going back to the house. And she dreaded stepping back into danger . . .

She finally made up her mind on Thursday, June 9. She took a train to London and travelled by bus across the city. And by 3.30 p.m. she was at number 88 — walking between the posts where the front gate had once been.

Now there was no rubbish in the front garden and the boarding at the windows had been replaced by glass. Other attempts had been made to brighten and improve the terraced house. The steps at the end of the cleared path were freshly scrubbed and the door, slightly ajar, had recently been painted in bright canary yellow.

All the neighbouring houses looked just as she remembered them but number 88 had been dramatically transformed. It was a building which had been snatched back from decay.

Through the windows of the front ground-floor room she could see a group of young people — all in their late teens or early twenties — who were kneeling silently, with their eyes shut, in a circle.

Wendy hesitated, anxious and disappointed. She had expected the house to be empty, just as it had been when she and Harry had first found it in February. She had anticipated merely walking in, of going quietly to the first-floor room where the floorboards were loose, of hurrying away, unseen, with the box. Now it couldn't be like that at all . . .

The youngsters were still kneeling, trance-like, apparently lost in some communal meditation. They might not notice her, she thought, if she were stealthy enough and fast enough. But, on the other hand, there might be more of them in other rooms. There might be some in the room where Harry had hidden the box . . .

She tapped with her knuckles at the door – tentatively, at first, and then harder.

Footsteps approached across the bare boards of the hall. Then the door was opened wide by a tall and immensely scrawny man with long hair and an unkempt ginger beard. His feet were bare and he was wearing tattered blue jeans patched with bits of floral curtaining. His eyes – dark and deep-set and staring with fierce intensity – were oddly disconcerting and he was older than the people in the front room. In his mid-thirties, maybe, or even nudging forty.

'Good afternoon sister,' he said. 'Jesus loves you.' His voice was deeply resonant and his accent was strongly east London.

'Who are you?' asked Wendy.

'Eliphaz,' he replied solemnly. 'Eliphaz the Temanite.'

'Look . . . I used to live here . . . a few months ago I was living here and I left something important behind . . .'

'The only thing that is truly important is Jesus. Has He entered your heart? He is waiting – waiting for you to invite Him in . . .'

'So I was wondering if I could just pop in and collect it . . .'

The man stepped back, gestured for her to follow, and Wendy noticed for the first time that he was holding a small Bible. 'Here in the Temple everyone is welcome,' he said.

Could this, Wendy wondered, be a trap? Harry had never told her what *they* looked like. Could this bizarre character – this Eliphaz or whatever he called himself – be one of *them*? Questions raced through her mind. Would she, if she went inside, disappear like Harry?

She had a great urge to run away, to forget the whole thing. Why should she go further into danger . . . it really wasn't her responsibility . . .

'Come on in . . . Jesus is here,' said the man encouragingly. 'And you need Jesus.'

Wendy pointed to the youngsters who were still kneeling in their silent circle. 'What are they doing in there?' she asked. 'All you people ... who exactly are you?'

'We are the Children of Heavenly Love,' said the man. 'We were sinners and we lived in the bondage of the flesh but Jesus Christ, the greatest revolutionary of them all, has entered our hearts and saved us from sin.' He closed his eyes, screwed up his face in apparent anguish, held his Bible high. 'Thank you, oh thank you, Lord Jesus,' he said. He opened his eyes, smiled, extended a hand in invitation.

'Eliphaz ...' said Wendy. 'Is that your real name?'

'It became my name when I entered into the love of Christ,' he said. 'Before I found the Lord I was called Jack – Jack Perkins. But now I am saved and the old me, the wicked me, has gone for ever ...'

No, she decided, he wasn't acting. No-one could *act* like that. Not unless he was someone like Michael Caine. This one just had to be a genuine Jesus freak ...

'That thing I mentioned,' she said. 'I left it upstairs ... under the floorboards for safety ...'

'You are more than welcome to come in,' said the man. 'Here in the Temple we do not wish to keep things which are the possessions of others.'

She followed him through the hall and up the stairs. And she was amazed by the transformation. The place had been cleaned and the walls had been painted. And the entire building had a curious atmosphere of tranquillity.

All three doors on the landing were open. Wendy indicated the front room. 'In there,' she said.

The man stopped, put a hand on her arm. 'I forgot to ask your name.'

Instant suspicion. 'Why do you need to know it?'

He smiled, shook his head sadly. 'There is fear in you, sister. You should accept the Lord and let Him help you ...'

187

'Why is my name important?' persisted Wendy.

Another smile. 'So that I can introduce you to my brothers,' he said. 'They will expect me to introduce you.'

Then Wendy noticed there were two young men in the room. Both, she would have guessed, were about eighteen and both were dressed in the style of the man called Eliphaz. There was no furniture, not even the old sofa which had been there, and the two of them were seated on the bare boards. They were studying Bibles, mouthing words silently as if trying to memorise them.

'Wendy,' she said quietly. 'My name is Wendy.'

Both youngsters immediately looked up and scrambled to their feet. They were smiling broadly and welcomingly.

'This is Wendy,' said Eliphaz.

He took Wendy's elbow, eased her firmly into the room. 'This here is Lazarus, one of our brothers from America,' he said. 'And our friend over here used to be called Arthur. But now he's filled with the Spirit and he's become Canaan. Canaan the Rechabite.'

'Jesus loves you, Wendy,' said Lazarus politely. 'Praise the Lord!' He spoke with the warm and homely drawl of the Deep South. On the knuckles of his right hand was tattooed the word 'love'. A matching tattoo on his left knuckles said 'hate'.

'Yes, Jesus surely loves you,' said Arthur who had become Canaan. Wendy could immediately identify his Birmingham origins.

They stared at her, now waiting for her to take the initiative, and their solemn sincerity made her feel oddly uncomfortable. 'Thank you,' she said. It sounded ridiculously inadequate and there was an awkward silence. She indicated the section of the floor where the sofa had been and turned to Eliphaz the Temanite. 'It should be just there,' she said. 'Under the loose boards.'

He nodded. 'You need help?'

'No . . . no, thank you . . . I can manage.'

188

They watched while she went down on her knees and started trying to prise up one of the boards.

'Wendy . . . do you know Jesus?' Lazarus put the question casually. He might almost have been asking about the weather.

'Sure.' She was pre-occupied with her work and she did not look up. 'Sure I know Him.' The board was fixed more firmly than she'd expected.

'I mean *really* know Him,' said Lazarus more vehemently. 'There's a whole heap of dudes out there in the systemite world, in all them fine churches an' all, who reckon they know Jesus but they wouldn't even recognise Him if He stopped them in the street . . .'

The board was now rising from the floor. Wendy wormed her fingers under it and started to tug.

'I tell ya . . . He was an unwashed hairy hippy from the slums of Galilee . . . but, ya gotta believe me, that cat was for real,' said Lazarus. 'And He still is today . . .'

Loud creaks as the bit of wood bent and finally burst away from the retaining nails. Wendy peered down into the darkness, put a hand down to grope around. Nothing. She must have picked the wrong board.

'. . . yes, He's here with us today . . . He's right here in this room . . . and, I tell ya, He's a mind-blower!'

Maybe it was a bit nearer the window. Yes, now she came to think of it, the board had been just behind the sofa. She moved across, started again.

'He's the ultimate trip, Wendy . . . and you wanna get right there with Him because there ain't much time left . . .'

This board was much looser. She jiggled it a little to get a better grip and then lifted it.

'. . . it's all right here in the Bible . . . how the seven vials of the wrath of God will be poured over the nations . . .'

There it was! She snatched up the box, got to her feet. 'Thank you,' she said. 'I'm sorry to have interrupted you.'

Eliphaz, she now realised, had placed himself squarely between her and the door. His face was coldly resolute and his arms were folded across his chest. 'That box is yours and whatever is in it is yours ... but I have to ask you one question,' he said. 'Does it contain drugs?'

Suddenly he seemed bigger than before. Bigger and more powerful. And her old fears about *them* came flooding back. She had been a fool to return to this house ...

Lazarus and Canaan the Rechabite seemed to be closing in on her, one on either side, and her stomach was churning with panic. 'I've got to go now.' She was struggling to control her voice, to stop it going all squeaky. 'Please let me go.'

'It's all here in the Book of Revelation.' Lazarus appeared to be unaware of what was happening in the room. He was preoccupied entirely with his own thoughts, with his convictions about the imminent End of Time. 'Listen to this ... the Bible gives facts and details ... it don't mess about ... "and the fourth angel poured out his vial upon the sun ... and power was given unto him to scorch men with fire ..."'

Eliphaz held out his hand. 'Give the box to me,' he said. Wendy shook her head. 'It's mine,' she protested. 'You said I could come in and get it.'

'"... and men were scorched with great heat, and blasphemed the name of God ..."'

'Does it contain drugs?' repeated Eliphaz.

'No!' she shouted. 'It's nothing like that!'

He stood aside to let her pass. 'Please forgive me for being suspicious.' Now his manner was contritely apologetic. 'We would have taken them if they had been drugs. We would have taken them and destroyed them. You have to realise that many of our brothers and sisters here were damaged by drugs ... in their days of fleshly bondage.'

'Then you're letting me go?'

'Of course – but please come back to see us again,' said Eliphaz. 'All God's children are welcome here in the Temple.'

'Let Jesus into your heart, Wendy,' said Lazarus as she walked to the landing. 'He loves you real good.'

'Hallelujah!' added Canaan the Birmingham Rechabite.

Eliphaz escorted her to the front door. 'Don't forget, sister, that you do need Jesus,' he said. 'God be with you.'

She ran from the house, along the street, around a corner to a telephone box. She dialled the number for Sceptre Television. 'Please may I speak with Colin Benson?'

'Hold on,' said the operator. 'I'm just putting you through . . .'

Terry Dickson had prepared a background-information sheet about Mars for Clements so that some of the details could be fed into the programme's links. It said:

Mars has a diameter about half that of Earth and is officially classified, together with Mercury and Venus, as one of the inferior planets in our sun's family of planets.

It is our nearest neighbour among the planets – being 12.6 light minutes away from the sun, compared with our 8.3 light minutes. You will see this in perspective when I point out that Neptune and Pluto are 250 and 327 light minutes from the sun respectively.

The principal significance of this is that Neptune and Pluto, together with the other giant planets, Saturn and Uranus, would be far too cold to support life as we understand it.

Conversely, Mercury and Venus – 3.2 and 6 light minutes from the sun respectively – would be too hot.

Mars is appreciably cooler than Earth, of course, but scientists have long been agreed that temperatures there could be endured by man: the problems, while serious, should not prove insurmountable.

The actual distance between Earth and Mars varies considerably — being anything from 35 million miles to 60 million miles. This is because Earth moves in an almost circular orbit while the orbit of Mars is much more eccentric.

The predominant red colour which has given Mars its popular name comes from regions very similar to many of the deserts known on Earth. Like, for instance, the Painted Desert of Arizona.

Green patches which vary in size and shape from season to season are believed to be caused by the growth of plants similar to rock lichens. I am advised that lichens can survive at lower temperatures than most terrestrial plants and require very little moisture. However, pioneering work in the deserts of the Middle East has proved that more valuable crops can be grown if a region is properly irrigated and tended. That could apply equally well to the desert regions of Mars so making it possible, at least in theory, for man to become self-supporting there.

On the planet as a whole there is no shortage of water or potential water. It has been known for thirty years, as a result of work done at Yerkes Observatory near Chicago, that the polar caps of Mars are composed of snow. This snow could be converted into water which could then be channelled as required.

The one question which has apparently still not been satisfactorily resolved is that of atmosphere.

Does Mars have air which we could breathe? The answer, quite frankly, is that no-one really seems to know. I've now spoken to a number of scientists who are confident that appreciable quantities of free oxygen probably did exist there at one time. It may well be that, as Gerstein has suggested, life-supporting atmosphere has been locked in the surface soil but I have been unable to find any other expert who is prepared to publicly endorse that suggestion.

Obviously the whole question of the possible colonisation of Mars, the central question you asked me to investigate, depends on the certainty that the planet has an atmosphere similar to Earth's. There appears to be no such certainty. Gerstein is being decried by most of his contemporaries in Britain and abroad and, without wishing to be rude about the man, I wouldn't fancy sticking my neck out professionally on his say-so.

In short, Chris, it's a fascinating theory but it doesn't quite add up.

Clements read the last few paragraphs through for the second time and snorted impatiently. 'Well, Terry love, it's my neck that'll be sticking out – not yours,' he said. 'Gerstein's got me convinced and I'm prepared to gamble on him.'

But he didn't need to gamble, not as it turned out. For, at that moment, Wendy was waiting to talk to Colin Benson . . .

Memo dated June 13, 1977, from Leonard Harman to Mr. Fergus Godwin, Controller of Programmes:

I have returned to the studios today after a week's sick leave and I am astonished to learn that it is apparently your intention to allow the screening of that interview with the former astronaut Grodin.

We have already discussed at length the unethical circumstances under which the interview was conducted and which resulted in Grodin expressing extravagant views. We were agreed, I thought, that Grodin's statements could not possibly be substantiated and that, if dignified by being included in a programme purporting to be serious, they could do considerable harm.

193

The whole of this particular *Science Report* programme, as I have told you on numerous occasions, is a blatant example of irresponsible sensationalism which will reflect adversely on the company's image.

Are companies in the rest of the ITV network and those abroad aware of the troublesome and, indeed, unsavoury background to this production? I can only assume not for, otherwise, I am certain they would not be prepared to buy it.

Once again, I urge you most strongly to withdraw this programme from the schedules.

Memo dated June 14, 1977, from Fergus Godwin to Leonard Harman:

I can no longer agree with you over the remarkable 'brain-drain' investigation which has been mounted by Clements and his team.

I grant that it is highly controversial and even frightening. It will also cause embarrassment in certain high places.

However, I have assessed the evidence which is now in the programme — the product, I might add, of diligent research and impressive dedication — and I feel we would be failing in our public duty if we were to suppress what appears to be the unpalatable truth.

Since we last spoke I have had the opportunity of studying Simon Butler's interview with Dr. Gerstein. Gerstein is a man for whom I have the greatest respect and no-one of his stature would lend his name to anything which, in your words, savoured of 'irresponsible sensationalism'.

There have been times, as you know, when I have been perturbed by the unexpected directions in which this investigation has moved. I now feel able to set all my reservations aside. Clements has my unqualified support.

I do not propose to reply in more detail to your query relating to networking and overseas sales for I consider that to be irrelevant in light of my present feelings.

Memo dated June 15, 1977, from Leonard Harman to Mr. Anthony Derwent-Smith, Managing Director:

You are already aware of my severe misgivings in relation to the *Science Report* programme, scheduled for network transmission on June 20, in which it is suggested that there is an international conspiracy to transport intellectuals and others to life on another planet.

I have made my opinions known on many occasions and I commend your attention, in particular, to the minutes of the Senior Executives' Meeting held on April 8. I warned then against what I recognised as a policy of expensive folly.

I am taking the unusual step of enclosing herewith copies of all correspondence between the Controller of Programmes and myself on the subject for I feel that, in view of the damage this production could do to the reputation of the company, this is a matter in which you might see fit to intervene.

I cannot urge too strongly that under no circumstances should this programme be screened.

Memo dated June 15, 1977, from Anthony Derwent-Smith to Fergus Godwin:

See the attached note and pile of bumph which reached me by hand today from Mr. Harman.

It is not my practice to become entangled in differences of opinion between my Controller of Programmes and any of his subordinates – particularly when I am approached in what I consider to be an underhand manner, with no copy of the note having apparently been sent to you. Nor do I intend to start intervening on this aspect of programme policy which I consider to be entirely your territory.

Please deal.

Godwin re-read the note and the one sent to Derwent-Smith by Harman. 'Cheeky bastard!' he said. He dialled on his internal telephone. 'Harman ... be in my office within two minutes. I'm going to mark your bloody card!'

Katherine White took the call in the *Science Report* office. 'No ... Colin Benson's popped out for a coffee ... who's this calling, please?'

'I must speak to him quickly,' said Wendy. 'It's urgent.'

'Can I take a message? Ask him to call you back?'

All Wendy wanted now was to get rid of the box. She anxiously scanned the faces of people loitering near the telephone box. Every wasted minute, she felt, put her in greater danger. If only she knew what *they* looked like ... 'Could you find him? It is desperately important.'

'I'll see if I can catch him in the canteen. Can I give him a name?'

'Tell him it's the girl who was with Harry,' said Wendy. 'Tell him I've got what Harry wanted to give him.'

'Hold on ...'

'Look ... I'm in a pay-box and I'm right out of change ...'

'Give me the number of the box and then replace the receiver,' said Kate. 'I'll call you right back.'

Wendy obeyed. She waited, her back to the door of the booth. And she was unaware of the man until he jerked the door open. He looked angry and beefily pugnacious. She gave a small scream, cowering away from him. He glowered at her with distaste. 'You planning on spending the day in here?'

196

'I won't be more than a minute . . . I'm waiting for a call.'

'Yeah?' He grabbed her arm, started to pull her. 'Well, I'm waiting to *make* one. So come on . . . out of it.'

'Please, this won't take long, really . . . .'

'Lady, this is a public box and I'm not hanging around all day while . . .'

At that moment the bell rang. Wendy shook away the man's hand, snatched up the receiver, heard Benson's voice. 'Yes, that's right . . . I was the girl with Harry,' she said. The man muttered aggressively, stepped out of the box and positioned himself immediately outside. Wendy spoke quietly, convinced that the man was trying to eavesdrop. 'I must meet you,' she said. 'Harry had something he wanted to give you and now I've got it. But I've got to be careful in case *they* are looking for me . . .'

They met an hour later at the spot where Benson had first seen Harry Carmell – outside the fruiterer's in the street market near the studios.

'You said *they* might be looking for you,' said Benson. 'Who are *they*?'

Wendy shrugged, pulled a face. 'Who knows?' she said. 'Goons, heavies . . . Russians, Americans, Germans, Outer Bloody Mongolians . . . what difference does it make?' She discreetly gave him the box. 'That's what Harry wanted you to have – he said something about it helping you see what was on some tape made by Ballantine. That make sense to you?'

'Not much,' said Benson. 'Wait here . . . . I'll have a shufti inside the box.' He hurried to the nearby men's lavatory, locked himself in a cubicle and opened the box. It contained a square printed circuit and he gave a low whistle of surprise. 'Well, I'll be . . .' He put it back in the box, re-joined Wendy.

'I've just remembered,' she said. 'Harry said you fit it to an IC40 or something and then you get a juke-box. Does that mean anything to you?'

197

'I must get back to the studios right away,' said Benson. 'See what sort of tune we can get out of the juke-box.'

'You don't need me any more?'

'Where'll you be?'

'Not sure – but not in London. There's too much heat in London.'

Benson tapped the box. 'Surely you'll want to know what all this adds up to . . . where can I contact you?'

'I'll contact you,' she said. And, as Harry Carmell had done months earlier, she hurried away and disappeared in the crowds.

Technicians at the studios had never before been presented with such a problem. They puzzled and experimented for the best part of an hour before finally getting it right. And then, in the darkness of the preview theatre, Clements and Benson watched in amazement as the pictures suddenly started spilling across the large screen.

'I don't believe it!' said Clements. 'Good God . . . I simply don't believe it!'

SECTION TWELVE

Every seat in the preview theatre was filled. All members of the *Science Report* team had been summoned there — to see what Clements and Benson had been watching only a little earlier. Fergus Godwin was also there, sitting next to Clements, and so were many other executives of the company.

Clements's eyes were sparkling with excitement when the house lights eventually came up. 'Well, Fergus?' he asked. 'What d'you think?'

Godwin frowned and nibbled at his bottom lip, baffled and reluctant to commit himself. 'What the hell can I possibly think?' he countered. 'If what we've just seen is authentic, if it isn't just an elaborate fake, then the human race has been conned rotten and we've got the most incredible television scoop ever. But ... I mean ... that *can't* have happened — it can't possibly be true!'

'But it fits in, doesn't it?' persisted Clements. 'It fits with everything else we've got ...'

'Have you checked with Jodrell Bank? With people who worked with Ballantine?'

'Well, no ...'

'Then do it. Do it now. And put the whole thing to NASA as well. If we used that in the programme and it turned out to be a stumer ... there'd be the most God-awful blow-back. And, I give you fair warning, Chris, I'm not prepared to carry the can.'

'But NASA are certain to deny it,' protested Clements. 'That stands to reason ...'

'Let me know when you've spoken to them.' Godwin got up, started to leave the theatre. 'And I also want to hear what Jodrell Bank have to say.'

Hendlemann, the man at Jodrell Bank, was friendly

199

and eager to be helpful. But, when he heard Benson's description of what was on the tape, he was utterly sceptical. 'Sir William never mentioned a word about it,' he said. 'And something of that magnitude ... he'd never have kept it to himself.'

Benson tried to smother his disappointment. 'But did he ever say anything to you, or to anyone else, about meeting a man called Harry something-or-other when he was at NASA last year?'

Hendlemann was apologetic. 'Not a thing. I'm afraid I'm not being much use to you, Mr. Benson ...'

'Would you ask around? Maybe he did mention this Harry to someone else at Jodrell Bank. I assure you, Mr. Hendlemann, it really is important.'

'You said earlier you thought it might throw some fresh light on Sir William's death ....'

'It's just possible.'

'Hm, in that case I'll do all I can. There was something about that crash which didn't quite add up, as far as I was concerned. Now I'm not promising anything, mark you, but I will ask around.'

'And if you do discover anything ...'

'I'll call you back either way. *That* is a promise.'

The NASA official, who refused to give his name, took a very different attitude. 'I heard some freaky notions in my time but this one sure caps the lot,' he said. 'You better face it, son ... someone's been pulling your leg.'

'Then you are stating categorically that the tape must be a forgery?'

'How could it be anything else? That must be the most stupid question I've heard this year.'

'And the information on it is not accurate?'

'Son, do me a favour, will you? I've been very patient but I'm a busy man and I really think this joke's gone on long enough ...'

'I'm taping this conversation and I want you on record as saying that the information is inaccurate – if it really is.'

'I'm sorry . . . I've wasted more than enough time on this already. There's absolutely nothing more to say.'

Benson was left with the dialling tone. The anonymous man in Houston had replaced his receiver.

'Blast!' said Benson. He was tempted to dial again, to try speaking to someone different at NASA. Not that it would be likely to make any difference. All the official spokesmen had presumably been briefed to trot out the same sort of line. Laugh the idea right out of court – that seemed to be the tactic. And Benson was sure it was no more than a tactic.

He felt he had detected some hint of uncertainty under the man's brash derision. And he felt, more strongly than ever, that the tape was genuine. But proving it – or, at least, proving it enough to satisfy Goodwin – that was another matter.

He put the receiver back in its rest and was contemplating going for a canteen coffee when the bell rang. Hendlemann again. And this time with excitement in his voice.

'I've discovered something quite astonishing, Mr. Benson,' he said. 'Sir William *did* meet somebody called Harry at NASA. He made a note about it in his diary while he was in America. I've been checking through that diary and it really is quite remarkable. He doesn't mention this Harry's surname but, listen, I'll read you the extract:

' "Harry gave promised help but is now frightened. Told me today – These bastards would kill us if they knew what we've just seen. Take a word of advice, friend, and destroy that damned tape.' "

'There!' added Hendlemann. 'Now what are we to, make of that?'

'Anything else in the diary?'

'Nothing that appears to be relevant.'

Benson thought fast. 'The tapes you use at Jodrell Bank . . . is there anything distinctive about them?'

'In what way?'

201

'Could you, by studying this tape, establish if it belonged to Jodrell Bank?'

'No ... but I might well be able to establish that it did *not* belong to us.'

'And if you couldn't do *that* ... it would, at least, reduce the chances of it being a fake ...'

'Most certainly.'

'Is it possible, Mr. Hendlemann, for you to come to London?'

'I'll leave immediately,' said Hendlemann. 'I'm very anxious to see exactly what is on that tape.'

Benson met Hendlemann at reception and took him to the preview theatre where Clements was waiting. The tape was laced-up ready for viewing once again. They sat in silence, watching and listening.

'Incredible!' said Hendlemann eventually. 'Absolutely incredible!'

'You think that might have originated at Jodrell Bank?' asked Clements.

'Let me examine the actual tape,' said Hendlemann.

Clements led the way to the projection box and Hendlemann produced an eye-glass through which he minutely studied the tape. He became so absorbed in his examination that he appeared to be oblivious of the men with him. 'Why?' he asked. 'Why didn't he tell me?'

Clements signalled to Benson not to interrupt. They waited while Hendlemann checked frame after frame. Then he closely scrutinised the leader section of the tape and finally he nodded his head emphatically and put his eye-glass back in his waistcoat pocket.

'Well?' asked Clements. 'What do you think?'

'I'm almost afraid to tell you this – but I have to,' said Hendlemann. 'I do believe, Mr. Clements, that this is the genuine article.'

They hurried him across to Godwin's office where he repeated his belief – and the reasons for it.

'Give me just one minute,' said Godwin. 'I'd like to

202

have the Managing Director in on this one.' He dialled Derwent-Smith's internal number, briefly explained the situation, replaced the receiver. 'He's joining us,' he said.

Derwent-Smith listened while Hendlemann again repeated all he had said. 'Fascinating,' he said. 'And this diary of Sir William's — may we see it?'

Hendlemann nodded. 'It's outside in my car.'

'Well, Fergus,' said Derwent-Smith. 'You're Controller of Programmes . . .'

'Yes, but this is different,' protested Godwin. 'This is one where I want your help — because if we put one foot wrong here there's going to be such a stink . . .'

'You mean you might want me to share the blame.'

'No, I just . . .'

Derwent-Smith stopped him. 'I think we should talk a little more to this mysterious girl,' he said. 'The one who so conveniently supplied us with the printed circuit.'

'But we don't know where she's gone,' said Benson. 'She refused to tell me.'

'And you just let her walk away. That doesn't sound too clever, does it?' Derwent-Smith turned to Clements. 'And what's your opinion?'

'Well, the girl was frightened and . . .'

'No, not the girl . . . the tape. Are you still keen on using it?'

'Absolutely,' said Clements.

'Good,' said Derwent-Smith. 'Fergus?'

'In view of what Mr. Hendlemann says, I'm for going ahead.'

'Fine,' said Derwent-Smith. 'I'm with you all the way.'

That particular week, although the Sceptre Television team did not then realise it, was an extraordinary one for disappearances — the sort of disappearances which might have been linked with Batch Consignments.

New Zealand — Monday, June 13, 1977. At 10.30

a.m. accountant Miles Thornton drove into the caravan-park near Tauranga in the North Island's Bay of Plenty. With him were his wife and two young sons — all looking forward to a break of a few days. This was one of their favourite spots, a place where they'd spent many holidays.

Thornton found, to his surprise, that there was no-one on duty in the prefabricated building which served as a reception centre. And, even more surprising, there was no sign of anyone in the park. There were cars there. Plenty of cars. But the whole place was completely deserted. Normally there'd have been people sprawled out on loungers, children playing ball-games between the rows of caravans. 'But the only living thing to be seen was a dog,' he said later. 'It was weird.'

More weird, in fact, than he realised at the time. Records later found in the abandoned reception centre showed that more than 200 people should have been there that morning, including twelve employees of the caravan park. There were no signs of violence, no signs of any struggle. But not one of those people has been seen since.

America — Tuesday, June 14. At 3.0 p.m. two coach-loads of young trippers — average age 19 — set off on a sight-seeing tour from Casper, Wyoming. They were last seen heading in the direction of Cheyenne. Seven hours later the vehicles were found empty by the side of a lonely road.

In the sand around the coaches there was a confusion of footprints. But they seemed to lead nowhere. A camera, a pair of binoculars and a girl's handkerchief were found. But, like the people in New Zealand's Bay of Plenty, those seventy-six youngsters were never seen again.

At 4.30 p.m. that same day a small passenger-cargo vessel, the *Amelio*, left Barcelona with 165 people on board. Intended destination: Tunis. The *Amelio* was last seen steaming into a light sea mist south of the Balearic Islands. There was virtually no wind and the water was calm.

The mist was a comparatively small patch, covering little more than about two square miles, but there is no record of the *Amelio* ever having come out of it. An eventual intensive air-sea search of the area resulted in a complete blank. Not even a bit of wreckage has ever been found. As one coastguard official put it: 'This is one of the absolute mysteries. It is just as if the sea had opened up its mouth and swallowed her.'

So there it was. More than 440 people disappeared in the oddest combination of circumstances during those two days in June.

It would be irresponsible for us to state that those people have now become 'Batch Consignment Components' for we have no absolute proof. We do suggest that, however, as a distinct possibility.

The Ballantine tape was, of course, the most astounding feature of that television production. It was authentic. Absolutely and startlingly authentic. But, as Godwin had feared, it did bring the most 'God-awful blow-back'.

Simon Butler introduced it and, as viewers will recall, all that could be seen at first was a haze of colours and uncertain shapes. There was a whirling blur of confusion — multi-coloured dust dervishes glimpsed crazily through a tumbling kaleidoscope — and nothing, nothing more.

Then the picture cleared and the camera seemed to be skimming low over a wild and barren landscape. No vegetation, no suggestion of life. Just mile after mile of wilderness and brown-red desolation.

Sounds of static. Then, faintly, of men cheering. And finally there were the American voices — from the Space Control Room at NASA:

FIRST VOICE: Okay ... try to scan.
SECOND VOICE: Scanning now.
FIRST VOICE: The readings ... where are the read-
ings?

At that moment, superimposed over the scanning of
the alien landscape, viewers saw the computer-printed
word 'temperature.' And, almost instantaneously, that
word was duplicated in Russian. Now there was a great
outburst of Russian voices. Excited, jubilant. And then,
once again, the second American voice came through
with great clarity: 'Wait for it ... w-a-i-t for it ... Come
on, baby, don't fail us now ... not after all this way ...'
Computer figures appeared alongside the words on
the screen. The temperature, they showed, was four
degrees Centigrade. More printed words – 'Wind Speed'
– in American and then Russian. And the first
American voice was shouting triumphantly: 'It's okay
... it's good, it's good.' A Russian voice, equally
ecstatic, carried the same message.
Then the computer print-out started giving the most
vital information of all – information, in English and
Russian, about the atmosphere of that strange and
distant territory.
The words and letters were appearing with agonising,
nerve-shredding slowness. As though they were being
formed, uncertainly, by some retarded, mechanical
child. There was a great silence of anticipation and of
dread. Then from the screen came the shrieks and
whoops of joy. The first American voice could be heard
shouting over the din: 'On the nose! Hallelujah! We got
air, boys ... we're home! Jesus ... we've done it ... we
got air!'
His yells of excitement, and similar ones from his
Russian counterpart, were drowned by the crescendo of
cheering. And, during a lull in that cheering, the second
American voice could be heard saying: 'That's it! We
got it ... we got it! Boy, if they ever take the wraps off

this thing, it's going to be the biggest date in history! May 22, 1962. We're on the planet Mars – and we have *air*!'

That was it. The end of the Ballantine tape. And millions of viewers, in many parts of the world, briefly wondered if they had misheard. Man on Mars in *1962*? No, surely, that was not possible ...

Simon Butler, his face sombre, assured them that it was more than possible. Here, from a transcript of the programme, are his actual words:

We believe that to be an authentic record of the first – and secret – landing on Mars by an unmanned space probe from Earth. We also believe the date given – May 22, 1962 – to be accurate.

Clearly, the blanket of total security by which this information has been covered could have been maintained only through the active participation of governments at a very high level.

Equally clearly, there must have been some powerful reason why the true conditions on Mars, suitable as they appear to be for human habitation, have been kept secret. Indeed, the effort which has gone into persuading the world at large that the opposite is true argues that some operation of supreme importance has been going on beneath this security cover.

We believe that operation to be Dr. Carl Gerstein's Alternative 3.

Whether a human survival colony has by now been established on Mars, or whether preparations are still in hand for its transportation from the Moon to Mars, we do not know. But we put out this programme tonight as a challenge to those who *do* know to tell us the truth.

He paused after spelling out that challenge, one hand resting on a model of Earth and the other on a model of

207

Mars, to underline its significance. The programme was over and the gauntlet had been thrown down. The next move was up to the government. And the governments of other countries – particularly those of the super-powers.

Butler knew, of course, about the behind-the-screen doubts and anxieties. He knew how Harman had tried to neuter the programme and, indeed, how he had come close to succeeding. He was only too aware that the company had taken a calculated risk in persisting with this programme, that what had been revealed would very likely be emphatically denied, that there could be ugly repercussions for Clements and Fergus Godwin. And, of course, for himself.

He was the anchorman, the man who – as far as the public was concerned – was right at the centre of the entire investigation. He was well-known and well-respected and that, from the official viewpoint, made him doubly dangerous. It would be remarkable if attempts were not made to discredit him, to prove that, far from being a responsible commentator, he had been party to an ill-conceived hoax.

At no time, however, had he considered opting out. He had always believed in the truth. He had always presented it professionally. And this particular truth was far too important to be suppressed.

He concluded with these words:

> We regret if the implications of what you have seen are less than optimistic for the future of life on this planet. It has been our task, however, merely to bring you the facts as we understand them – and await the response.

The response started almost before he finished speaking. Switchboards at newspaper offices and regional television stations were flooded with calls from frightened people, from people desperate for re-assurance.

Those people got their reassurance. They got it because of the statement drafted by Harman. But that statement was a lie.

SECTION THIRTEEN

There is nothing new, of course, in the concept of men using the moon as a launch-pad for a new life on Mars. H. G. Wells, who correctly anticipated so many technical triumphs of the space-age — triumphs which seemed ludicrous to most people in his day — was expounding it back in 1901.

Here, from his classic *The First Men In The Moon*, is a segment of dialogue between two space travellers:

'It isn't as though we were confined to the moon.'
'You mean —?'
'There's Mars — clear atmosphere, novel surroundings, exhilarating sense of lightness. It might be pleasant to go there.'
'Is there air on Mars?'
'Oh, yes!'
'Seems as though you might run it as a sanatorium . . .'

So Wells, once again, has been proved right.

A number of leading journalists, maybe remembering Wells and his track-record as a prophet, did not automatically believe the Harman denial. They were puzzled by it, and were possibly thrown a little by it, for it had the ring of authenticity. And after all, they reasoned, what possible motive could a reputable television company have for claiming they had just presented a tissue of untruths? And yet . . . Alan Coren, writing in *The Times* on June 21, was one of the first to throw doubts on the validity of the Harman statement:

The seeming preposterousness of the story, on the other hand, was totally acceptable. The preposterous-

210

ness of the times have seen to that. Why should the madness of the NASA programme not be linked to the madness of Watergate, to create a Nasagate in which life is discovered on Mars, but the information is suppressed for governmental ends?

That was a shot in the dark by Coren – a shot guided by instinct as much as by insight. But, as he will realise today, it was uncannily on target.

But, in the final analysis, it was all to make little difference to Harman. Remember what was said at the meeting of the Policy Committee on August 4, 1977:

A TWO: But what about the regional officer concerned?

A EIGHT: You're right there. He should have stopped that television crap. He's proved himself to be utterly unreliable. He failed and failed badly and, what's worse, he could let us down again. The man, without any question, is a liability and I propose an Expediency.

R TWO: Seconded.

R EIGHT: Those in favour? ... Then that is unanimous. The method?

A THREE: How about a telepathic sleep-job ... maybe with a gun ...

R EIGHT: That seems sensible ... it's too soon after Ballantine for another hot-job ...

Harman, on that day in August, was being sentenced to death. The date of his death, however, was not so easily settled. That, as Dr. Hugo Danningham has now explained, would depend on Harman's biorhythmic sensitivity cycle – on the unseen assault being synchronized with his moments of extreme vulnerability.

James Murray of the *Daily Express* is another level-headed and highly-experienced writer who does not readily accept the obvious – particularly when it is given to him in the form of an official Press statement.

211

He has a reputation for seeking the facts *behind* the statement. And so, despite the 'knock-down' treatment being given to the programme on the front page of his own newspaper, he courageously stuck to his assessment of Butler, Benson and the others:

> They plausibly linked natural phenomena and real events in space to come to the inevitable conclusion that there was a monumental international conspiracy to save the best human minds by establishing a new colony on Mars ... So all these scientists and intellectuals slipping abroad to the 'Brain Drain' were really being shipped to Mars on rockets via the dark side of the moon.

Murray, in other words, recognised the truth even though he did not have the facts completely to substantiate that truth.

Men like Coren and Murray worried Harman. They were helping to perpetuate the doubts and suspicions he had tried to smother. And he was frightened that they might start digging deeper, that they might eventually be able to present the full and horrendous truth. Just as we are now doing in this book.

The men of the Policy Committee had put no great priority on this particular murder. Alternative 3's chief executive officer in Britain had already been instructed to suspend Harman from his secret regional duties — and to recruit his successor. Harman *would* die. They knew that with certainty. He would die without revealing what he knew. And that was all that really mattered.

Other men, for other reasons, were disturbed by the realisation that the Alternative 3 sensation was not to be swiftly buried. They were particularly unhappy about Philip Purser's *Sunday Telegraph* suggestion that the investigation might have been a 'fiendish double bluff inspired by the very agencies identified in the programme'.

They were among the Members of Parliament, the overwhelming majority, who were not privy to the facts about Alternative 3. Some have since claimed that they *suspected* the truth but they certainly did not *know* it. Yet they had the task of coping with much of the terror which spread so insidiously after that television transmission.

Most people, as we have said, were only too eager to believe Harman's denial. But a sizable minority appreciated the full significance of what had been revealed. These were people, in the main, who had already been uncomfortably aware of the Doom-Day prospect outlined by Gerstein, the sort of people who were only too aware of the mammoth cover-up which the 1968 Condon report had provided for so-called Flying Saucers.

There were those who vaguely remembered what the *Evening Standard* had said about the $500,000 Condon study:

> It is losing some of its outstanding members, under circumstances which are mysterious to say the least. Sinister rumours are circulating ... at least four key people have vanished from the Condon team without offering a satisfactory reason for their departure. The complete story behind the strange events in Colorado is hard to decipher ...

The validity of the suspicions in that *Evening Standard* article suddenly seemed to be confirmed by other statements later made public – quite apart from President Carter's apparently remarkable about-turn on the subject of Flying Saucers.

Professor G. Gordon Broadbent: 'At the very highest levels of East-West diplomacy there has been operating a factor of which we know nothing.'

Would a man of Broadbent's calibre make a statement of that nature lightly?

Apollo veteran Bob Grodin: 'The later Apollos were

213

a smoke-screen ... to cover up what's really going on out there ... and the bastards didn't even tell us!'

Why, if there was nothing to hide, should he make such a curious statement?

More and more snippets of information started being remembered and re-quoted — some from old newspaper files, some from records leaked from NASA.

Here, for instance, is a verbatim transcript from a taped conversation which Scott and Irwin had with Mission Control during their moon-walk in August, 1971:

SCOTT: Arrowhead really runs east to west.

MISSION CONTROL: Roger, we copy.

IRWIN: Tracks here as we go down slope.

MISSION CONTROL: Just follow the tracks, huh?

IRWIN: Right ... we're (garble) ... we know that's a fairly good run. We're bearing 320, hitting range for 413 ... I can't get over those lineations, that layering on Mount Hadley.

SCOTT: I can't either. That's really spectacular.

IRWIN: They sure look beautiful.

SCOTT: Talk about organisation!

IRWIN: That's the most organised structure I've ever seen!

SCOTT: It's (garble) ... so uniform in width ...

IRWIN: Nothing we've seen before this has shown such uniform thickness from the top of the tracks to the bottom.

NASA has never explained those tracks — or who made them — although there are now grounds for the belief that they were left by a giant Moon-Rover vehicle of American–Russian design.

That is just one more example of how information about *real* space progress is being kept strictly secret. Dr. James E. McDonald, professor of meteorology at the University of Arizona and senior physicist at its

Institute of Atmospheric Physics, has been a vociferous critic of this secrecy.

In *The Enquirer* on February 19, 1967, he said: 'The U.S. Air Force has been scandalously blinding the public as to what is really going on in the skies. The Air Force investigations have been absurd, superficial and incompetent ... and scientists all over the world had better stop accepting the ridiculous Air Force reports and start investigating the problem themselves at once ... it's a problem demanding truly international investigation.'

So, with that sort of background to this latest television investigation, is it surprising that there were people not impressed by the denial? Or that those people should start demanding information from their Members of Parliament?

Michael Harrington-Brice is typical of those M.P.s. He says: 'I was put in an impossible position. For weeks after that programme went out I was getting deputations at the House, demanding that the government should issue a formal denial. I tried to bring pressure for that to be done, for a government denial would have helped alleviate the understandable anxieties of my constituents. However, it was not possible to pin down anyone in authority.

'I tried to put down questions about Alternative 3 but they were invariably blocked and what is particularly odd is that there now appears to be no official record of those questions.

'I also tried to raise the matter privately with Ministers but I was invariably told that Alternative 3 was a subject they were not prepared to discuss.'

What, at that stage, was Harrington-Brice's personal opinion?

'I formed the distinct impression that something really unusual was happening behind the scenes, that we in Britain were on the periphery of some secret venture being controlled by the super-powers.

'Nothing specific was said, you understand, but hints were dropped. I was obliquely given the message that it would be sensible for me to stop probing.

'It would be quite wrong, however, for me to pretend that, at that time, I had any information to confirm the accuracy or otherwise of the allegations made in that programme.'

Another Member of Parliament, Bruce Kinslade, was also seeking an official investigation into the statements made during the television programme – according to his private secretary.

On Wednesday, July 6, Mr. Kinslade, as you may recall, was hit by a lorry while crossing a side street near his home in Kensington. The lorry did not stop and has never been traced. And Mr. Kinslade died almost instantaneously. The inquest verdict was 'accidental death'. That verdict, for all we know, may have been accurate . . .

Letters continued to arrive at Television Centre. Letters which confirmed that more people, having had time to reflect, had reservations about the denial – or flatly refused to accept it.

The President of the prestigious Hampstead H. G. Wells Society wrote: 'In my experience I would estimate that there was a lot more truth in your programme than the majority of the public realise.'

A woman living in Southcroft Road, London S.W.16, summed up the attitude of many in her thoughtful letter:

With reference to your 'Alternative 3' programme which was shown on Monday, 20th June, several newspapers the following day declared the programme to be a hoax, and your spokesman was quoted as saying, 'Everything was based on what *could* happen.'

I and many other people feel strongly that this was not a hoax, and that this ridiculous claim is just another attempt by the government to hush things up (as seems to be the case with UFOs and the Bermuda Triangle). Everyone has a right to know what is going on; we all have to live on this planet, and space exploration should benefit us all.

It greatly incenses me to be continually kept in the dark when any discovery is made. Pressure was obviously put on you, but it does you no credit to show up the production team as charlatans. No, I cannot believe it was a hoax for the following reasons:

1. Would you really have included references to Ballantine's death as a hoax – at the expense of his family's feelings?

2. The ex-astronaut was obviously a highly intelligent man and well-educated. He had seen something that caused the dreadful deterioration we had to witness.

Please realise that the majority of your viewers are discriminating adults who can think for themselves. Let us have the truth of the matter.

That July also brought evidence of other aspects of the disaster looming inevitably nearer for this world. *The Times, July 26:*

A frightening picture of the accelerating world population is given in the 1977 World Population Report, published this week by Population Concern.

The report points out that if the present rate of population growth had existed since the birth of Christ there would now be 900 people for every square yard of Earth.

Half the fuel ever used by man has been burnt in the past 50 years.

The world's population is now more than 4,000 million and increasing by 200,000 every day.

Two hundred thousand *extra* people on this crowded planet every single day! That is 73,000,000 a year. And that will result, in only three years, in more *additional* people than the entire present population of America!

Those figures emphasise the magnitude of just one of the survival problems facing mankind – with this planet's water and other natural resources becoming progressively more scarce. And that is in addition to the inevitable 'Greenhouse Armageddon' described by Gerstein.

Is it, then, any wonder that the men behind Alternative 3 were anxious to accelerate their operation? Was it not obvious to them that time was running out – possibly even faster than they had earlier anticipated?

During the autumn of 1977 the subject of Alternative 3 began to drop out of the headlines. We know from Trojan that there was mounting activity behind the scenes – and that there was talk of attempts being made to sabotage the Alternative 3 operation. But the public, for a while, was allowed to forget.

Then, on Thursday, September 29, Dr. Gerard O'Neill – the Princeton professor who had given that astonishing interview to the *Los Angeles Times* in July – again came boldly into public prominence. This time he had been interviewed by Angus Macpherson, space correspondent of the *Daily Mail*, and the headline said: THE WONDERFUL WORLD OF 2001 IS OUT THERE WAITING.

Macpherson, respected as one of the world's most authoritative science-fact specialists, wrote:

Flying to London today is another scientist who is perfectly serious about his prediction of what faces the human race as we approach the start of the 21st century. But American physicist Dr. Gerard O'Neill holds out the promise of a totally different future . . . a brave new world in space. The choice, as he sees it,

218

is between George Orwell's 1984 and Arthur Clarke's 2001.

'Tell humanity there's no hope and everyone applauds you. But tell them there is a way out and they get furious,' says Dr. O'Neill, who has worked for seven years on a mind-stretching scheme for the emigration of most of us into artificial colonies in outer space.

He has been brusquely dismissed as a pedlar of nonsense by Jacques Cousteau, whom he greatly admires, and there was hurt as well as humour on the lean face under its trendy Roman fringe as he told me: 'Jacques is terribly worried about the pollution of the ocean and the destruction of its life.

'He thinks we ought to be doing more about it. So do I. Environmentalists are really very negative. They're so obsessed with Earth's problems they don't want to hear about answers.'

O'Neill's own answers are that we not only can colonise the solar system – but *must*, if human life a few generations from now is to remain civilised or even bearable.

O'Neill's colonists would get away from the start from the space suits and cell-like space stations of science fiction ...

O'Neill is coming to London to present his prediction of space colonisation to the British Interplanetary Society.

The BIS is a legendary forum for glimpses of the future. Its members have seen a Moon-landing ship unveiled, looking eerily like the Apollo LEM, but some thirty years before it.

And they were the first to hear Arthur Clarke outline a visionary scheme for a global chain of communication satellites.

This could be a similar bit of history making ...

For most of the generation that gaped at the first Moon landings it has become a madly expensive

219

confidence trick — a game of golf on a useless rockpile that only two could play and that cost £500 a second.

All this is desperately myopic, declares O'Neill, for the denizens of a planet whose 4,000 million inhabitants face the prospect of being two to three times as crowded by the early years of the next century.

'In fact, we found in space precisely the things we are most in need of — unlimited solar energy, rocks containing high concentrations of metals and, above all, room for Man to continue his growth and expansion . . .

'A static society, which is what Earth would have to become, would need to regulate not only the bodies but the minds of its people,' he told me. 'I refuse to believe Man has come to the end of change and experiment and I want to preserve his freedom to live in different ways.

'I see no hope of saving it if we remain imprisoned on the Earth.'

Macpherson pointed out that O'Neill is 'consulted respectfully — if a shade warily — by Government officials, Senate committees and State governors.'

The article showed that O'Neill was visualising the future along slightly different lines to those approved by the men of Alternative 3. It also indicated that O'Neill was not aware — and possibly is *still* not aware — that the Alternative 3 'future' had already arrived.

Macpherson wrote:

His colonies are planned as vast cylindrical metal islands drifting in orbit, holding inside a natural atmosphere, trees, grass, rivers and animals — a capsule of a warm Earthlike environment.

He sees them reaching half the size of Switzerland, ultimately, housing 20 to 30 million people and sustained by the inexhaustible energy of space sunshine.

Yet their construction, he insists, would need only the technology we already have ...

The article finished with these thoughts:

For most people of the pre-space generation, probably, the moment when the magic finally went out of the adventure came a year ago when the dream of life on Mars was dispelled by the Viking spacecraft.

But for O'Neill that was another plus for space. The best thing we could have found was nobody there.

The colonisation of the new frontier can take place without repeating the shaming history of the Indian nation – or even the bison.

'Perhaps nobody's there, anywhere, after all. Perhaps there isn't a Daddy to show us how to do things.

'It's a bit frightening ... but it gives us a lot of scope.'

We discussed the content of that article with M.P. Michael Harrington-Brice. What, in view of his own researches, was his opinion?

He said: 'Dr. O'Neill is arguably the most brilliant man in his own line in the Western world and I am certain he is right in saying the technology is already available for a project such as he envisages.

'However, he is apparently working on the assumption that the information *officially* released about conditions on Mars is true and I would certainly hesitate before making that assumption.

'If what was shown on the Ballantine tape was the *real* truth – and I have seen no evidence which convinces me it was not – then the whole situation changes dramatically.

'Obviously it would be far easier and cheaper to colonise a suitable and empty planet, to which we have got comparatively ready access, than to build gigantic, artificial islands in the sky.

'It would be grossly impertinent of me to say that Dr. O'Neill is wrong for he is a man of immense international stature. However, I can't help wondering if the political facts, the facts of East-West co-operation, have not been kept from him. There is certainly nothing in what he says which convinces me that Mars is not the venue for Alternative 3.'

Harman, we learned later, read that article in the *Daily Mail*. He read it on the morning of publication – on September 29. He did not know then, of course, that he had exactly 48 days left to live.

A cryptic message from Trojan. Brief, typed, unsigned: 'Surprise development rumoured. Sabotage possible. Will send details if and when available.'
We puzzled over the message but we did not try to contact Trojan. That was the arrangement. He always took the initiative. It was safer that way.

SECTION FOURTEEN

They call it Archimedes Base. And that's where the trouble, the really big trouble, flared so violently.

Archimedes is a walled crater-plain on the western border of the Mare Imbrium, the Moon's 'Sea of Shadows'. It has a diameter of about 50 miles and, unlike the nearby Aristillus crater, it has a relatively smooth ground surface. That is why, according to information from Trojan, it was developed as the principal transit camp on the Moon – the place from where people were normally lifted for the final leg of their journey to Mars.

Man cannot survive in the natural atmosphere of the Moon. NASA said so years ago and NASA, in that instance, was telling the truth. So most of Archimedes Base was hermetically sealed under a transparent bubble inside which air and temperature was controlled to the levels usual on Earth. The construction had taken two years and had been a fantastic triumph of space engineering.

Conditions under the bubble were similar to those visualised by Dr. O'Neill for his artificial worlds of the future. Men and women could live there comfortably for indefinite periods – secure inside a domed and gigantic greenhouse.

There were two huge airlocks in the southern section of the bubble. Shuttle craft arriving from Earth and from Mars entered through these locks before taxiing to the centrally-sited Arrival Terminal. A series of roads ran from the terminal to the stores and service areas and to the three separate 'living-quarter villages' – one for pilots and resident personnel, one for 'designated movers', and one for 'batch-consignment components'.

And over it all was a spread of camouflage, reminiscent of that used during World War Two, to ensure that Archimedes Base could never be seen by unauthorised observers on Earth.

There was another transit camp, the original one on the Moon, in the crater known as Cassini but that was now considered too small. Most of its equipment and furnishings had been moved to Archimedes. For Archimedes was the bustling centre of activity ...

Trojan's cryptic message about possible sabotage was soon followed by this report:

> Stringent security ensures the complete segregation of Designated Movers from Batch-Consignment Components until after disembarkation in the new territory.
>
> They are transported in separate craft and, while awaiting transportation, they are quartered in different areas of Archimedes Base. This is as a result of an order from the Policy Committee.
>
> It is felt that among the Designated Movers there may be those who initially harbour reservations about the morality of the mental and physical processing considered necessary for Components.

'Components'! Let us not be confused by the jargon euphemisms. Trojan uses them. Trojan, like most others in Alternative 3, has been brain-washed into accepting such words as normal. He is revolted by what has been done, by what *is* being done, but he has unwittingly absorbed the obscene distortion of language. So, just for a moment, forget 'components'. Trojan means *people*. He is writing about slaves, about men and women who have been mutilated mentally and physically, who have been programmed to obey orders. And who have been condemned to a life of sub-human degradation.

His report continued:

224

These Designated Movers can have their doubts put into 'proper perspective', after they have become acclimatised to life in the new territory, by representatives of the Committee in Residence. They can, according to official reasoning, be persuaded to recognise the necessity for such processing and to realise that the ultimate survival of the human race must take precedence over the fate of a limited number of low-grade individuals.

Consider the appalling significance of that paragraph! It means, if 'official reasoning' is right, that Ann Clark and Brian Pendlebury and others like them can be taught to regard fellow humans as expendable beasts of burden. It means, surely, that natural compassion must be systematically eradicated, that the minds of 'designated movers' are also moulded to match the needs of Alternative 3. Orwell's vision of 1984, it seems, has already come to fruition – millions of miles from Earth.

Trojan's report then went on to detail the curious circumstances which resulted in Earthly efforts to undermine Alternative 3. And which eventually culminated in carnage at Archimedes Base . . .

Bacteria are far more tenacious than humans when it comes to clinging to life. They survive the seemingly impossible. They can apparently retreat into a form of hibernation for centuries. For millennia even. Then, when conditions are right, they wake up, as it were, and they flourish. That is apparently what happened on Mars.

The 'dynamic changes' recorded in 1961 and described by Gerstein provided the ideal conditions. And across the silent wastes of the empty planet there was a great awakening of the minute unicellular living organisms. They developed and they spread. They were too small to be seen but they were there, waiting, when Man first arrived . . .

These were alien strains of bacteria, pernicious and voracious strains never before encountered by humans,

225

but they were not numerous enough noticeably to damage the imported and carefully-cultivated crops. Not until late 1976. That, as we now know, was the time of the great blight . . .

Attempts were made to fight them with bactericides and even by bacteriophages which involved the introduction of ultra-microscopic organisms normally parasitic to bacteria. But the Committee in Residence realised it was a losing battle. And that was when the super-powers decided they needed The German.

The German, whose name we have agreed to withhold, is possibly the most imaginatively successful bacteriologist in the world. That is accepted by his contemporaries in the East and the West. He has probably achieved more than any other man in his sphere – not only in combating bacteria but in harnessing them into the service of man. That was why he was needed so urgently in the new territory . . .

But he refused to go. He was seen by the Alternative 3 regional officer and, eventually, by the West German Chief Executive Officer. They argued with him, offered him every possible inducement, but he remained adamant. Certainly he would respect the confidences he had had entrusted to him but he had work to do, work on Earth, and he had absolutely no inclination to become involved in Alternative 3.

They did recruit his principal assistant, an American in his mid-thirties, who travelled as a designated mover in February, 1977. He went willingly, enthusiastically even. But he is another man whose identity it would be unfair to reveal for, if he is still alive, he is today being hunted. He is being hunted by agents of the East and the West.

He will certainly have changed his name by now, and probably his appearance as well, but he must know that for him there can be no permanent hiding place. He is the man chiefly responsible for founding the guerrilla group known as Anti-Alternative. He was also responsible for the eventual disaster at Archimedes Base. We call him The Instigator.

It soon became apparent to the Committee in Residence that The Instigator, although competent and experienced, lacked the intuitive flair needed for the new-territory task. They still needed The German. But The German was still refusing ...

Urgent meetings were convened in the Hall of the Committee in Residence. There were consultations with the Policy Committee on Earth, with key men in Department Seven. And eventually a decision was reached. The German liked and respected The Instigator. He had confidence in his judgement. And if any man could persuade The German to become a designated mover it was The Instigator. He should go back to Earth, they decided. He should go back to talk to The German. That, as it turned out, was their biggest and most disastrous mistake ...

They had made one serious miscalculation over The Instigator. They had failed to realise that he still had not got the plight of the Components into 'proper perspective'. Maybe that would have changed if he had been allowed more time for there had been others, many others, who had needed months to become completely accustomed to living with an enslaved sub-species. All of them had eventually accepted that this was part of the essential balance. But The Instigator had not been allowed time, not enough time, and he was tormented with secret guilt. What right, he wondered, did he have to be one of the Chosen, one of the Superior Select? He was racked with disgust and with doubts and he knew then that, somehow, he had to shatter the component-system ...

And then they told him they were returning him to Earth.

There was a stop-over at Archimedes Base on his return journey and he was temporarily housed with a new group of designated movers awaiting transportation to the new territory. They knew nothing, these people, about the components – quartered, as usual, in a different 'village' – who were being condemned to spend the rest of their lives as slaves. He told them. He told them exactly what was happening and exactly what to expect. He described the kidnappings and the mutilations being carried out on Earth – for *their* benefit and comfort. And they were not ready for such horrendous information. They were normal people, highly-intelligent and sensitive, and they had not yet been exposed to the skilled and persuasive arguments of the Committee in Residence. They were uncertain about whether to believe him. It all sounded so lunatically outrageous. Yet this man was strangely convincing ...

A small party of them decided to establish the truth. They decided surreptitiously to visit the village he'd described. And that is what sparked the holocaust at Archimedes Base ...

The Instigator did not contact The German when he returned to Earth. He fled into hiding. And then, with a small group of trusted collaborators, he founded his action group, Anti-Alternative. This group, unlike organisations such as the IRA or the PLO, could make no public statements for such statements could lead to them being rooted out and destroyed. They dedicated themselves to disrupting, by guerrilla tactics, all work connected with the exploration and exploitation of space. Their actions, they felt, might force an eventual re-think on Alternative 3.

On October 1, 1977, the *Daily Telegraph* carried a story, written by Ian Ball in New York, which was headlined: SATELLITE ROCKET No. 2 BLOWS UP. It said:

A second communications satellite was reduced to debris over the Atlantic yesterday after another spectacular rocket failure at the Cape Canaveral space centre in Florida.

228

Within two and a half weeks, the failures have destroyed communications satellite projects, one European, the other American, worth a total of $91.4 million (about £54 million).

An Atlas Centaur rocket, carrying a $49.4 million Intelsat 1V-A satellite built by Hughes Aircraft, was destroyed minutes after its launching late on Thursday. The failure was similar to the September 13 explosion of a Delta rocket carrying a $42-million European Space Agency orbital test satellite.

'We had indications of trouble in the engine area within seconds after lift-off,' said the Atlas Centaur launch director, Mr. Andrew Stofan. 'At 55 seconds the Atlas lost control and broke up. It flipped, broke apart, and then the Atlas blew up.'

The remainder of the Centaur stage was destroyed by an Air Force range safety officer, ending the mission four miles high and four miles down the range. The debris from rocket and satellite fell into the ocean.

In roughly the same area of the ocean, an Air Force recovery team has been searching for debris from the Delta rocket.

The next Intelsat 1V — a launch scheduled for November 10 — and other Atlas Centaur launches have been postponed until an investigation into the latest failure is completed.

Similar problems were being experienced by Russian space-teams. On October 11, 1977, the *Guardian* carried this Reuter report from Moscow:

Two Soviet Cosmonauts failed yesterday to dock their Soyuz-25 craft with the Salyut-6 orbiting laboratory.

Mission commander Vladimir Kovalyonok and flight engineer Valery Ryumin, thought to be planning a long stay aboard the new space station, were ordered back to Earth after abandoning the link-up.

Tass, announcing the latest in a series of troubles to affect the Salyut series, said there had been 'deviations from a planned docking regime' during the approach while the Cosmonauts' Soyuz-25 capsule was 120 yards from the station. The Soyuz-25 failure has come as a blow to Soviet space chiefs
. . .

So that is what happened. Did it happen because of The Instigator? That is a question we cannot answer. We simply do not know. We *do* know, however, that the catastrophe at Archimedes Base can be traced back directly to The Instigator. And *that* was incomparably more devastating.

Leonard Harman died at ten minutes past two in the morning on Wednesday, November 16, 1977. He died, wearing his pyjamas, in the dining-room at his home.

His widow, Mrs. Sarah Harman, gave this evidence at the inquest:

My husband had been depressed and rather withdrawn for some time, possibly for six months or more, but he never confided any reason to me.

I knew there had been some friction between him and Mr. Godwin, Mr. Fergus Godwin, at the studios and at first I thought that was possibly making him feel the way he did. But the trouble at the studios, whatever it was, seemed to pass over and still my husband was no better. I urged him on several occasions to see a doctor but he told me that it was nothing serious and that I was not to fuss.

I never, at any time, thought he might be likely to take his own life.

On the Tuesday evening, I mean the evening of the 15th of November, we watched television and then went to bed as usual just before midnight. I didn't notice anything particularly unusual about him. He behaved just as he normally did.

230

We read in bed for a while and it must have been nearly one o'clock before we settled down for sleep.

Just before two o'clock I was disturbed by him getting out of bed. I assumed he was going to the bathroom. But then he seemed to be gone a long time and I can't really explain why but I began to get rather worried. I had a feeling that something wasn't quite right.

I called out to him but there was no reply so I got out of bed. The bathroom door was open and, because of the street lights outside, I could see that he was not in there.

Then I heard a movement from downstairs. I called out to him again but still there was no reply. By this time I thought that he must be feeling unwell and that he'd probably gone down to the kitchen to make himself a hot drink. He'd done this once or twice before and it had always soothed his stomach.

I decided then to go down and make the drink for him. But he wasn't in the kitchen. The house was completely silent. I called out to him again but there was still no reply. I was a bit frightened by this time because I couldn't possibly imagine what he could be doing.

There weren't any lights on, not until I switched on the one in the hall, and my husband had never done anything like this before. He'd never walked in his sleep or anything.

Then there was a sort of scuffling noise from the dining-room. I went in and he was standing there in the darkness in the middle of the room. I switched the light on and spoke to him but he didn't seem to hear. His eyes were open – they were staring straight at me – but he didn't seem to be aware of me or of anything else. It was as if he was in a trance.

He had a gun in his hand, a little pistol, and he put the barrel to his head and pulled the trigger. And that's all that happened. The next second he was dead.

Mrs. Harman also told the coroner that her husband had not owned a gun, that he'd never had one in the house. But the coroner reached his own conclusion. Wives, in his experience, didn't necessarily know everything about their husbands.

The verdict was 'suicide'.

Disaster hit Archimedes Base on a cataclysmic scale. The Arrival Terminal ... the service centres ... the buildings of the three villages ... they were all ravaged and wrenched from their foundations by the sudden and cyclopean clash of uncountable tornadoes. They crumbled and disintegrated, these buildings, as they juddered and somersaulted high in the air. And people spilled from them. The living and the dead – they all looked the same in that great spasm of destruction. They were all flailing limbs and buckled, distorted bodies. Many of them exploded far above the ground and bits of them whirled around in the dust and the debris before being sucked out into the eternal blackness of space.

And all of it, we now know, had been sparked by a gentle and compassionate marine biologist called Matt Anderson. He had meant well. He had been inspired by the highest motives. By consideration and humanity, by raw and spontaneous pity. And he had unleashed a nightmare.

That is clear from documents analysed by Trojan. Very little else, however, is certain. There were few survivors and their accounts were so disjointed and confused. The full facts, now, will probably never be known.

Here, however, is what we have been able to piece together:

Anderson, a thirty-three-year-old single man from Miami, Florida, was one of the designated movers at Archimedes Base who listened to The Instigator. He was one of the small group who secretly visited the segregated Components Village. He talked to the people there, heard enough to realise that The Instigator had been telling the truth. It was grotesque and barbaric but it was, unquestionably, the truth.

That whole party of designated movers was scheduled for transportation to the new territory that night. And everything would have been different if they had all gone. There would have been no disaster.

They would certainly have posed a bigger 'conscience problem' to the Committee in Residence but, in time, the Committee would have converted them into accepting the necessary realities of Alternative 3.

But Anderson did not travel with the others. He stumbled on the return journey from the village of the slaves. He stumbled and hurt his spine. And it was decided that he was not fit to travel, that he should stay for a while at Archimedes Base.

Ten days later he slipped unseen from his room and again visited that village. It was not difficult for there were no guards. There was no need for guards around the village. The people temporarily there had been instructed to remain in their quarters. And they had been programmed to obey, unquestioningly, every order they received.

Anderson wanted to talk to them at length, to understand them, to see if he could possibly help. And that was when he got his great shock. By then there was a new Batch Consignment in the village and in that Batch was a man he knew, a man who, years earlier, had been a colleague at school.

The man recognised him, could obviously think fluently and intelligently, but all the vital personality had been gouged out of him. His bearing and his attitude showed that he knew and accepted his position. He was a slave. That was when Anderson knew he had to take action . . .

Trojan's report says:

233

Two of the Components who did survive have revealed under interrogation that they heard Anderson talking to the man on two occasions, on that first day and later when he returned with details of the plan for the intended evacuation. This is principally how Department Seven has been able to establish much of what did happen before the disaster ...

There was an aerospace technician in the latest group of designated movers, a highly-qualified man who had been trained by NASA, and Anderson, it seems, sought him out and explained the whole situation. He told this man of the atrocities to which they were all, unwittingly, a party. He elaborated on how they had been lured towards a debased and de-humanised future, on how they would be battening for the rest of their lives on the misery of the mutilated slaves. He convinced him it was their duty to rescue the people from the village, to return them to their families on Earth – and to ensure that this traffic in human life was stopped for ever.

Trojan's report continues:

The main depot for craft on the Earth-run was south of Archimedes Base on the far side of the mountain range known as Spitzbergen. Most long-range vehicles were maintained and parked there and smaller craft were used to convey passengers to and from Archimedes, rather in the style of airport buses on Earth.

There were invariably a number of these smaller craft on the tarmac at the Archimedes Arrival Terminal and the plan was for Anderson and Gowers, the aerospace technician, to steal one of these craft and use it to evacuate as many of the Components as possible.

Another sympathetic designated mover, briefed on the technicalities by Gowers, would operate one of the airlocks in the southern section of the bubble to allow them through. They would then travel to the main depot where, by force if necessary, they would commandeer a vessel in which to make the journey back to Earth.

So that, apparently, was what was meant to happen. But it all went wrong. Horribly and hideously wrong. Gowers found a suitable craft and he checked it, established that it was fuelled and ready for flight. And Anderson was in charge of discreetly marshalling the people in the village of slaves, of supervising their march to the Terminal.

Everything went well at first. There were a hundred and fifty-five slaves in the village at that time and the small craft could accommodate only eighty-four of them, so Anderson selected the youngest, including his former schoolmate, for in his opinion they ought to have priority. When he returned to Earth and publicly exposed this sick side of Alternative 3 there would be such an international outcry that the other slaves would also be returned to their homes. Yes, and those who had already been taken to the new territory. The vast majority of human beings would never tolerate the obscenities being committed in their name. That, according to the evidence from Trojan, is what Anderson really thought.

There was no problem in sifting aside those who were not to be immediately saved, although all the people in the village now knew exactly what was being planned, for, of course, the slaves had been programmed into automatic obedience.

Trojan's report went on:

One of the surviving Components later interrogated said that Anderson told them: 'There are few guards and so it is unlikely that any serious attempt will be made to prevent us leaving this Base or, indeed, this planet.

'However, those of you chosen for repatriation

235

must remember that, in these circumstances, it is better to kill than be captured. The lives and freedom of many people depend on us getting back to Earth and so you must be prepared to kill anyone who tries to stop you. That is an order.'

In fact, six of Alternative 3's resident personnel were soon killed. They were trampled down and kicked to death by the slaves, near or in the Terminal, when they tried to stop the party reaching the craft. They were left broken and bleeding on the ground and the slaves, with no show of emotion, walked over them and climbed on board. Then the engines fired into life and Gowers, seeing the opening-lights winking around the airlock on the left, eased them upwards.

The craft hovered briefly in the still air, thirty or forty feet above the tarmac, and then the inner lip of the airlock rolled aside like a transparent stage curtain. Their path was now clear and Gowers depressed a switch to start the forward thrust. The horror, at that moment, was just seven seconds away . . .

Trojan's report picks up the story:

A senior technician at Archimedes Central Control, one of the permanent staff who did survive, has made a statement in which he describes how he was alerted by shouting and screaming from the direction of the Terminal. The angle of his view prevented him from observing what was happening there but then he did notice the unexpected opening of the airlock door. He knew that if the outer door were also to open, possibly because of some malfunction in the equipment, the Base would be subjected immediately to acute decompression.

He saw no traffic and no traffic was scheduled for departure. So, assuming there was a serious fault and that the shouts were probably ones of warning, he pressed a master-control button. This was on a board designed to activate a fail-safe system, over-riding all

236

others, and his action resulted in the airlock door snapping instantly back into position.

An experienced pilot could have coped with the problem by taking avoiding action and returning his craft to the Terminal but Gowers was not an experienced pilot ...

Gowers, in fact, was almost at the door when it closed. Suddenly, straight ahead of him and all around him, there was just a transparent domed wall. He felt trapped, like a fly under an upturned tumbler, and he panicked. He swerved the craft violently upwards to the left and then, in desperation, he over-compensated and jerked it into a fast and erratic zig-zag course. The craft, now bucking viciously, surged towards the roof. Gowers, hopelessly out of control, snatched wildly at the control stick, sending the craft into a lethal whip-lash dive. It exploded into one of the walls of the dome, spewing fire and wreckage and blazing bodies, and it smashed a devastating hole in the transparent surface.

The entire base, where the air was artificially maintained at Earth pressure, immediately decompressed. It was as if some mammoth and malignant vacuum-cleaner was greedily sucking everything into its mouth. Litter-cans and small vehicles and the six men who'd been trampled to death. And the savagery of the maelstrom shattered heavy objects against the dome, rattling them and bouncing them until they too punched their way through and were swirled out into the outer blackness. And the new holes brought new snatching whirlwinds. And the buildings groaned and surrendered and shot up, disintegrating, in that monstrous cannonade of havoc.

That day brought death to every Designated Mover at Archimedes Base. There were twenty-nine of them — scientists, technicians and medical specialists — mainly from America and Russia. And not one survived. They

237

were brilliant men. Carefully selected men. Today they are mere particles of dust. Drifting through the uncharted wastes of eternity.

However, as we have indicated, there were survivors. Two of the people known as Components lived through the holocaust and so did five of the resident staff. If they had perished the events of that terrible day at Archimedes would probably have remained a mystery for ever. There would possibly have been reports from observatories of a strange and momentary flare of activity on the moon – activity which might have been presumed to be the result of some unknown natural phenomena. And that would have been all. But because of these seven survivors, because of the information they gave to Department Seven and which Trojan has passed to us, the truth can be recognized.

These seven lived because at the time of the devastation they happened to be insulated in rooms where the atmosphere was independently maintained – and they escaped to the obsolete base at Cassini.

Cassini Base, we understand, is now being redeveloped. It will once again become the principal transit camp on the moon. The Alternative 3 operation suffered a serious set-back at Archimedes but it has certainly not been abandoned.

No voyages are being made from Earth at the moment for there is much work to be done at Cassini but people are still being watched and assessed as potential Designated Movers. And, according to Trojan, plans are being made for the imminent round-up of more Components.

Maybe there are men and women in your town, possibly in your street, who will disappear, suddenly and inexplicably, in the near future . . . men and women already ear-marked for an astonishingly different existence on that far-distant planet.

They would already have gone, those people, if it had not been for the obstinacy of The German. And for the concerned compassion of The Instigator. They would already have joined those who, if biologist Stephen Manderson is right, are now on a planet where no squirrel will ever scamper. And where no nightingale will ever sing.

There is just one final point for us to make. On the back cover of this book you will note one word which you may consider puzzling: 'speculation'.

Why 'speculation'? That is a valid question ... especially in view of the fact that so much of our evidence, particularly that quoted from newspapers, was already a matter of public record.

Well ... we did mention that politicians tried to suppress this book, that two in Britain sought injunctions to prevent its publication. And we did explain that we were forced into a 'reluctant compromise'.

Need we say more?

Warner now offers an exciting range of quality titles by both established and new authors. All of the books in this series are available from:
Little, Brown and Company (UK) Limited,
P.O. Box 11,
Falmouth,
Cornwall TR10 9EN.

Alternatively you may fax your order to the above address. Fax No. 0326 376423.

Payments can be made as follows: Cheque, postal order (payable to Little, Brown and Company) or by credit cards, Visa/Access. Do not send cash or currency. UK customers: and B.F.P.O.: please send a cheque or postal order (no currency) and allow £1.00 for postage and packing for the first book, plus 50p for the second book, plus 30p for each additional book up to a maximum charge of £3.00 (7 books plus).

Overseas customers including Ireland, please allow £2.00 for postage and packing for the first book, plus £1.00 for the second book, plus 50p for each additional book.

NAME (Block Letters) ....

ADDRESS...

....

☐ I enclose my remittance for _____

☐ I wish to pay by Access/Visa Card

Number ⬚⬚⬚⬚⬚⬚⬚⬚⬚⬚⬚⬚⬚⬚⬚⬚

Card Expiry Date ⬚⬚⬚⬚